B.

X

# CIRCLE C
# C
# MOVES IN

# CIRCLE C MOVES IN
## A Western Novel

## BRETT RIDER

SAGEBRUSH
Large Print Westerns

First published in Great Britain by Harrap
First published in the United States by Macrae-Smith

Published in Large Print 2010 by ISIS Publishing Ltd.,
7 Centremead, Osney Mead, Oxford OX2 0ES
United Kingdom
by arrangement with
Golden West Literary Agency

**British Library Cataloguing in Publication Data**
Rider, Brett, 1879–1971.
   Circle C moves in.
   1. Western stories.
   2. Large type books.
   I. Title
   813.5'2–dc22

ISBN 978–0–7531–8513–1 (hb)

Printed and bound in Great Britain by
T. J. International Ltd., Padstow, Cornwall

To
Lenore, Kit, Linnet
and Leo
Best of Pals

# CHAPTER ONE

# Warned Off

The sun was suddenly below the mountain ridge, and Donal Cameron halted his horse and looked back into the long valley now lying deep in twilight. A campfire winked through the growing dusk. He could see Old Sinful, busy at the chuckwagon. Beyond the campfire, too far for his eyes in that gathering darkness, were other men, bringing up the slow-moving herd.

The cook's unmelodious voice reached up the slope to the accompaniment of clattering pans. The young cattleman's rather grave face relaxed somewhat as he listened. Old Sinful was fond of that song, and the outfit had heard almost too much of it during the long drive up from the Brazos.

> "They say there'll be a great roundup
> Where cowboys like dogies will stand,
> To be counted by those riders from Heaven
> Who are posted and know every brand."

A vague shape moved in from beyond the campfire. Donal heard the newcomer's voice, loudly protesting.

"You sure ride that song hard. Sounds awful doleful to me."

The cook hotly denied that the words were doleful. "They give me a sort o' peaceful feelin'," he said. "I ain't wearin' no brand, Rusty, but I figger that when the Day comes, them Heavenly Riders 'll spot me for a maverick an' git a Hallelujah iron slapped on my tough old hide."

"No cowman with good sense'll waste time with an old mossyhorn like you," jeered the rider. "Where's the boss gone, Sinful?"

"He lit out for San Benito," answered the cook. "From what he said he figgers to git us some grub. This here chuckwagon's about as clean as Mother Hubbard's cupboard. You boys is goin' to eat light tonight."

There was a brief silence, broken by the cowboy's resigned and bitter voice. "Sinful — I reckon you can keep right on with that doggone song. Ain't nothin' can get me more down than I feel right now."

Donal's horse moved up the trail, a steep climb that in some twenty minutes brought them to a wide stretch of mesa well covered with a growth of piñon trees. The horse picked up speed, but the night was black about them before the young cowman saw the glimmering lights of San Benito.

He gazed about with some surprise as he rode down the dusty street. Long streamers of bunting flaunted from the brightly-lighted fronts and draped the balcony of the new two story hotel.

2

It came to Donal that it was the Fourth of July. He grinned. He had forgotten about the Fourth. One day had been just like another on the long drive from the Brazos.

These evidences of the national holiday had nothing to do with his growing amazement as he continued to gaze about him. Changes had come to San Benito since his visit three years earlier. The town was then hardly more than a trading post, run by an old Scotchman by the name of Angus Cameron.

The trader had shown an enormous interest in the young Texan who too was a Cameron. It was from Angus that Donal first learned about the valley of the Rio Seco.

The trading post was still there, a long building of thick adobe walls that rose shoulder-high above the flat roof and were pierced with loopholes. Old Cameron had had marauders in mind when he built his store. Renegade whites, as well as the warrior broods of Mangas Colorado and the more noble Cochise.

A high log stockade had originally encircled the big store but the section fronting on the street had been removed. The rear portion now used as a corral was cut off from the street by a split-rail fence, laced with barbed wire.

Donal reined his horse in front of Cameron's store. Angus was the only man he knew in San Benito. He could get the news from the old trader.

He swung from his saddle, tied the horse to the long hitch-rail and paused to look back at the new shoddy frame buildings he had just passed. Numerous horses drooped at the tie-posts in front of the saloons, and more riders came drifting up the street. A springwagon with a leathery-faced ranchman holding the reins jolted past in a cloud of dust. A woman sat beside the driver and three giggling young girls were squeezed in the back seat.

More wagons and buckboards and riders were suddenly filling the street. Most of them headed for the big livery barn that stood some two hundred yards beyond the hotel. Others tied up at the hitch-rails. A buckboard in which sat a young man and a girl swung into the alley that led to the corral behind the store.

The driver checked his team as he saw the stranger. "Looking for Angus?" he asked.

"You've guessed it," replied Donal. "The store seems to be locked up. The doors are padlocked."

"You'll find Angus in Albuquerque," said the young man.

"Gone for good?"

"Nope. Laid up in a hospital. Angus got shot up a week or two back." The man in the buckboard smiled. "You won't kill that old-timer with just one bullet. He sheds off bullets the way a duck sheds raindrops."

"I'm mighty sorry to hear about it," said Donal.

The other man smiled again. "If you're a friend of his, I'm glad to be knowing you. My name is Bluett Clover, but folks mostly call me Blue Clover. My wife," he added. His elbow lifted in a nudge at the girl by his side.

"It's mighty nice of you to tell me about Angus," Donal thanked him. "My name is Cameron."

4

The Clovers looked at him in astonishment.

"Meanin' you're a relative?"

"No relation," said Donal with a shake of his head. "I brought up a bunch of cows some three years ago for a man near Silver City. Angus sold us supplies we needed."

"Was thinking you'd the look of a cowman," Blue Clover said. "One of 'em my own self," he added with an engaging grin.

"The brand stands out plain on most of us," laughed Donal.

"Yeah." Blue Clover looked at him thoughtfully. "We always put up the team in the old corral here. Angus don't charge us a cent, 'cept for the hay we use."

"Is the corral open?"

"Sure it's open, to any friend of Angus Cameron's. The gate is kept locked, but Roderick Dhu is back there. He runs things in the corral." Young Clover put a match to the cigarette he finished smoothing into shape. "Why don't you come along and get a good feed into your horse?"

"I was planning to get some supplies and head back to my outfit." Donal spoke worriedly. "I guess I'll have to try that store down the street."

The pair in the buckboard exchanged looks. "You won't be buyin' supplies in this town tonight." Blue Clover chuckled. "Ain't you knowing this is the Fourth? That's why so many folks are in town. There's a big dance tonight. Lucy and me have come in fifteen miles for that dance."

5

Donal hid his disappointment. Nothing for it except wait until morning. No sense returning to the camp empty-handed. "All right," he said good-naturedly, "I'll be obliged if you'll lead me to your friend Roderick Dhu."

The Clovers drove on down the alley. Donal followed with his horse. He was surprised to find that Roderick Dhu was a slim Apache youth.

"Rod is Angus Cameron's adopted son," Clover informed him. "He's lived with Angus since he was a papoose."

The young Apache greeted Donal with a pleasing dignity, told him that Angus had spoken of his visit three years before. "I go on bear hunt when you here that time," he explained. His speech was touched with a brogue that could have come only from his Scottish foster-father.

The Clovers went off to find friends at the hotel. Donal waited to question the Apache about getting the needed supplies from the store. Roderick Dhu shook his head. He would open the store fast enough, only there were no goods to sell a customer. Donal gathered that Angus was having serious troubles. Somebody was out to ruin his business. Wagons carrying merchandise from Albuquerque had been waylaid two times running and the entire shipments stolen. It was on the last haul that Angus had been shot and his freighter killed.

"Maybe soon I go on warpath," said the young Indian darkly. "Angus say to me, *no, no*, when I tell him I go on warpath for bad men who make this trouble for him." His black eyes were hot.

**6**

Donal wanted to ask him about the boom that had come to San Benito. He decided to wait. He was hungry, and there was a restaurant down the street, next to the new hotel.

The board sidewalks were thronged with ranchers and their women in for the dance. Donal made his way across the street to the restaurant. Two men stood in low-voiced conversation on the hotel porch. The taller of the pair looked sharply at him, and something he said to his companion made the latter turn his head in a prolonged stare. He was a small, thinnish man, with hard bright eyes set in a mask of a face, and wore a star pinned to his shirt.

Donal paused at the restaurant door and glanced back. The two men were still watching him. Donal was conscious of a flare of anger. He pushed into the restaurant.

A waitress, the only one in the place, hurried to his table as he pulled out a chair. "You're lucky," she began; "the door would have been closed in another five minutes. Everybody is going to the dance at the hotel." She drew back slightly as he looked up, and he sensed that the anger in his face must have startled her. He felt unaccountably sorry. Something about her attracted him.

She stood silent, waiting for his order.

"Hope I'm not keeping you from the dance." He spoke awkwardly. "Maybe I can find some other place —"

She shook her head. "The saloons serve a free lunch, but that's not enough for a hungry man."

7

"I'm hungry, you bet," Donal admitted with a grin. "What have you got that's quick?"

The waitress told him with businesslike crispness.

"I'll take the steak," said Donal, "and the apple pie and coffee."

She hurried off to the kitchen. Donal watched her. He liked the trim look of her — the way she walked. She was pretty, too.

She was back in a few moments with bread and butter and a glass of water. "Stranger here?" Her smile was friendly again. "Don't think I've seen you before."

"Three years since I was here," he told her. "The town has changed. Hardly know the place."

"I haven't been here long myself," confided the waitress. She shrugged her shoulders. "Maybe it was a better place when you were here three years ago."

Something in her voice made him look at her sharply. "You don't like San Benito?"

"Not so much." She refilled his water glass, stood watching him make a cigarette.

"It's a good country," Donal said. He sensed the girl was lonesome and wanted to talk.

She looked at him, her expression enigmatic. "You've come to stay?"

"You've guessed it," smiled Donal. He told her about the herd brought up the trail from the Brazos.

She looked troubled. "I'd push those cows some other place a long way from here," she said.

"For what reason?" Donal was startled.

"You'll find out if you stay." She hesitated. "It's none of my business, but I'd hate to see you — get killed!"

**8**

"Who'll do the killing?" His tone was amused.

"How do I know?" She fingered nervously at her apron. "I'm not joking."

"I don't scare easily," Donal said with a short laugh.

Her smile returned. "I'm sure of that. Anybody can see you're the sort of man who will fight." Her face sobered. "My father was that way, too — not easily scared." Her low voice faltered. "Didn't stop them from — killing him."

Donal stared at her, shocked, wordless, filled with a vast compassion. She gave him a crooked little smile, turned hastily away. "Your steak will be ready by now." She sped toward the kitchen.

Somebody pushed in through the street door — the tall man whose stare Donal had resented. He stood for a moment, his gaze going past Donal to the kitchen door. Apparently the girl heard and recognized his step. The door opened, framed her peering face.

"Bring me a cup of coffee," the newcomer said. He moved toward a table near the wall.

"Yes, Mr. Daker" — the girl's dark head withdrew.

The timid note in her voice drew a frown from Donal. He wondered which would come first. This arrogant man's coffee, or his own steak.

He was conscious of a quick pleasure when the kitchen door opened and the girl appeared with a loaded tray. She deftly placed the steak in front of him and filled his coffee cup from a small pot which she placed on the table.

"I'm making the apple pie hot for you," she said in a low voice. "Hope the steak is good."

"Hurry up with my coffee, Isabel." Daker's voice was surly. "I'm in a rush."

She threw him a quick nod, sped back to the kitchen. Donal tackled the steak. It was a good steak and he was ravenous. He looked across at Daker. Cowman stood out from every inch of his big frame. No mistaking the breed. A cattleman in a big way, judging from his looks. Donal was familiar with the type. Arrogant, overbearing, impatient of opposition.

The waitress was swiftly back with the demanded cup of coffee. Daker said something. She put in sugar and cream for him. Donal saw that her slim body had taken on an odd tenseness as she bent over the table. He heard Daker's voice, a low rumble. "How about that proposition of mine, Isabel?"

The girl shook her head and it was obvious that her answer displeased the man. His rumbling voice loudened. "About time you make up your mind. No sense — you staying here in this place slinging hash for all the bums that come in."

Her voice reached Donal clearly, agitated, almost pleading: "I can't make up my mind now, Mr. Daker. You must give me more time to think it over." She went quickly back to the kitchen. Her face was pale.

Daker drained his cup and got out of the chair. There was a dark angry flush on his sunburned face. He was a bear of a man, rugged and big-framed, perhaps in his early fifties. There was a touch of gray under the wide-brimmed hat which he had failed to remove.

He stood there, glowering, then his gaze swung toward Donal. It was apparent that he wanted to vent his spleen on somebody. The young stranger would do.

Donal looked up as Daker approached. The man's animosity seemed to well out of him like a red mist. "When did *you* get into town?" His voice was harsh.

"An hour or so ago. Not that it's any concern of yours."

"Don't give me any lip, young man."

Donal stared up at him, lowered his look to the big hand hovering over holstered gun, fingers spread wide apart. He eased his own long legs cautiously under the table.

"Where are you from?"

"That's *my* business."

"Where are you headed for?"

"The same answer will do." Donal's own gun slid up with a swift motion of his hand, lay there on the table, fingers wrapped around the butt. He watched the other man closely.

"That was quick work." Grudging admiration was in Daker's voice. "Tough, huh?"

"I can take care of myself," Donal said.

Daker's hand came away from the gun in his belt. His expression relaxed somewhat. "I know who you are. You're that young Cameron I've been hearing talk of."

"That's my name."

Daker bent toward him. "You figure to run cows in the Rio Seco country. I heard about it . . . been on the lookout for you."

"It's no secret," Donal said.

Daker's face reddened. "I'm giving you some good advice. Keep those cows moving till you're a long way from the Rio Seco, young man. We don't need you in these parts."

He gave Donal no time for a rejoinder, went stamping out to the street.

The pretty waitress had evidently been watching. She hurried from the kitchen. "I heard him!" She was visibly disturbed. "I tried to warn you about this place. I'd do what he said — go a long way from this part of the country."

"He talks big." Donal shrugged his shoulders. "Big talk doesn't scare me."

"He *is* big! Jim Daker is the biggest cattleman in the district — and he hates nesters."

"I'm no nester," retorted Donal. He flushed.

"Mr. Daker hates anybody who comes to this range. He doesn't want newcomers. He — he's dangerous."

Her concern for his safety warmed him. He gave her a slow smile, said casually, "My name is Donal Cameron . . . mostly Don — among friends."

She dimpled. "I'm Isabel Lee."

"I heard Daker call you Isabel." Donal looked down at his plate. "I couldn't help hearing what he said."

Her answer lifted his head in an astonished look.

"Mr. Daker wants to adopt me as a daughter."

"*Adopt* you!"

"He is sorry for me." She faltered. "My father and young brother were killed, and Mr. Daker is sorry for me — he says."

12

Donal looked at her keenly. She had said something earlier about her father. *Not easily scared . . . didn't stop them from killing him.*

"My father had a small cattle ranch," Isabel went on in a low voice. "He was told to leave, and because he refused we were burned out, and —" Her voice choked.

"I see," Donal said gently. "Don't talk about it." He looked at her thoughtfully. "Why don't you let Daker adopt you? He must be a rich man."

Isabel shook her dark head. "I can't make up my mind. Something keeps me from — from it." She returned to his own problem. "I hope you'll take Mr. Daker's warning. You will only run into trouble if you try to locate in the Rio Seco country. No matter if you do fight back . . . you just have no chance."

He changed the subject. "I'll be seeing you at the dance," he said.

"No! no!" Her tone was horrified. "You must leave town — tonight."

Donal got out of his chair. "I'll see you at the dance," he repeated. He stood there, smiling at her. "I'm going over to the hotel for a room and a chance to wash off some of this trail dust."

She made no answer, just looked at him, her eyes wide, her lips parted.

"You'll be there, Isabel?"

She nodded her head. "Yes, I'll be there — Don."

Donal's smile broadened. "I haven't danced for a coon's age," he confided. "I'm sure lucky tonight, Isabel."

He was gone. The girl stood there, staring at the swinging door. Her look went slowly down to the table. Suddenly she was smiling, and hurrying toward the kitchen with the gathered dishes.

The man behind the desk in the hotel lobby gave Donal a morose look. "Ain't you got eyes?" he wanted to know.

"You're looking at them now," retorted Donal.

"If you'll use 'em," said the clerk, "you'll see that sign proclaimin' loud there ain't no beds left for nobody."

"Don't see any sign." Donal's glance roved about the lobby.

"Doggone!" The clerk's tone was sheepish. He spat into a tall brass spittoon. "Looks like some dumb fool has gone an' walked off with that sign. Figgered to be funny, I reckon."

Donal grimaced. "The fact remains the same . . . no beds left."

"The shoutin' truth," agreed the clerk. He spat again into the spittoon, looked at the tall stranger speculatively. "Cowman, ain't you?"

"Bringing a bunch up the trail," admitted Donal.

"I'd like a dollar for every dogie I've done had a rope on," said the clerk. "Reckon I'd be ridin' for Jim Daker right now if it hadn't been for this —" His eyes slanted a glance down at his left arm. "A feller wearin' a hook for a hand ain't much good with a rope."

14

"I knew a man down on the Brazos who had one of those things," Donal told him. "Hooky Joe, we called him."

"I'm just plain Hook," grinned the clerk. "Hook Saval. Got tangled with a mess of bob wire one night when my bronc took a notion to play peek-a-boo with the stars. Time I gets untangled my hand is clean sawed through the bone. Finished the job with my jackknife."

"You're a tough hombre," admired Donal.

The ex-cowpuncher caressed his grizzled mustache with the shiny hook. "I reckon they don't come tougher," he admitted complacently. "Ridin' herd on a doggone hotel just don't set good in my craw, but Jim Daker ain't to be balked when he gets a notion."

"Daker owns this hotel?"

"Sure he does. Owns the Daker House an' doggone proud of it he is. We ain't hardly ready for bus'ness yet, but these Fourth o' July doin's kind of pushed us to open ahead of time."

"Daker owns the new store, too?"

"Jim is pardners with Al DeSang in the store," replied Hook. "Al runs the store an' the saloon over on the other corner, the Longhorn. Al owns the Longhorn. Got some good-lookers in his dancehall." The clerk paused, added reflectively, "Why don't you bed down at the feed barn? You can tell Billy Winch I sent you. Billy runs the San Benito Feed and Livery Stable."

Donal thanked him for the suggestion. People were thronging into the lobby, pushing toward the long room in the rear. The dining room, Donal guessed. The place was brightly lighted by big kerosene lamps swung from

15

the beams of the unfinished ceiling. Red, white and blue bunting draped the walls.

Hook Saval saw his look. "Dinin' room ain't open for bus'ness yet. Not till we get the tables an' chairs in from Albuquerque. She's all right for the dance, though. We done fixed the floor awful slippery." He stared at Donal thoughtfully. "Was you aimin' to come to the big dance, feller?"

Donal admitted the thought was in his mind.

"You'll want to get a ticket," Hook suggested. "Gents five bucks a head . . . ladies free."

"Didn't know I had to get a ticket."

"I can fix you up." Hook fished out a ticket from a desk drawer, looked at him inquiringly.

The young cattleman thought ruefully of his dwindling funds. But he had promised the pretty Isabel Lee he would see her again at the dance. He pulled out a five dollar gold piece and rang it on the desk. "There's your money, Hook."

The clerk handed over the pasteboard, hesitated, leaned toward him confidentially. "I like your looks, young feller. If I was you, I'd keep them cows of yours movin' till you've got 'em a long ways from here. This country ain't healthy for a feller lookin' for new range."

"Thanks for the tip." Donal turned away and pushed through the crowd toward the street door. He was conscious of a hot resentment. Hardly more than an hour in this town, and three people had warned him to be on his way out. Not a healthy country for a newcomer, old Hook Saval had told him. Donal's jaw set in hard lines. He carried good medicine for *that* sort of bad health.

The young cattleman came to a standstill on the hotel porch that still gave out the smell of fresh pine lumber, and thoughtfully made and lit a cigarette. He was not going to be scared away from the Rio Seco. The plan had been with him for three years, ever since the time he brought up the Bar 77 trail-herd for the Silver City man. He had fallen in love with this Southwestern New Mexico, and he had worked and scraped and saved for the small herd of cattle that now wore the Circle C on their hides. He was determined to make that brand well-known in the Rio Seco country. He was here, now, and he was going to stay. This was *his* country.

# CHAPTER
# TWO

# The Mislaid Gun

The problem of a place to sleep still remained to be settled. Donal started up the street in a direction opposite to the one that would have taken him to the San Benito Feed and Livery Stable. If it was to be a straw pile he knew of a better plan than seeking the hospitality of Hook's friend, Billy Winch.

Two men pushed out of the Longhorn Saloon. The look of hard, almost fierce resolve on the face of this stranger drew brief inquisitive glances from the pair as they crossed the street toward the hotel.

Daker men, Donal guessed. Daker would be the sort who hand-picked the members of his outfit. He would be intolerant of inefficiency, and these lean, hard punchers who had just passed him wore the earmarks of top hands. There was something formidable about the older man, with his harsh face and insolent self-assurance. A man to be wary of, Donal reflected as he kept on his way toward the Trading Post corral. He knew the type, ruthless, predatory — and dangerous.

He passed a small frame building, its new pine boards still paintless. Above the door was a sign that indicated the place was the office of the town marshal.

**18**

A man stood in the doorway, the same individual he had noticed talking to Jim Daker on the hotel porch.

The marshal jerked him a brief nod. "Howdy!" His voice was thinly nasal, his face an expressionless mask.

Donal said, "Howdy," went on his way, conscious of the man's unwinking stare following him. He felt in his bones that he was not going to like the marshal of San Benito. There was a prickly, deadly look to the man.

Again he found Jim Daker in the picture. This was Daker's town — the marshal was Daker's man, and he would keep the sort of law and order decreed by his boss.

Roderick Dhu opened the gate of the stockade corral.

"I'm looking for a bed," Donal told him with a grin. "Got plenty of clean straw, Rod?"

"Plenty straw," replied the Apache. "You no need straw for bed. You friend of Angus . . . same name with Angus and me. You sleep on good bed in house." A smile lit his dark face. "Angus like you sleep on his bed. He talk a lot about you . . . he say you what he call his clan."

"I'm in luck," Donal said gratefully. "I'll want to wash up, Rod. I'm going to that dance."

The Apache youth led him to the back door of the big store building. It opened into a roomy kitchen with a hard earthen floor. A large brick range stood in one corner and there was a homemade sink with a hand-pump. An old Mexican woman looked up from a pan simmering on the fire.

"This is our friend, the one the old señor talk about," introduced the Indian. "He will sleep here tonight."

The old woman smiled. "*Si, si.*" — She turned back to the simmering pan.

Donal followed the youth into a small, dark passage and found himself in Angus Cameron's bedroom.

"I bring hot water," Roderick Dhu said.

"Cold water is good enough," demurred the young cowman. The pitcher on the homemade washstand was full, he observed.

"Manuela always have plenty hot water," insisted the Apache. "I bring tub for you to have good wash all over." He opened a drawer in the washstand. "Here is razor — soap."

Donal rubbed his bristly chin. "Maybe you are talking good sense, Rod."

"Sure." Roderick Dhu's swarthy face showed amusement. "We make you look fine for this dance. Maybe you meet plenty girls."

"That's right." Donal's pulse quickened as he thought of Isabel Lee. "Bring on your hot water, young friend."

In less than half an hour he was out in the kitchen again. Manuela smiled approval. "This young man is beautiful," she said in Spanish to the Apache. "He has the grand manner."

Donal's eyes twinkled. "*Gracias, señora.*"

The Mexican woman gave him an embarrassed smile. "You speak my tongue, sir? I did not know."

"All my life I have had many friends among your people," Donal told her in Spanish. "Many thanks for the good hot water. I am so clean I squeak."

Roderick Dhu said thoughtfully, "You are now fix up fine for the dance. The girls will look at you, but if you wear that gun you will have looks not so nice from Rede Sems."

"Who is Rede Sems?"

"He is the town marshal, also he is more dangerous than a rattlesnake." The Apache's black eyes hardened. "A bad hombre to tangle with."

"I can leave my gun with Hook Saval at the hotel desk," Donal suggested.

"Better you leave the gun with me," advised Roderick Dhu.

"Hook seems like a decent old-timer," argued Donal. "I like him."

"Hook Saval works for Jim Daker," the Apache said softly. "There is talk that Rede Sems also takes his orders from the same boss."

"Meaning what?"

"Angus teach me all I know," Roderick Dhu said. "He teach me to speak good American and he teach me arithmetic like two and two make four."

"I savvy." Donal smiled. "Hook Saval plus Rede Sems equals Jim Daker."

"Or maybe Al DeSang who is a big man in this town and Daker's partner." The Indian shook his head. "Add 'em any way you like, you get bad medicine. Maybe I wrong. Maybe you stand all right with Jim Daker and Al DeSang." His eyes narrowed in a keen look.

"Daker told me I wasn't wanted in this town," admitted Donal. "I don't know DeSang. Haven't met him yet."

"He is smart," Roderick Dhu said noncommittally, and then gravely, "If you smart you no go to that dance."

"I've made a promise to be there. I don't break a promise, Rod."

"I like you, Don," the Apache said simply. "You are my brother."

"We are brothers," agreed Donal. His stern face relaxed in a warm smile. "*Adios*, Rod. See you later."

"You no leave gun with me?" The Indian's tone was disappointed.

"I'll take a chance with Hook," Donal told him amusedly. "I might need that gun in one big hurry."

The scraping of a fiddle touched his ears as he made his way along the deserted street toward the hotel. The dance was on. Isabel Lee would be thinking he had lost his nerve and obeyed Jim Daker's orders to get out of town. Don quickened his stride.

He paused on the porch steps, listened to the caller's voice lifting above the shuffle and stamp of feet.

"First couple out and swing to the middle,
Shake your big feet to the tune of the fiddle."

Donal grinned, pushed up the steps and through the lobby door.

22

Blue Clover saw him from the entrance to the dance floor. He came up, a broad smile on his face. "Wasn't expectin' to see *you* over here, Don."

"Don't often get a chance to swing my big feet to the tune of a fiddle," chuckled the Texan.

> "Take that new one an' swing her 'round,
> A prettier gal just cain't be found —"

Donal caught a glimpse of Isabel, flushed and laughing-eyed. Her partner was the big, ruthless-faced man he had noticed crossing the street. He was aware of a sharp, jealous twinge, was aware, too, of a flat, toneless voice.

"Take a look at that sign, mister, or maybe you cain't read."

Donal turned, met the town marshal's unwinking stare. Rede Sems flexed a thumb at the placard tacked to the desk.

### GENTS MUST LEAVE GUNS
### WITH DESK CLERK

"Sure!" Donal said good-naturedly. He unbuckled his belt and moved to the desk.

"I'll keep her safe for you," promised Hook Saval. There was approval in the brief scrutiny he gave the .45 in the holster.

"I'll get you acquainted," Blue Clover offered. "You'll have to kind of horn in, Don. There's two fellers for every girl."

23

"I've already picked one out." Donal's eyes were on Isabel. "The one in the pink dress."

Blue saw his look, shook his head dubiously. "Watch your step with her. Lew Trent is all set to get his rope on that one."

"Who is Lew Trent?" Donal was watching the trim, graceful girl in the pink dress.

"Lew is foreman of the Rocking D — Jim Daker's outfit." The young ranchman's voice was troubled. "Ain't wanting to speak out of turn, Don, but you're new here. Trent don't like competition no more than his boss does."

"Much obliged, Blue."

"No sense in you getting tangled with Trent too quick," insisted Clover. "He can make a lot of grief for you."

"I'll take a chance," smiled Donal.

A tall, well-built man approached the desk. His appearance was striking, drew Donal's attention. An expensive white Stetson covered well-barbered black hair, and he wore a long black coat and fawn-colored trousers that were tucked into shiny black boots. A big diamond glittered in his tie and he had the quiet manner and smooth affability of a professional gambler.

"Hello, Hook." His broad white teeth gleamed under a heavy black mustache as he looked at the placard. "You know I never wear a gun, Rede," he said to the town marshal.

Sems made no reply, but Hook winked knowingly. "Meanin' you don't wear 'em conspicuous-like, huh, Al?" He stared pointedly at the man's left breast.

24

"You talk too much," the newcomer said curtly. He turned away, halted as Blue Clover spoke to him.

"Want you to meet Don Cameron, Mr. DeSang. Don come in for supplies . . . found the stores all closed."

DeSang smiled cordially. "Sorry, Cameron. Guess we can fix you up in the morning."

"How early do you open?" asked Donal.

"Seven o'clock," DeSang answered.

"I'll be around," Donal said. "Want to get an early start."

"Glad to have met you," DeSang assured him. "Daker was speaking of you," he added with an amused lift of dark brows.

Donal shrugged, made no answer. He felt that the man was trying to draw him out.

DeSang's smile widened. "I wouldn't let Daker scare you," he said. "Daker hates nesters, but you're not a nester."

"No more than he is," Donal rejoined. With a curt nod he turned and followed Blue Clover to the dance-floor.

"Head gents forward an' back once more," bellowed the caller, "forward ag'in as you did before —"

Donal saw his chance, stepped in, hands reaching for Isabel. Her eyes widened, her color heightened, as she met his smiling look. The caller's strident voice filled their ears.

"A prettier gal just cain't be found —"

"I'd given you up," Isabel said a bit breathlessly.

"I wasn't missing this chance for a dance with you," Donal replied.

"I was hoping you had left town." The girl darted an apprehensive glance at the Rocking D foreman. "You shouldn't have come."

"You really wanted me to go?"

"No — no . . . yes — oh, yes!" She was confused, distressed.

"Fifty-fifty, anyway I like to take it," Donal said with a laugh. And then, almost harshly, "I'm staying for keeps, Isabel. This is *my* country."

The caller's voice scaled downward. "An' seat your pardner in the old armchair," he commanded huskily.

The fiddle stopped with a squeak and they moved to one of the wooden benches against the wall. Lew Trent followed them.

"Ice cream in the room back yonder," he said to Isabel. His unsmiling eyes apparently failed to see Donal. "Allow me the pleasure." He crooked an inviting right arm.

"Your mistake," Donal said softly. "The lady is my partner."

The tall Rocking D man's head turned in a slow look at him. His eyes were very bright — and hard. "I don't make mistakes, mister."

"Please!" The girl spoke in a low, frightened voice, and her hand went to Trent's arm. "Thank you, Mr. Cameron — and good-bye — if I don't see you again before you leave town." She threw Donal an appealing look as she moved away with Trent.

**26**

Donal stood there, angered, resentful. The girl was again warning him, almost begging him, to leave town. He met Lew Trent's backward glance. There was a threat, a deadly promise, in that stormy look.

Surprise spread over Hook Saval's face as Donal approached the desk. His grizzled brows lifted inquiringly. "Leavin' the dance some early, son!"

"Need some sleep, Hook." Donal forced a smile. "You know how it is, pushing a bunch of cows up the trail."

"Used to think there was no place to sleep 'cept settin' there on a saddle," chuckled Hook. "You don't need to tell me, young feller." He was scrutinizing the array of gun-belts piled on the floor behind the desk. "Now where in blazes has that Colt of yours gone an' hid itself!"

Donal leaned over the desk for a look. "The belt has a square silver buckle with my Circle C mark on it," he said.

"I know —" Old Hook spoke fretfully. "Seen that mark on the buckle when you handed her over to me." He met Donal's look. There was a hard light in the young Texan's eyes. "Could have sworn I put that Colt 'longside the others."

"It's not there now." Donal's tone was chilly.

"It sure ain't." Embarrassment brought a flush to Hook's leathery face. "Looks like some doggone polecat's been snootin' 'round while I was gone."

"You've been away from the desk?" Donal spoke sharply. "How long were you gone?"

"Wasn't gone for more'n ten minutes. Went up to my room for a fresh plug of terbaccer. Rede Sems said he'd keep his eye on things till I got back." Hook broke off with a relieved ejaculation. "Doggone! Here she is — layin' in the cubby shelf." He reached under the desk and pulled the missing gun-belt into view. "Must have stuck her in there my own self kind of unthinkin'."

Donal buckled on the belt. "I was scared for a minute, Hook. Hated to think you were up to some trick." He gave the other man a hard look.

"Wouldn't blame you for thinkin' a lot of hell," declared Hook. "Am sure sorry, son. Must be my mem'ry is goin' plumb to seed."

"No harm done," reassured Donal. "Well, so-long, if I don't see you again."

"Pullin' out early?"

"Just as soon as I get my supplies," Donal told him.

Hook hesitated, said slowly, "I ain't knowin' your plans, son, but good luck to you, even if you *ain't* makin' dust from these parts."

"Thanks." Donal held out his hand. "We'll shake on that, Hook."

Rede Sems was standing on the hotel porch as he emerged from the lobby. The little marshal's unwinking gaze swung to him, followed him down the steps. Donal halted, sent a look back at the man. "You ought to know me next time, Sems," he said.

"Yes," laconically replied the marshal.

"You'll be seeing a lot of me," Donal said. "I'm in this country to stay."

28

The flare of the big swing lamp lay full on that mask-like face, drew cold gleams from the strange eyes. The malignant impact of that wordless look sent prickles through Donal. Not fear, rather a deep anger, a vast dislike. Roderick Dhu was right about Rede Sems. The man was more dangerous than a rattlesnake. There would be no warning when he struck.

The young Apache must have heard his approach. Donal found him waiting at the open corral gate. "Soon back," Roderick Dhu said.

"Want to get an early start in the morning."

"No have good time at dance, huh?"

"Good enough." Donal's tone was curt, and, refraining from further comment, the Indian led the way through the kitchen to the bedroom.

"*Buenas noches*," he said from the doorway.

"Good night, Rod."

The Apache hesitated, his face troubled. "Too bad Angus not here. Angus tell you lots. He is smart and knows men's hearts."

Donal was touched by the youth's ill-concealed anxiety. "I'm learning fast, Rod. Don't you worry. I can take care of myself."

A shadow of a smile flitted across the Apache's dark face. "You smart, too, like old Angus." The door closed behind him softly.

Donal stood there, fingers tugging at the buckle of his belt. He hung it over the back of a chair, stared thoughtfully at the gun in the holster. Something queer about Hook forgetting where he had put the belt. The old man's surprise had been genuine.

He went over the scene carefully. The belt was not lying on the floor with the others. Hook admitted he had been absent from the desk for at least ten minutes. Perhaps longer, Donal shrewdly guessed. And he had asked Rede Sems to keep an eye on things.

Slowly a picture came to Donal. The town marshal behind the desk, alone in the deserted lobby, the array of filled holsters on the floor.

The young cattleman's face hardened. He jerked the long-barreled Colt from the holster, broke it open and emptied the chamber. He let out a grunt, stared angrily at the five empty shells in his palm.

The story was there. Rede Sems had taken advantage of the opportunity, switched blanks for the loaded cartridges. He had probably been in a hurry, warned by Hook's approaching footsteps, and hastily stuffed the belt into the cubby shelf under the desk.

The marshal's cold-blooded purpose was clear. He was planning a murder, a killing he intended to take place before Donal could leave San Benito the next morning.

Donal dropped the blanks into his pocket and carefully reloaded the gun. He wondered why Sems had not forced the issue during the brief encounter on the hotel porch. He knew that Donal's gun was empty, could have killed his proposed victim without risking a return shot.

He could think of only one plausible explanation. Rede Sems wanted the killing to take place in front of witnesses. An attempt to arrest him on some trumped-up charge, some outrageous trick that would force Donal to draw the gun he thought was loaded. Sems would have calmly shot him to death, claimed he was in his rights in defending himself while in the performance of duty.

Donal sat down on the homemade bed and pulled off his boots. It was a lucky break, Sems putting the belt in the wrong place after tampering with the gun. Donal would never have known of Hook's absence from the desk, would have had no reason to be suspicious. He smiled mirthlessly. The marshal was due for a surprise.

# CHAPTER
# THREE

# Murder Intended

Manuela greeted him with a smile when he appeared in the kitchen early in the morning. She had breakfast waiting for the señor, she informed him.

Donal looked ruefully at the sunlight slanting through the windows.

"I should have been on the way an hour ago," he grumbled.

"You sleep like a baby," the Mexican woman said in Spanish. "Like one who has no troubles on his mind. I had not the heart to awake you."

Donal thought of the mislaid gun. He smiled. "When did you ever see a cowman who had no troubles on his mind?"

She looked at him, nodded wisely. "You are a cool one," she said. "You have the eyes of a man who is not disturbed by danger."

He chuckled. "I want to buy a pack outfit," he said to Roderick Dhu who appeared in the doorway. "Can you fix me up, Rod?"

The Apache assured him there were several pack animals in the corral. Donal could have his pick.

"I'm mighty sorry to have missed Angus," regretted the Circle C man.

"You will be in again, soon?"

"You bet," promised Donal. "I've a lot to tell him. Hope he doesn't catch any more bullets." He got up from the table. "Well, let's take a look at those pack-mules."

It was past seven o'clock when he rode up the street with a sleek, mouse-gray mule at the end of a lead-rope. The street was surprisingly lively, considering the festive doings of the previous night. Ranchers and their families, making ready for the journey home, cowpunchers drifting past on their horses.

Donal espied Blue Clover and his wife entering the restaurant. He felt a twinge of regret as he thought of Isabel Lee. He would have liked to see her. The glimpse of the restaurant as he passed told him the place was crowded. There would have been small chance for a few words with the pretty waitress.

Two men came down the steps of the hotel porch and made for the restaurant. He recognized Lew Trent as one of the pair. The Rocking D foreman seemed about to halt as he met Donal's look, then with a word to his companion he turned into the eating-house. The other man craned his head in a keen stare as he followed. It was plain that he was marking the stranger who had had the temerity to dance with Lew's girl.

Donal's mouth twitched in a thin smile. The big Rocking D foreman would find that he didn't have the run of the yard when it came to Isabel Lee.

He rode on past the two saloons where men were pushing in and out of the swing doors. Some of them moved on unsteady legs, still feeling the effects of their Fourth of July celebration. Donal's gaze roved sharply, on the watch for Rede Sems. The marshal was not visible.

The San Benito General Merchandise Store stood on the corner below the hotel. Donal tied his horse to the hitch-rail and mounted the steps. A man watched him from the wide entrance. He nodded a greeting.

"Good mornin', suh." He was a small, rotund person and wore a white goatee and a Prince Albert coat. "Are you looking for Al DeSang, suh?"

"Not especially." Donal paused. "Want to get a few supplies. Are you the manager here?"

The man slapped limply at the cigar ash on the waistcoat that bulged over a protruding stomach. "No, suh. Soper is my name. Judge Soper, attorney-at-law." He beamed genially under his broad-brimmed hat. "We have been celebratin' our grand an' glorious Fourth, suh. Too bad you did not arrive in our fair town sooner, suh."

"I was here last night," smiled Donal. "Lively time in town last night, Judge."

"The Fourth is not the only time this town is lively," asserted Judge Soper. "This town is fair and square on the map now Al DeSang is running things. Al is making money hand over fist. A smart man, suh, and a very good friend of mine."

"I thought Jim Daker was the boss of San Benito," commented Donal.

34

"Daker thinks of nothing but cattle," Judge Soper replied. "An important man, suh, and most able in his line, which is cattle. He hates nesters, by the way." The judge nodded solemnly. "You didn't tell me your name, suh."

"Cameron," Donal informed him. He looked at the judge intently. It was obvious he had been drinking. He reeked of whisky, and the pudgy hand holding the cigar was shaky.

"Cameron? You say *Cameron*, suh?" Soper blinked protuberant eyes. "H-mm, the young man Jim Daker has been telling me about." He shook his head gravely. "You are a bold man, suh. I gather that Mr. Daker does not want you in this country. There is no range here for you, suh."

"I'm not asking for your opinion, Judge." Donal spoke coldly.

"It's my duty to warn you, young man."

Donal shrugged, went into the store. He was annoyed, and somewhat disturbed by the encounter. He had the feeling that the judge had deliberately waylaid him for some mysterious reason. He was again being warned off. Soper must have known who he was, which meant that Daker had probably put him up to it.

In less than half an hour he had purchased his supplies and was riding down the street with the laden pack-mule on a lead-rope. The Clovers came out of the restaurant, and at the young ranchman's hail, Donal checked his horse.

"On your way, huh?" Blue Clover crossed over to the middle of the street. "Good luck to you, Don. Be seein' you again, sometime."

"You bet —" Donal broke off, was suddenly tense. The man crossing from the opposite side of the street was the sinister little town marshal.

Blue Clover said softly, "Watch out, Don —"

The town marshal's thin, nasal voice interrupted. "Climb down from your saddle, Cameron, and keep your hands in sight." He stood in a half crouch, hands pressing low to both holstered guns.

There was a stillness in the street. Three men coming out of the saloon opposite the hotel halted abruptly, faces turned in rigid attention. Out of the corner of his eye Donal glimpsed Lew Trent framed in the restaurant doorway. The startled face of Isabel Lee appeared at the Rocking D man's shoulder.

"You heard me, Cameron. I ain't waiting for no palaver." The marshal's voice cut through the stillness like the whining blade of a knife.

"I'm not getting down, Sems." Donal spoke quietly. "Why should I?"

"I'm taking you to jail," Sems said. His fingers spread over gun-butts.

"What for?" Donal watched him closely. As yet he had made no motion to reach for his own gun. He caught Blue Clover's frantic whisper. "Don't start nothin', Don! He's a killer."

Somebody pushed through the hotel door. Jim Daker. His huge frame froze to a standstill on the high porch. He stood there, silent, attentive.

**36**

The pieces were fitting into their proper places in the picture. In those fleeting seconds Donal knew he had correctly interpreted the meaning of the empty shells found in his gun. The town marshal thought he was confronting an unarmed and helpless man. The needed witnesses were present. He could safely kill his intended victim and there would be no blame attached to him.

"I am riding on my way, Sems," Donal said laconically. His horse swung sideways under the light touch of spur. "Don't try to stop me."

Sems was suddenly jerking at his guns.

Not one of the tense watchers saw the movement of Donal's hand. It was too incredibly fast. They only knew that his .45 was belching noise and smoke.

Sems spun crazily around, the gun in his right hand exploding as it fell from his grasp. He tried to pull himself back into position and lift his other gun. Donal's pack-mule, panicked by the shots, made a frantic half-circle at the end of the lead-rope and let fly with both heels that caught Sems neatly on the place he used for sitting purposes. The town marshal flew through the air, landed sprawling on his face in the dust.

Somebody laughed, old Hook Saval, framed in the hotel entrance. "That jenny mule sure kicks nice," he loudly declared.

Donal's quick look at the crowd told him that the danger was over for the moment. These men were smiling broadly. It was apparent that the town marshal was not any too popular in San Benito.

37

His look went briefly to the restaurant door. Isabel Lee's hand was on Lew Trent's arm and she was saying something to him in frantic undertones. The Rocking D man freed himself with an impatient gesture, went clattering down the boardwalk. Apparently the girl had dissuaded him from going to the marshal's aid.

Donal holstered his gun, drew in the slack of the mule's lead-rope and rode up to Sems who was getting painfully to his knees. Jim Daker and Hook hurried across from the hotel porch, were in time to hear Donal's curt words.

"I think these blanks belong to you, Sems," he said. He tossed the five brass shells into the marshal's face.

Hook Saval was making angry noises in his throat. "The skunk!" he ejaculated. "So that's what he done behind my back!"

Sems got to his feet. His right hand hung limp and bloody. "You were lucky this time," he said. "Next time — not so lucky." He flicked a glance at his two guns, lying several feet apart in the dusty street.

"I could have killed you," Donal told him. "Pick up your guns if you want, Sems. We'll shoot it out man to man — only this time it's fair play."

The marshal gazed up at him, then again glanced at his guns.

"You've got one good hand," encouraged Donal. "I'm giving you your chance, Sems."

Rede Sems stood there, looking like a man too thunder-struck for words. He went red and white in swift succession, then still silent he turned and walked slowly away.

"You're acting mighty high-handed with this town's peace officer," grumbled Jim Daker, breaking the silence.

Donal looked at him for a moment, his eyes frosty. "Was he obeying *your* orders, Daker?"

The cattleman's head jerked back as though he had been struck a blow, and then slowly an angry flush spread over his face. "I don't like that sort of talk, young man."

"As for that I don't like your town marshal trying to murder me," retorted Donal. "I don't like a lot of things in this town."

"I didn't put Sems up to this," denied Daker in a choked voice. "I told him I didn't want you 'round here, but I didn't tell him to kill you."

"He knew you wouldn't do any crying about it if his trick had worked," drawled Donal.

"Maybe not," frankly admitted the owner of the Rocking D. "I'm sticking to what I told you, Cameron. There's no room for you here. If you've got good sense you'll keep traveling a long way from these parts."

"My answer still stands," replied Donal curtly. "There is room for me in this man's country. Neither you nor anyone else can scare me out of it." With a parting gesture he rode up the street with the laden pack-mule.

Roderick Dhu rose up from behind a big flat boulder as he passed the stockade corral. There was a rifle in his hands.

"I will watch that snake," he called out softly. "Keep going, my brother. It is best for you to be on your way."

"*Adios*, Rod," Donal called back. His expression was thoughtful as he rode on. Rede Sems would have lived no longer than it took for the Apache's bullet to reach him.

# CHAPTER
# FOUR

# Circle C Reads Sign

The creek flowed between low banks covered with a thick growth of trees. There were cottonwoods and alders, and dense tangles of brush. Here and there the sunlight played on the dappled trunks of sycamores. A mile or two down, the banks drew wide apart, allowed the stream to spread in shallows that moved lazily through a tule-covered marsh before the current drew in deep and narrow for the swift plunge down the gorge to empty into the Rio Seco.

Donal checked his horse. "Tule Creek, according to the map," he said to Rusty Cross.

Rusty stared at the spreading marsh. "Never saw a prettier layout," he commented in a satisfied voice. "Circle C will sure go places."

"Won't be easy," Donal said soberly. "We may have to do some fighting — to hold it."

"Don't go to raisin' my hopes, Don," chuckled the other man. "I was sort of scared that maybe we'd get soft with a sweet-lookin' spread like this. I'm sure sold on this New Mexico country."

"You boys won't have a chance to go soft," Donal assured him. "Jim Daker is going to be a tough nut."

"I've got teeth that can crack any nut," bragged Rusty. He was a brown-faced man, perhaps a year or two older than Donal, with straight black hair and snapping black eyes that seemed to be ever on the alert. "You've got an outfit that just don't savvy how to back up from any man."

"That's right," agreed Donal.

"Hand-picked from the best in the Brazos country," boasted Rusty. "Take Brasca . . . he don't want sugar in his coffee if he can get lead. And Wes Coles — that cow-poke is so tough bullets just slide off his hide. And old Bearcat — he ain't happy unless he's hung up a couple of rustlers before breakfast."

"Don't forget yourself, Rusty," laughed his boss.

"I don't ever take a back seat no time," modestly asserted the cowboy. "No more than Rubio does. That Mexican is sure sudden death when he gets on the prod. He's an hombre to tie to in a pinch." Rusty's smile widened. "Reckon Old Sinful has us all beat at that, when it comes to bein' *real* tough. Just got one fault . . . his doggone doleful singin'."

"Sinful is a good cook," reminded Donal.

"Cain't be beat," generously conceded Rusty. "Reminds me — I saw a flock of ducks liftin' out of the tules. I reckon to bag some of 'em for Old Sinful to fix up for us. Give us a change from that everlastin' beef."

The pair rode across the flats toward a straggling growth of cottonwoods in the bend of the creek. Long before they sighted the chuckwagon hidden in the fringe of green they could hear the cook's unmelodious voice lifted in song.

42

"The darned old mossyhorn," grumbled Rusty. "He's got no call to be feelin' down in the dumps."

"Don't get him wrong," advised Donal good-naturedly. "You should know by this time that Old Sinful is feeling fine when he sings that song."

"He sure must be feelin' awful good," admitted Rusty. "Never heard him put so much bleatin' into that funny noise he calls his voice."

The cook swung his head in a brief glance as they rode up to the chuckwagon, then returned his attention to the pot simmering over the fire. "Waal, boss, we done crost the Jordan, an' here she lays, as sweet a spread o' range as I ever did see."

"When do we eat?" interrupted Rusty. He sniffed hungrily.

Old Sinful fixed a cold look on him. "When I get good an' ready," he replied. He smiled wickedly. "If you're so doggone eager, young feller, you can go snake some of that dead alder wood over here. I'm nigh out of fuel."

"You can burn wood faster than the devil can roast a sinner," grumbled the cowboy as he rode off toward a fallen tree.

"It's for your own good," called the cook. "Never seen a outfit get away with more food than you boys stow into your stummicks." He grinned at Donal. "Was lookin' at that 'dobe house back yonder in the trees. Reckon 'twas *some place* a long time before the Mex war was fit."

"Been there close on two hundred years," Donal told him.

"Looks it," dryly commented the cook. He spat into the fire, reached for an onion and began slicing it into the simmering kettle. "Likely ha'nted, but we'll run 'em out, 'long with the cobwebs an' scorpeens an' such." Old Sinful chuckled contentedly. "Yes, sirree, we'll make a bang-up ranch house out of that ol' place."

"You bet." Donal smiled. "We've got a job of work on our hands, but not too big for Circle C."

"Them green apples you fotched over from town come in right handy," observed the cook. "I'm fixin' up a fresh apple pie for the boys. Sort o' celebratin' the end o' trail for us."

"We'll rise up and call you blessed," declared Donal.

"Waal" — Old Sinful spat into the fire again — "I been called a heap o' names in my time. Reckon a new one ain't goin' to harm me none."

The sun was dipping low to the distant mountain peaks. Already the shadows were beginning their crawl up the lower slopes. Donal swung his horse, rode out of the grove of trees to a low rise a few hundred yards away. He reined to a halt, sat there in his saddle, fingers busy with cigarette paper and tobacco.

His eyes glowed as he studied the scene, cattle leisurely getting their fill of the nourishing grass. The Circle C herd, a small one, but it would grow. There was plenty of grass-covered range, miles of range, and always plenty of water in Tule Creek when the springs dried up.

Two men rode toward him. Old Bearcat and Rubio. They drew their horses to a standstill, greeted him with contented nods.

"Wes and Brasca figger to take first watch," Bearcat said. "Won't be no trouble with them cows tonight with their bellies full of that grama grass."

"Those cow mooch 'appy," Rubio declared. He was a middle-aged, graying Mexican, inclined to paunchiness. There was a touch of Indian in the saddle-colored, deeply-lined face under the tall steeple hat. His eyes, alert and smiling, relieved the harshness of his expression.

"I'm riding over for a look at the old house," Donal told them. "You come along, Rubio."

"Most time to eat," Bearcat reminded. He went on down the rise, toward the spiral of smoke that lifted above the trees.

Donal glanced at the Mexican riding by his side. "You know this country, you told me." He spoke in Spanish.

"It is a long time ago," Rubio answered. "Many years ago — when I was a boy. It is different now."

They circled around a fringe of cottonwoods and came to a halt. Set back in a big grove of trees was a large adobe house. There were other smaller buildings of the same rough adobe construction, and the remains of several corrals in a large clearing now overgrown with weeds and underbrush.

"Yes," murmured the Mexican. "It is different now."

"You knew Fidel Salazar?"

"Yes, I knew the old señor. Hard times came to him. He was in much trouble always. A good man, but not smart enough for the gringos."

**45**

"We'll make the place a good ranch again, Rubio." Donal's tone was confident. "Won't be done unless we put up a better fight than old Salazar did."

They got down from their horses. Donal heard a startled exclamation from the Mexican.

"*Señor!* Somet'ing move!" Rubio changed to Spanish. "It was like a shadow — over there where the sunlight lies low on the wall."

"I saw nothing." Donal looked curiously at the Mexican. "Your nerves are jumpy."

Rubio's swarthy face had a grayish look to it. "No, no. You know me. I do not fear any man." He hesitated. "It is only that one hears talk about old Don Fidel. It is said that he is seen sometimes — walking here." Rubio crossed himself devoutly. "Look! Again I see that thing that moves on the wall. I do not like this."

In spite of himself, Donal was conscious of a prickle of apprehension. It was in his mind that something far more dangerous than the ghost of the murdered Fidel Salazar might be lurking within the walls of the old house.

He drew back behind a clump of tall bunch grass. Rubio crouched by his side, and for several moments they watched the wall where the lingering sunset rays played.

"I see nothing," Donal finally said. "It is your fancy . . . these tales of the old don have gone to your head."

The Mexican denied the charge. His eyes had not deceived him. Something had moved. Twice he had seen the shadow flit across the wall. "It is the old master," he whispered. "He looks for his wife, for his son and the little ones who were his son's children." He crossed himself again. "It is true . . . the master comes back from the grave — always seeking them."

"Don't be a fool," grumbled Donal, and then, "You were here when it happened, Rubio. Is it true they were killed by Apache raiders?"

"I was a small boy," the Mexican replied. "All that night I hid inside a cave the creek waters had dug under the bank. There was much noise and burning haystacks. It was terrible. Don Fidel — all of them killed."

Donal drew his gun. "It's no ghost, Rubio. If you really saw something just now I'm going to have a closer look. You can wait here."

"No, señor." The Mexican's tone was offended. "I go wit' you."

The two men moved cautiously through the rank growth of brush. The twilight was deepening rapidly under the huge cottonwoods. The old house became a gray, shapeless mass in that dusk. Only the twitterings of small birds in the trees broke the stillness, and the faint scuffle of leaves under their boots.

Donal halted, looked quizzically at his companion. "Nobody in that house," he said. "Not even a ghost."

A tongue of flame suddenly flared through the gathering darkness, the crashing report of a rifle shattered the evening quiet.

Their startled ears caught the whine of a bullet, the impact of lead boring deep into the tree behind them. They sprang apart, crouched in the tangle of brush. Donal heard Rubio's low whisper: "A very live ghost, that one." He relapsed into his broken English. "Thees mooch beeg joke on me."

"I take it we're not wanted here." Hot anger made Donal's voice brittle. "That was a close thing."

"I felt death kiss my cheek," the Mexican said. "May he burn in hell with no prayers said for his soul, this one who hides there."

Donal grew aware of distant shouts. The men at the chuckwagon had heard the rifle shot.

The Mexican laughed softly. "Old Sinfool — he make mooch beeg noise. He theenk maybe we mooch dead hombres."

The sound of drumming hoofs came to their ears, drew around the elbowing line of cottonwoods. Donal glimpsed the vague shapes of horsemen. He called out a sharp warning. The fast-moving shapes merged into the mantling darkness of the thicket, and in a moment the two men heard Rusty's voice.

"We savvy, boss."

Donal kept his gaze intently on the house, now hardly visible in the deep shadows. There was a man there, a man with murder in his heart. He thought of Jim Daker, but Daker would not stoop to this sort of cowardly killing. Rede Sems, perhaps. The town marshal's pride had been laid open to the bone. Disarmed by his proposed victim, sent sprawling in the dust by the heels of a pack-mule — a laughing-stock for all eyes.

Donal was not satisfied with this solution of the mysterious attack. A more sinister reason lay back of the murderous bullet. And the answer was to be found somewhere behind those aged adobe walls. Or was it?

He heard Rusty's cautious voice behind him. "What's up, Don?" The cowboy crawled alongside.

Bearcat came up, a soundless moving shape. "We'll smoke the skunk out pronto," he said. "If he walks on two legs he'll look purty danglin' from one of these trees."

Another shape crawled into view. Old Sinful, his large beefy face set in hard, belligerent lines, his long Sharps rifle in lowered hand. "Where's he at?" he wanted to know. "I'll blow his light out proper." The cook's voice was outraged. "There I was, all keyed up good to make that apple pie when he starts his shootin'. Made me go ruin as good a pie crust as a man ever sot tooth into."

Bearcat swore softly. "Worse'n murder," he complained indignantly. "I vote we swing him."

"We'll have to catch him first," reminded Donal. "All right, boys . . . fan out through the trees. If he's still in the house we'll have him trapped." He considered for a moment. "Rubio — you take a stand near the rear patio wall. He may try a break through the gate there."

The stillness was again heavy under those trees. Not even the twittering of a bird, nor the stir of a fallen leaf underfoot, as the Circle C men cautiously surrounded the lonely house. No painted warrior could have moved with more stealth than these wary and experienced fighters.

Donal crept forward, pausing once behind the trunk of a tree, ears straining to catch any betraying sound.

**49**

He reached the wide front door, a massive affair strapped with hand-wrought iron and still hanging as truly as on the day it was set in place between those three-foot adobe walls.

He pushed gently with the toe of his boot, crouched back against the wall, gun ready, as the door swung open. He waited a brief moment.

Nothing happened. No sound, no stirring of feet. He stepped inside, moved swiftly to the right of the doorway. His silhouette against the background of night might draw a bullet if the man was still in the room.

He stood there, listening, longing for a lantern. He began to realize the futility of a search without some sort of light.

A faint sound touched his ears. Something was moving, a swift, light patter on the earthen floor. Donal relaxed. Rats. The old house would be full of rats.

He recalled Rubio's words. *A shadow where the sunlight lies low on the wall.* The picture began to take form in his mind. The man had not been in the house when he fired the shot. He must have been outside, concealed behind the bushes. The last flashes from the sun behind him had thrown his shadow on the wall when he craned around the bushes for a look.

Donal went quickly outside and peered down the path that ran between the side of the house and the thick tangle of shrubbery. Grapevines, still clinging to a framework of poles.

He heard Rusty's voice from somewhere close behind. "Saw you slip out of the house and head into this path." The cowboy slid into view. "Bearcat says he

**50**

heard some feller ridin' away fast. Was pointin' for the hills yonder."

"Our man," conjectured Donal. "Wish we had a light, Rusty."

"Not much use, now the feller is on the run from here," commented Rusty.

"Give the others a call." Donal began tearing at the dried branches of the grapevine. "I've an idea the man was skulking in these vines. Rubio saw a shadow moving. Anybody back here could throw a shadow on the wall with the sun behind him." He put a match to the hastily-fashioned torch and walked down the path. "Look close for sign, Rusty." The torch flared brightly in his hand.

They bent low, studied the ground as they moved slowly along. Rusty grunted. "There's his tracks —" He straightened up, a puzzled look on his face. "What would he be layin' here for? How would he know you'd be along for a look at the house?"

"Let's hunt for more sign," Donal said. "I only know he took a shot at me."

Bearcat, followed by Rubio and Old Sinful, came on soundless feet. The cook glowered at the faint imprints of boot heels. "No sense me foolin' 'round here. I'm gettin' back to camp before my dinner is burned to hell." He vanished into the darkness, muttering eloquent words.

Rubio brought a second torch and the others followed the footprints further down the path. They came to an opening between the vines. Donal stooped and picked up an empty brass shell.

"Was shootin' a .44 rifle," Bearcat said.

"Doesn't tell us much." Donal dropped the shell into a pocket.

"Looks like this feller was hangin' 'round for some time," Rusty Cross observed. "There's close to a dozen cigarette stubs layin' here."

Donal's face was thoughtful as he straightened up from something he had been scrutinizing. "Do you boys notice anything special about these tracks?" he asked.

"*Si*." Rubio looked at him. "Thees hombre ees lame."

"That's right," Donal said. "We've got something to go on. We have to watch out for a man slightly lame because one leg is shorter than the other."

A deep laugh rose in Bearcat's hairy throat. "Ol' Clubfoot, huh! Reminds me of a b'ar used to come raidin' us down on the Box 7 . . . Ol' Clubfoot we called him. Too smart for us he was. Never could get him."

"We'll do our best to get *this* Old Clubfoot," Donal said grimly. "All right, boys. Let's head back for camp. And you might do some hard praying about that apple pie Old Sinful claims is ruined."

"A-*men!*" fervently exclaimed Rusty Cross. He pushed his gun back into its holster with a jubilant slap. "I'm bettin' on Old Sinful to wrastle with that apple pie till he's like a proud conquerin' hero plumb on top of a pie crust that's all puffed up with its juicy insides."

"Don't say no more," begged Bearcat. "You got my mouth to waterin' fast enough to irrigate the Jornada."

# CHAPTER
# FIVE

# The Spanish Grant

There was a chill in the air that made the horses hump their backs and step along gingerly as Donal and Rusty rode across the flats through the gray dawn. They passed the bedding ground, where a lone cow patiently stood while her offspring eagerly took breakfast from her. She rolled apprehensive eyes at the two horsemen. She was a gaunt, rangy beast with lance-sharp horns, obviously one of the breed that had helped found a mighty empire of cattle.

Rusty's eyes took on a thoughtful squint as he looked at her. "She's all Texas longhorn," he commented, "but that little one she's nursin' is going to be some different when he grows up. Look at his white head — just like his pa's."

"You can't beat that Hereford cross," Donal said. "You'll see nothing but white-faces on this ranch if you stay long enough, Rusty."

"Wasn't thinking to head back for the Brazos," Rusty confessed. "I'm liking this New Mexico country, Don. It's a man's country."

Donal gave him a keen look. "There'll always be a place for you with Circle C. Say yes — and you're the foreman right now."

"The vote is unanimous, and the vote says yes." Rusty reddened with pleasure. "I'll do my best by you, Don. Don't mind saying that I was kind of hoping you'd give me the chance. I don't crave nothing better than to boss Circle C for you."

They halted their horses on a high knoll from where they could watch the slow drift of the grazing cattle, and a silence fell between them as the red gold of the sunrise flamed over the saw-toothed hills.

Donal spoke softly. "Our first dawn on Circle C. I'm mighty glad to be here, Rusty, and glad you're with me."

"Same with me," replied the new foreman simply.

As if moved by the same impulse the two men leaned from their saddles, grasped hands in a hard shake. It was a compact they were making, a compact of unswerving loyalty, each to the other.

A rider moved toward them from the camp hidden in the cottonwood trees. "Rubio," Rusty said. "He ain't taking no time out for sleepin'. He was up most of the night, riding herd." His face sobered. "What do you make out of that business last night? Has me puzzled what that feller was doing at the house."

"Wish I knew the answer," replied Donal.

"Could have been some jasper holed up from the law," speculated Rusty. "Lots of fellers on the dodge and that old place makes a good hideout."

"How about those cigarette stubs?" reminded Donal.

"That's right." Rusty grinned. "Those stubs showed he'd been waiting there for some time — and for *some* purpose." The new foreman's eyes were angry. "Only one reason for him waiting there . . . a shot at you."

"I've been warned off."

"Daker will find out we don't scare easy," Rusty said.

They rode down the slope toward the approaching Mexican. He lifted a hand in greeting. "I watch thees cow," he said. "I dreenk coffee — mooch coffee. Feel fine."

"*Gracias.*" Rusty kept his horse moving, but Donal halted. He saw that Rubio had something on his mind.

The Mexican looked worried. "I do not like that business last night," he said in Spanish. "You must be careful. We are not wanted here."

"What do *you* make out of it, Rubio?"

"I do not know." The Mexican shook his head. "Thees contry 'ave bad time," he went on in his mongrel English. "Mooch pipple die — like Salazars."

"We'll have to change things," Donal said. He stared hard at the Mexican. "You want to say *adios* — be on your way?"

Rubio straightened in his saddle. "I do not run away from trouble," he said in Spanish. "I stay here on this ranch always — if you will have me. I am not so young," he added simply.

"You're due to collect a lot of money from the Circle C payroll," chuckled Donal. "All right, Rubio. You'll have charge of the ranch yard when we get settled." He rode on down the slope, warmed by the beatific look on the Mexican's face.

After breakfast at the chuckwagon he saddled a fresh horse and rode over to the house, accompanied by Rusty and Bearcat.

"Too many trees," observed the foreman as they dismounted and tied their horses. "Must have been an awful long time since any folks lived here."

"A lot of years," Donal said. "Your grandfather wasn't born when that house was built, Rusty."

"Goin' to be a heap of work clearin' out the dead wood," commented Bearcat. "These here corral are fair choked with brush. Won't be no use till we get 'em cleaned out."

They made their way through the tangle of garden and went into the house, but a careful search failed to find any signs to show it had been used as a hideout.

Another door opened into a large patio, formed by two wings that ran back from the main building and cut off from the yard by a high wall of adobe brick. A wide corridor extended around the three sides, with doors opening into the various rooms. The garden was choked with brush and weeds.

They passed through the patio gate and came to the grapevine arbor and began a close inspection of the tracks left by the lame marauder.

Donal, crouched on his heels, muttered a low exclamation. "This right boot has an iron strap on one side of the heel."

"Should make it easy to spot the feller," commented Bearcat. "Lame in one leg an' wearin' an iron strap on his right bootheel."

They followed the tracks for some fifty yards to a thicket of young cottonwoods choked with a heavy growth of brush.

"Had his horse tied here," Donal said.

"Only one set of tracks," Rusty pointed out. "He was on a lone prowl. Sure is queer business," he added.

There was nothing more they could do and abandoning further search the trio returned to their horses. Rusty rode up a high knoll that rose about a hundred yards back of the corrals. "I reckon that's the Rio Seco yonder," he called out.

Donal and Bearcat rode up the hill and gazed at the fringe of green that marked the banks of the river. Here and there, between the breaks in the trees they glimpsed the flashes of sunlight on water.

"Seems kind of loony, calling it the Rio Seco," puzzled Rusty. "No sense to it . . . means dry river."

"Once in a while it's a long time between rains," Donal said.

"You said there was always water in Tule Creek," reminded Rusty.

"Tule Creek is fed by big springs high in the hills. Melting snows, I reckon. But when Tule Creek empties into the Rio Seco the water sometimes sinks below the sand in dry seasons."

"A feller wouldn't think that river ever was dry, the way she looks now," declared Rusty.

"You'll see her dry if you stick around," laughed Donal. "Onate was the first man to come this way," he went on. "That was a long time ago. He took a caravan of settlers up the Rio Grande from Old Mexico."

"Sure." Rusty nodded. "I've heard of that Onate hombre. He's the feller that put Santa Fe on the map."

"Something like that," agreed Donal. "Those Spanish pioneers always had a few padres along, and they had a way of putting names to things. My idea is that when they crossed that river it was in a dry season when it was a sandy wash. So they called it the Rio Seco — dry river."

Bearcat and Rusty admitted the explanation seemed reasonable. They were familiar with the vagaries of rivers in the southwest.

Dust drifting back off the camp drew their attention. Rusty said worriedly, "Somebody riding this way in a hurry."

They put their horses to a run down the hill and, as they reached the yard, Old Sinful, followed by Wes Coles and Brasca, tore up at a fast gallop.

"Gang of fellers headed this way," shouted the cook as he dragged his horse to a halt. He was riding bareback.

"Most a dozen of 'em," added Brasca, a lean, hard-looking man with a shock of yellow hair under his Stetson. "Don't like their looks, so we figgered it good sense to join up with you."

Wes Coles, a chunky, round-faced man in the middle thirties, gave Donal a grim look. "It's a hostile party, boss. I'm advisin' we get ready for 'em." For all his cherubic face, there was something formidable about Wes Coles when the twinkle left his eyes. And there was no twinkle in them now.

58

The trailing dust cloud was already past the chuckwagon and heading fast for the house. Donal spoke sharply. "Spread out in the trees . . . keep out of sight . . . you'll know what to do."

Wes Coles and Brasca swerved their horses into the concealing brush that grew thickly near the patio wall. Old Sinful and Bearcat rode into a dense thicket of young trees. In less than a minute they were behind cover.

Donal looked at his foreman. "I think our callers will be from the Rocking D," he said softly. "I wasn't expecting that affair of last night, but I was looking for a visit from Jim Daker."

"Here they come." Rusty's eyes narrowed to slits as he stared. "The big fellow will be Daker, I reckon."

"The big boss in person," Donal assured him.

"Looks like a grizzly bear, and sure on the warpath," muttered the Circle C man. "Nine of 'em, Don, counting Daker."

The riders drew to a halt less than ten yards from the waiting men. Daker, mounted on a tall bay horse, leaned forward, hands resting on the pommel of his saddle.

"I told you to keep your cows moving away from here." His voice was harsh, his face forbidding, dark with the anger that burned within him. "You're not wanted in the Rio Seco."

"I like it here, Daker." Donal spoke coolly. "Good range — plenty of water. Just what I'm looking for." He added in a low aside to Rusty, "Keep your eyes on the man next to Daker. He's the foreman, and tough."

**59**

"You heard what I said." Daker's voice rose. "You're moving on — you and your cows. I've given you fair warning."

"Did you send a messenger last night, Daker?" Donal asked the question softly.

"Messenger?" Daker looked puzzled. "No, Cameron. I sent no messenger."

"I'm glad to know it," Donal said. "I'd hate to believe you kept murderers on your payroll."

"What do you mean?" asked Daker angrily. "What are you driving at?"

"Somebody hiding in the brush took a shot at me last night."

"Don't know a thing about it," fumed the owner of the Rocking D. "When I don't want a man campin' on my range I tell him so to his face. I don't send bushwhackers after him."

"*Your* range?" Donal's tone was ironic.

"Don't get fresh, young man. You heard me. I said *my* range, and I'm telling you for the last time to clear out."

"I won't be the first you've said that to," Donal retorted.

"Not the first," admitted Daker with a wintry smile. "They all move on, Cameron. You'll do the same if you have good sense."

"I'm staying," Donal told him quietly. "There's room for me in this man's country."

The cattleman's hands tightened over the saddle horn. "Don't be a fool!" Rage choked his voice. "You're

**60**

on Rocking D range, and I'm here to run you and your outfit off of it."

"Not *your* Rocking D range, Daker, or maybe you don't remember Fidel Salazar."

Daker's head lifted in a startled look. "*Salazar!*" He spoke in a low, hardly audible voice. "*Salazar?*"

"He used to live in that old house." Donal gestured at the gray adobe walls. "Fidel Salazar."

"Salazar has been dead a long time," Daker said in a stronger voice. "What has he got to do with you trespassing on my range?"

"Salazar used to own this land," answered Donal. "I'm the owner, now. This is *my* range, Daker, not Rocking D range."

"You're crazy!" exploded Daker. "I've run my cattle here since before you were born."

"There was nobody to stop you," retorted Donal. "Things are different now."

Daker stared at him. Bewilderment, indecision, a growing anger was in the look. He seemed bereft of words.

"You know what I mean," Donal went on. "This land is an old Spanish grant . . . been in the Salazar family for nearly two hundred years, perhaps longer."

Lew Trent interrupted him impatiently. "What's the use of wastin' time with this fool palaver, boss?" His eyes signaled the cluster of riders.

"Keep your hand away from your gun, Trent." Donal's voice lifted sharply. "That goes for all of you," he added.

Something in his tone held the Rocking D men rigid in their saddles.

"If you want gun-smoke you'll have more than you bargained for," Donal told them in the same taut voice. "You won't have a chance."

Obeying his gesture, the shocked Rocking D men looked from side to side. Dismay spread over their faces.

"Got us covered," muttered one of the riders.

"We sure have, mister," bawled Old Sinful from the concealment of the thicket. "I ain't missin' you at this distance with my ol' Sharps. Got her lined up purty for blowin' a hole through a pair of you with one shot."

"I'm good for two more of 'em," announced Bearcat.

"Got you beat," chuckled Wes Coles. "Count three for me. How's it with you, Brasca?"

"Got my sights lined on the big feller that's so anxious to start the fireworks," Brasca answered.

The Rocking D men glared helplessly at those unwavering rifle barrels poked at them from the bushes. They were nicely trapped.

Jim Daker broke the silence. "You're a smart man, Cameron. Smarter than I knew." Grudging admiration was in his voice. "You can't make it stick if it *is* a good bluff."

"You're wrong," Donal retorted. "This is no bluff, Daker. Get that notion out of your head."

"You can't make it stick," repeated Daker. "I'm no fool. I know the law."

"I was telling you that this land is an old Spanish grant —"

"Not since the Mexican War," interrupted Daker. "This is United States country now." He snorted. "Those old grants don't mean a thing."

"Wrong again," smiled Donal. "Owners of Spanish grants were allowed to record their holdings with the government after the war. I looked up the records. Fidel Salazar established his rights as lawful owner."

"That don't make *you* the owner," sneered Daker. "Anyway, Salazar is dead, been dead for years, and this land is open range — *my* range."

"I'm trying to tell you that this land is not open range. It is not government land at all. It's deeded property. No man can set foot on it without my permission."

Something like panic looked from Daker's eyes. He glanced at Lew Trent. The foreman's face was shocked, angry. "Let's get out of here," Trent muttered.

Daker ignored him. "Maybe it is what you say, about the Salazar grant," he said to Donal. "My fault for not looking into the thing myself. I'm still claiming it doesn't make you the owner. You ain't a Salazar. As far as I know there ain't a Salazar left. If I'm right, this land has gone back to the state."

"I've got a deed to this land, Daker. Salazar is dead. He left no children. You know they were killed in that Indian raid."

Daker nodded. "I know about the raid. That's why I say there's no Salazar left to claim ownership."

"Salazar left a sister. She lives in Albuquerque. I've seen her. She was glad enough to get the eight thousand dollars I offered her for a deed." Donal paused, added significantly, "That deed is on record."

"I'll fight you," Daker said furiously. "Deed or no deed, I'll fight you. I've been running my cows on this range since before you were born."

"Listen, Daker, I'm giving you the boundaries of my Circle C." Donal drew a paper from his pocket, glanced at it. "All the way from the Honda, running five miles west of Tule Creek down to the west fork of the Rio Seco, and running twenty miles east of Tule Creek to the Comanche."

"You can't do this to me!" Daker shouted.

"It's already done. You've had a good time of it, Daker, playing the cattle king in these parts." Donal's voice hardened. "Listen — Circle C has moved in for keeps, and Circle C will hold every inch of range described in the Salazar grant. Keep that fact in mind, and we can be good neighbors."

"Or damn bad enemies," bawled Old Sinful.

"Shut up, Sinful!"

"Was just warnin' him in plain langwidge," grumbled the cook.

Jim Daker spoke again, more quietly, almost pleadingly. "I've got to have access to Tule Creek. My Loma Paloma range ain't worth a hoot if my cows can't get to the creek when the springs dry up."

"I said I'd be a good neighbor," responded Donal. "You won't find me unreasonable."

Daker was silent and it was Lew Trent who spoke. "You do a lot of talking, Cameron. I hear you come from the Brazos country. I'm telling you out loud that you're up against a hard outfit when you try to buck the Rockin' D. We'll chase you out of this country . . . clear back to the Brazos."

Somebody laughed. Rusty Cross. "Listen," he said, "your talk just don't scare us a-tall."

There was a brief silence. Only the creak of leather as the Rocking D men stirred restlessly in their saddles.

Donal sensed a critical moment. These Rocking D men were fighters, loyal to the man who had their names on his payroll. Donal held them in respect. The men on his own payroll possessed that same loyalty to the man they served. Such loyalty was the unwritten code of the range.

"What do you say, Daker?" He asked the question quietly. "If there's trouble, it's up to you."

Indecision looked from Daker's eyes. "You're smart, Cameron." Again the grudging admiration in his voice. "I've got to think it over." His head turned in a look at the menacing rifles. "You're holding all the cards right now."

"Nothing more for me to say," Donal said. "You've paid your call. If you come again, come as a friend."

Daker looked at him fixedly. "You've got nerve, young man. I'll grant you that, and I don't mind admitting it's the kind of nerve I like. I'm that way, too." He gave Lew Trent a nod. "Let's go."

"One moment —" Donal lifted a hand. "How about that visitor last night?"

"Don't know a thing about it," burst out Daker. "I don't send killers to lie in wait for a man." His indignation was genuine.

"I've heard talk," Donal said grimly. "I've heard that men who don't move on when you tell them — get killed — their homes burned."

"What happens to men who try to horn in on my range is their own fault," Daker replied. "All I do is tell them to move on, Cameron. I don't clutter up my mind with what happens to them."

"No —" Donal's tone was cold. "You just give your orders. What happens afterward doesn't bother you. Isn't that right? You shut your eyes, close your ears and think you're the great cattle king whose word is law."

"I'm not liking your talk," rumbled Daker. The ruddiness faded from his face, gave him a haggard look.

"It's hard talk," admitted Donal. "The truth hurts your pride and you don't like it."

Daker shook his head, pulled savagely on bridle reins. "Let's go," he again said to Trent.

Rusty Cross shook his head gloomily as he watched them. "We ain't finished with this business," he prophesied. "That Trent feller is tough. He was ready to shoot it out if Daker had said the word."

"It was touch and go," agreed Donal.

"The Rocking D is a big outfit," Rusty reminded him. "Only seven of us, counting Old Sinful."

The cook overheard him. "Countin' Old Sinful, huh!" he exploded wrathfully. "I resents that sort o' way o' figgerin', you doggone young maverick. Let me tell you I was followin' war-trails before you was dried behind the ears."

"Rusty wasn't meaning a thing," hurriedly soothed Donal. "He means you've got more important things on your mind. You're the cook for this outfit and can't be always reaching for your Sharps."

"Mebbe so," grunted the mollified cook. "Not that I ain't partial to a leetle excitement once in a while."

"You'll get plenty," chuckled Bearcat. "We ain't seen the last of that outfit."

Donal stared at him, straight brows drawn in a frown, then he turned to his horse and swung up to the saddle.

The grimness of that look silenced further comment. There were only seven of them, as Rusty had pointed out. A small outfit, compared to the Rocking D. True enough they were seven good men. But so were the Rocking D riders good men, and the Rocking D could boast more than five times their number.

Wordless, their faces grimly thoughtful, Circle C followed the young boss back to camp. Each man of them knew the defy had been given. There was no retreat now.

# CHAPTER
# SIX

# A Message from
# Circle C

The weeks slipped by, busy days at Circle C. The old house of the Salazars lost its look of desolation along with its dust and cobwebs. The brush and weeds that choked the corral were uprooted and burned. Rubio was familiar with the mysteries of making adobe bricks and managed satisfactory repairs where needed.

No further protest came from Jim Daker. Apparently he was resigned to the situation. Donal made a shrewd guess that the owner of the Rocking D must be looking into the records of the Salazar grant. Donal did not worry. His own exhaustive search had satisfied him. The title vested in him by the deed from Fidel Salazar's sister could not be assailed. Nevertheless Donal was taking no chances. This country he had chosen to make his own was still a hostile land. For the moment the sky seemed fair, but far down on the horizon the storm clouds still threatened. No telling when the lightning would strike. And the first blow would be at Circle C's small herd.

Fortunately there was plenty of good feed close to the house. The cattle were safe enough with one man riding herd during the hours of daylight while the rest of the outfit worked feverishly at the task of getting the ranch buildings and yard in order. Nightfall found the herd crowded into the corrals, an alert lookout on watch until dawn flushed the eastern sky.

Blue Clover rode over from his ranch in what was known as the Little Bend country, where the Rio Seco made a southerly loop before turning again on its meandering course to the Rio Grande.

"You've sure got a nice spread here, Don," he admired. "Don't savvy how you done it, and don't savvy how you can hang on to her. Jim Daker has been running his cows on this Salazar range before you and me was born. Just cain't see Jim Daker settin' still while you horn in on him like you done."

"He's done some shouting," admitted Donal. "He's been over . . . brought quite a bunch with him. Didn't stay long."

"You've got me guessin'," declared Clover. "Been plenty of fellers wanting to locate theirselves a spread in this country." He shook his head. "Most of 'em found things too hot . . . pulled up stakes and cleared out."

Donal looked at him searchingly. "What happened to the men who didn't — move on?"

The Little Bend rancher seemed reluctant to talk. "I'm not one that likes to say much, Don."

"I savvy." Donal pondered for a moment. "Was Isabel Lee's father one of the men who couldn't be scared away?"

"Never had the straight of that bus'ness," answered Blue Clover. "There was talk that a bunch of Apaches done it."

"Do you believe that?"

"No." Blue scowled. "I ain't the only one who don't believe it was Apaches." He hesitated, added uneasily, "Wouldn't want you to say nothin' about what I think. I've got my Lucy to look out for. But maybe you don't savvy, not having a woman."

"I won't repeat what you tell me," Donal assured him. "Tell we what you know, Blue."

"Well — there's talk that them raiders wasn't real Apaches. Reckon you can guess what I mean."

Donal nodded. "I think I can, Blue. You mean they were renegades, masquerading as Indians."

"Yeah, I reckon so." Clover shrugged. "Ain't hard to savvy what I mean."

"I can't see Jim Daker back of that kind of devil's work," declared Donal.

"The Rockin' D is a mighty hard outfit." Blue Clover spoke sullenly. "Daker wouldn't be knowing all the things that went on. He just lets out there's certain folks he don't want 'round. He don't bother himself about what happens. Leaves it to Lew Trent, and you've seen that hombre."

"You mean Daker turns his face the other way," Donal said in a low, hard voice.

"Keep it under your hat," cautioned Blue. "I was only wanting to warn you."

"Thanks." Donal's smile was grim. "Circle C won't be caught napping."

"You've got more than the Rockin' D to buck," warned Blue. "Lot of rustlin' the last couple of years. Daker claims he's been hard hit. Al DeSang is hollerin', too."

Donal looked at him, surprised to hear DeSang's name.

"He runs the DS, up in the Comanche hills east of here," explained Blue. "DeSang has a big spread, and getting bigger."

"I didn't know he was in the cattle business," commented Donal.

"He's a smart man," observed Blue. "DeSang didn't have much when he landed in San Benito. Now he's pardners with Jim Daker in the big store, owns the Longhorn Saloon and got his irons in a lot of other things. I reckon he's making money fast. Old Soper's his sidekick."

"A good friend of DeSang's, he told me," Donal said.

"Him and DeSang are as thick as thieves," confirmed Blue. "Soper is an awful boozer, but I reckon he's useful to DeSang . . . pretty good lawyer." Blue slid from his perch on the corral fence. "Well, Don, got to be headin' for home or Lucy will be pullin' my hair." He grinned, added hospitably, "Drop over sometime. Lucy'll give you a bang-up meal. She's a top hand cook."

"I'll be seeing you," promised Donal, genuinely pleased.

"You can bring Rusty Cross along with you," invited Clover. He chuckled. "Lucy has a sister stayin' with us that Rusty won't find hard to look at."

71

"I'll hold her out for bait," laughed Donal.

He stood for a few moments, watching until the cottonwoods hid roan horse and rider from view. The talk with Clover had aroused a sudden longing to see Isabel Lee again. She would have heard by now that he was still in the Rio Seco country, despite her urgings to keep moving until a long way from Jim Daker's domain.

He went back to the house, his thoughts on Blue Clover's reluctant account of the brutal outrage that had left Isabel Lee without home or family. Anger burned within him. It was plain that Clover held no belief in the Apache angle. Clover had heard enough talk to know for a fact that the raiders were renegade whites in the guise of Indians. Such things were known to have happened.

He found himself reluctant to believe the shocking conclusion. The thing was too hideous. Jim Daker might be hard and ruthless, but not devil enough to instigate so dreadful an affair. He tried to push the thought from him. Again he heard Blue Clover's hesitant voice: *He don't bother himself much about what happens.*

Rubio was pushing a homemade mop over the hard-packed earthen floor of the big room. Donal gave him a brief glance, went out to the patio and sat down on a bench fashioned from twisted branches of mountain mahogany. It was an old bench, probably the handiwork of some Indian retainer of the Salazars long before Zebulon Pike had found his way across the mountains to Santa Fe.

A considerable amount of furniture still remained in the old house. Homemade stuff, probably dating from the days of the first Salazar. No doubt but what later generations of Salazars had brought in more elegant furnishings from Santa Fe, or from the City of Mexico, but these had long since vanished under vandal hands. For the moment there was enough for present needs, although Donal had in mind several things he planned to have Angus Cameron bring from Albuquerque in his freight wagons.

He lit a cigarette, his thoughts on Isabel Lee again. He recalled her perturbation when learning of his plans to locate in the Rio Seco country. *I'd hate to see you get killed.* The falter in her low, sweet voice. *My father was that way, too . . . not easily scared . . . didn't stop them from killing him.* Yes, she feared he would share her father's fate. Jim Daker hated nesters, Isabel said. Jim Daker was dangerous, a man with no mercy in him.

Donal squinted thoughtfully at his cigarette. He was puzzled by the girl's apparent belief that Daker was in some way involved in the murder of her father and young brother. If such was her thought of the man, how could she even bear the thought of becoming his adopted daughter? She would not hesitate to reject the offer if she *really* believed Daker guilty. The thing was a conundrum and turn it this way or that he could find no answer.

The longing to see the girl again began to possess him. He was aware of a loneliness that surprised him. There was no sense in it, not with the companionship he already enjoyed. There was nothing dull about the

Circle C outfit. These men were the kind he had spent most of his life with.

He snubbed the cigarette underfoot and stared musingly at the enclosing walls of the ancient *casa* of the Salazars. *His* house now, and achingly empty of what should be in it. He knew now the reason for his sudden loneliness. He wanted to hear the sound of voices in that house. Not men's voices, not Old Sinful's lurid exhortations addressed to the vast adobe range built into the kitchen wall, not Rubio's softly-murmured love songs. What he yearned to hear was the voice of a woman inside that house.

Donal got to his feet, stared around, a scowl on his face. A woman! That was the answer. Old Sinful would have other duties when roundup time came. He would be away with the chuckwagon. Somebody must take his place in the kitchen. A woman — a cook — a housekeeper!

He thought of Manuela, the pleasant-faced old Mexican in the kitchen of Angus Cameron. He would go to San Benito and have a talk with Manuela. She would find a good woman for him.

The scowl left his face. He made and lit a fresh cigarette, revolving the plan carefully in his mind. Angus Cameron was probably back from the hospital. He wanted to have a talk with Angus, and there were things to order for the house.

He pushed through the patio gate in search of Rusty Cross, tinglingly aware of an odd stir within him. Isabel Lee was in San Benito. He would see her.

74

He found Rusty helping Bearcat set up posts for the new corral fence. The two men looked hot and dusty, and not very happy.

"Never took to real hard work like diggin' post holes," Bearcat grumbled. "I was born thataways — plumb lazy." He grinned, wiped his perspiring face with a shirt sleeve.

"Lazy ain't the word," jeered Rusty. "You're just plain useless when it comes to handlin' a shovel."

"Ain't noticin' that you lean on that shovel too hard," retorted Bearcat. "What I mean is that shovels ain't part of a cowman's eddication. I ain't mindin' followin' a bunch o' cows up the trail through hell an' high water, settin' in the saddle so long that I feels like I've growed fast to the leather. Ain't mindin' none if we runs into a war party of Injuns an' has to do some fightin' to save our skelps. All in the day's work for a cowman." Bearcat shook his head gloomily. "Shovels was just left out of my eddication."

"It's tough, all right," sympathized Donal.

Bearcat grinned, spat on his hands and gripped the offending shovel. "Hell, boss, you know I'm only pertendin' to beef. When thar's work to be done you cain't beat a top hand like me —" He broke off with a startled grunt, flung the shovel from him and ran with short, choppy steps to his horse.

The others had heard the distant shots. Almost as quickly as Bearcat, Rusty was in his saddle and following across the yard on the dead run. Donal made for the barn, still lacking a roof above its adobe walls. He always kept a horse saddled, ready for any emergency. It was a rule never to be broken, for each man of the outfit to have a horse ready for instant use.

He hastily drew the cinch tight, slipped on bridle and led the horse out. Old Sinful, carrying his Sharps rifle, emerged from the patio. Rubio appeared, buckling on his gun-belt. Their faces were grimly expectant.

Donal rode toward the two men. "You two stay close to the house," he told them. "Can't leave the place unguarded."

They nodded, disappointment in their faces. "Sure," grunted the cook. "We'll keep our eyes peeled."

The few moments' start had given Rusty and Bearcat a considerable lead. Donal caught a glimpse of them vanishing around a low ridge nearly a quarter of a mile distant.

Two more shots touched his ears. Closer this time, and a puff of smoke lifted from the barranca on the near side of the ridge. Donal swerved in that direction, sent his horse plunging across a stretch of sandy wash that lay at the barranca's mouth.

He knew the cattle were grazing beyond the ridge, where Rusty and Bearcat had ridden. The two men could cope with any trouble there. He was not worried about the herd. It was that first shot that had alarmed him. There were grim possibilities. A skulking ambusher, lying in wait on the slopes for a chance to pour bullets at the unsuspecting Brasca and Wes Coles.

Donal loosened his gun in its holster, eyes warily roving as the horse scrambled through a heavy growth of piñons. The two shots he had just heard indicated that either Brasca or Wes was in hot chase. The last shot had sounded like a .45 Colt. All the Circle C men carried Colt .45's. The first and second shots had come from a rifle. The ambusher would be using a rifle for the work he had been sent to do.

He brought his horse to a standstill, stared intently at a thick clump of scraggly piñons. Something stirred there, the glint of sunlight on metal. A rifle, lifting in the hands of a concealed man. Donal whirled his horse, flung himself from the saddle, and as he landed prone behind a big slab of rock he heard the vicious screech of a bullet, the crashing report of a gun.

He crouched there, the big slab of rock between him and the lone rifleman. Piñon trees flanked him on either side.

Another shot broke the stillness. It came from lower down the hill, on the side that sloped to the flats beyond the ridge. Something crashed through the chaparral. A horse, and moving fast.

His attention went back to the rifleman crouched in the brush above him. Silence lay heavily there. Donal hoped the ambusher had not slipped away. He wanted that man.

He crept forward, gun in hand, managed to bring the concealing clump of piñons into view. Despite his caution, the man must have heard him. The rifle barrel poked out, roared. A bullet spatted against the boulder. Donal guessed the man was shooting blindly on the chance of a lucky hit.

He tried a shot on his own account, aiming at a point directly behind the curling smoke. He heard a groan, a threshing of piñon branches, and suddenly the ambusher staggered into view, took a curious weaving step and collapsed.

A yell floated up from the lower slope. Brasca's voice. Donal sent back an answering shout and went slowly to the dead man sprawled face down by the piñon tree.

A brief look was sufficient. He had never seen the man before. He straightened up and, after a moment's thought, stooped again and scrutinized the man's boot heels. They were badly worn on the sides, but otherwise were ordinary boots. No sign of the iron strap that had marked the tracks of the man with one leg shorter than its mate.

Brasca made an appearance. "He ain't the lame feller," he said as Donal looked up. "The lame jasper got clean away."

Donal stood staring at him. Brasca understood, said quickly, "Wes took a slug through his hat. Wasn't hurt, but he's sure peeved about the hat." The cowboy began to make a cigarette. "They was layin' for us up on the slope. The lame jasper and this feller here."

"I'd liked to have caught the lame one," grumbled Donal. "We could have learned things from him . . . found out what's back of this prowling and spying."

"I took after 'em," Brasca said. He grinned, added casually, "Forgot to say that the bullet that holed the hat dropped the horse and left Wes afoot. He was all tangled up with that daid bronc and yelled for me not to mind him. At that the coyotes got a good start on me."

"Much obliged for breaking the bad news so gently." Donal's tone was ironic. "Was that your shot I heard?"

78

"He was goin' too fast," grumbled Brasca. "Couldn't get close enough for a fair shot. Found his tracks where he'd left his horse. Same kind of tracks we found down at the house . . . iron strap on his bootheel. He was the feller all right."

Donal's look went to the dead man. "He'll have a horse somewhere close," he said. "Scout around, Brasca. We'll rope the body to that horse and turn it loose."

"Smart idee," admired the cowboy. "Good way to get him back to where he come from. The horse will head straight for home fast enough."

"A message for them," Donal said grimly. "A message from Circle C."

# CHAPTER
# SEVEN

# A Man's Job

San Benito drowsed under a hot noonday sun. A mongrel dog that had sought the coolness of a mudhole under the watering trough in front of Billy Winch's livery barn lifted a sleepy look at Donal as he rode past.

The red horse was inclined to halt for a drink at the trough. Donal pushed on. There was plenty of water in the big stockade corral at the top of the street. He was in a hurry to see Angus.

Few people were astir, a freighter, making his way to the little restaurant, a fat Mexican in faded blue overalls, swilling buckets of water on the boardwalk in front of the Longhorn Saloon, a rancher and his sun-bonneted wife climbing from a buckboard across the street.

Donal's eyes roved alertly. He had not been in town since his encounter with the marshal. He had a hunch that Rede Sems was not one to forget.

The new hotel now boasted a coat of dazzling white paint. Several men lounged in the shade of the porch. The town marshal was not among them.

His pulse quickened as he passed the restaurant. He had a vague hope that he might catch a glimpse of

Isabel Lee. He was disappointed. The outer door was shut and the window shades drawn to keep out the baking heat.

A man appeared in the open doorway of the town marshal's office. Rede Sems!

Donal tensed in his saddle. To his surprise he saw a deep flush break over the little law officer's face. Rede Sems was blushing. He nodded curtly, said, "Howdy, Cameron," and abruptly turned his back.

Marveling a bit at the town marshal's almost painful embarrassment, Donal continued on his way to the stockade corral. He could hardly believe his eyes. That deadly little man blushing like a schoolboy caught in mischief.

Some glimmer of the truth came to him. Sems' fellow-townsmen had witnessed his humiliation at the hands of a stranger and the heels of a mule. The affair had left a rankling wound, a festering sore that made the man all the more dangerous. Sems would be waiting for his chance to even the score.

The shutters were down from the windows of Cameron's Trading Post, the big doors wide open, and old Angus himself standing there, great bony face wreathed in a wide smile.

"Aye, 'tis the young Cameron!" His more than fifty years in the southwest had made little change in the trader's manner of speech. He still spoke with the tongue of his Highlander forebears. "Welcome you are, lad. 'Tis bonnie to see you."

"The same to yourself, Angus," grinned the young cattleman. "I'm putting up my horse for a feed, and then it's a long talk between us."

"Aye —" Angus limped out to the porch, leaning heavily on a stout cane of polished manzanita wood. "Roderick Dhu will be at the gate to let you in, lad. We've been looking for you these minutes past."

"I sent no word I was coming!" Donal gave him a surprised look.

Angus chuckled. "Rod's been on the watch for you these days. Morning and noon he rides to Indian Head — that's the peak yonder. Overlooks the valley. With his glasses he can see the trails. Aye, 'tis two hours ago he sighted you."

Donal rode into the alley that led to the corral. Roderick Dhu stood by the open gate. His hand lifted in a welcoming gesture. "It is good to see my brother," he said. His eyes glowed. "You have not run away, as some said you would. My brother is brave."

"Thanks, Rod." Donal slid from his saddle. "We Camerons don't scare easily."

"You bet," responded the Apache, pleased at being included in the clan.

He went off to the stable with the horse and Donal made his way through the alley to the front entrance of the store.

"Over here, lad," called the trader from his desk at the far end of the long room.

"Dark in here, after that blazing sunlight," Donal said as he pulled out a chair and sat down. "Cool, too."

"These 'dobe walls are close on four feet thick," Angus informed him. "The heat does no bother us." He chuckled reminiscently. "I was no thinking of the heat when I built the place. 'Twas a long time back, lad. Nobody in this town but me, and there wasn't even a town. Just Cameron's Trading Post."

"You're an old-timer, all right," Donal commented. "You know this southwest country."

"Aye, I know the country," assented the trader. "I was freightin' into Santa Fe before Doniphan got there with his army. Trapped all over before I went into the freightin' business." Angus lit a stubby pipe and puffed contentedly. "Knew what I was about when I built this place. Those thick walls were no just to keep out the heat. I made 'em big to keep the redskins out, and all the other hellions that thought they could come raidin' me."

Donal gazed around at the well-stocked shelves. It was apparent that Angus had managed to get his freight wagons moving again.

The trader saw his curiosity. "Roderick Dhu told you about the trouble I've been having. I beat 'em, lad. Nobody is going to run *me* out of this country. We Camerons can fight." His eyes twinkled. "You're one of the clan, lad, from what I've been hearing since I got back from the hospital. Took Sems' gun away from him, kicked him in the pants." Angus let out a booming laugh.

"It was the mule kicked him," Donal drawled. "How's the leg, Angus? Heard you got shot up."

"The leg is fine, considerin'," replied the trader. "The sawbones wanted to cut it off, but I told him I'd get his scalp if I didn't die first." His shaggy brows drew down in a frown. "I'll be doing a hobble step the rest of my life. But I'm lucky, lad — and thankful."

"Any idea who it was shot you?" asked Donal curiously.

"I could name him," replied Angus cautiously. "I'm bidin' my time, lad. There are more ways than one to trap a wolf. I should know, havin' trapped many score of them in my time." He abruptly changed the subject. "How does it go with you, lad? You have put it over, from the talk that drifts in."

"Thanks to your tip about the Salazar grant," Donal hesitated. "Some queer business going on, Angus."

The trader listened attentively to the account of the mysterious lame man, the later attempt to ambush the Circle C riders.

"I'm not knowing any man whose legs don't match," Angus said when Donal finished. "I've been away this past month at that hospital. This town is growing fast, filling up with a rare lot of border scum. Your clubfoot man is likely new to San Benito, brought in special for the job of killin' off such as you and myself. 'Tis plain we're no wanted here."

"Jim Daker doesn't want me here," Donal said. "He doesn't fit into the picture, though. I don't see him as that sort. He is overbearing, arrogant, and hates nesters, but he's not the kind of man who'd plot cold-blooded murder."

Angus puffed hard on his pipe. "I'd like to have been there when you told him about the Salazar grant."

"He took it hard," admitted Donal.

"First time he's been stood up to." The trader's booming laugh filled the store.

"How about yourself?" asked Donal. "How about that new store Daker and DeSang have started?"

"I have said my piece to them," admitted Angus placidly. "I did no lay a soft pedal on my tongue."

Donal looked around the empty store. "I don't see any customers."

"It is an off day," explained Angus. "You need no worry, lad. I've no been losing trade to the San Benito General Merchandise Store. The Cameron Trading Post has been doing business here since long before you were born. Every rancher within a hundred miles comes to old Angus when he has money to spend for goods." He knocked the ashes from his pipe, recharged it from a bag of soft buckskin. "DeSang is welcome to the town trade."

"I'm told he's making money hand over fist," Donal commented. "What do you think of him, Angus?"

The trader looked down his big nose. "He is a downy bird, and so crooked a snake gets tied up in knots trying to follow his tracks."

"You don't like him?"

"I like him the same way a good Christian likes the devil," Angus confided with another wry smile. "I'm not telling you wrong when I tell you to watch your step where DeSang is concerned."

"How about Judge Soper?"

"Drunk or sober, he's tied hand and foot to Al DeSang," replied the trader. "A sharp rascal, lad, and sometimes not as drunk as he seems. I'd no tell him what you don't want the wrong man to hear."

"You don't think much of this town," accused Donal.

"Nothing wrong with the town," grumbled Angus. "'Tis the folks . . . slimy, scheming folks."

"Daker doesn't seem that sort," argued Donal.

"He's so pumped up with pride he can no see things right," retorted Angus. "Daker thinks he runs this town, but it is Al DeSang who is the real boss. DeSang is so crafty he leads Daker by the nose and the poor fool no the wiser."

"Rede Sems is Daker's man. At least that's my impression."

Angus snorted. "DeSang lets Daker think so. I happen to know it was DeSang who brought Sems here, got Daker to make him town marshal. Rede Sems takes his orders from DeSang. Something for you to remember."

Donal stared at him. "You're giving me ideas," he murmured. "By the way, has Daker an interest in DeSang's DS ranch?"

"Daker wouldn't stand for a partner in a cow ranch," Angus answered emphatically. "To tell you the truth, I'm some puzzled at DeSang going into the cattle business. I'd no think Daker would like it." He stared thoughtfully at his cold pipe. "I hear that DS cows are verra fast breeders, from the size of the calf crop."

"Meaning what?" Donal pricked up his ears.

**86**

"It's a puzzle you can work out for yourself, lad," Angus said blandly. "Cows are *your* business."

"I'm learning things," commented the Circle C man dryly.

"'Tis well that you do," Angus said. "You'll no find it easy, lad. You've taken on a man's size job, as you have already guessed. There's only one law that counts as yet in this Rio Seco country. The law of the .45."

"We'll have to work for better things." Donal spoke thoughtfully. "We won't get law or justice that way. We've got to establish a *real* law in this man's country, or there'll be no justice for a decent citizen."

"*Your* job," Angus said laconically.

"Don't be too hopeful," laughed the young cattleman. "I've plenty on my hands right now."

"You'll do it," prophesied Angus. "I'm seeing changes in the Rio Seco, now that Circle C has moved in."

"That reminds me —" Donal's look went to the hall door that led to the kitchen in the rear of the store. "Circle C needs a housekeeper, a combination cook and housekeeper."

Angus noticed his look. He shook his head. "You'll no steal Manuela away from me," he declared firmly. "You are a Cameron, like myself, but I'll no let you have her."

Donal grinned. "I was only thinking that Manuela might find me some woman who'll take on the job."

"Likely she can." Angus reached for his cane and got out of his chair. "I'll take you into the kitchen —"

**87**

It appeared that Manuela knew of a treasure by the name of Marica Torres.

"She is not young, señor, but also she is not too old."

"I won't want a young one," Donal assured her.

"She is my half sister, and her cooking is even better than mine."

"One cannot believe such a tale," chuckled Donal. "It will be enough if she is only half as good as you."

"Her husband is dead, but she has a son who is already seventeen and a man who knows cows and horses like an old one." Manuela cocked her head in a questioning look.

"He is hired," Donal told her promptly. "Circle C can use him."

Manuela was pleased. "That will be good," she said in a satisfied voice. "Marica will want Pasqual with her. She will not be lonesome."

It was arranged that Roderick Dhu would find Marica and bring her to the store. It seemed that she lived in the Mexican quarter near the town.

"You'll have a bite to eat?" suggested Angus hospitably.

"I'll be back later," Donal replied as he turned toward the door. "Thanks just the same, Angus." The thought of Isabel Lee hurried his stride, quickened the beat of his heart.

# CHAPTER
# EIGHT

# Jim Daker's Iron

Considering the hour, business was surprisingly dull in the little restaurant. A lone customer, the freighter Donal had noticed earlier, was morosely contemplating a slab of pie on the plate before him. His eyes lifted in a look at the newcomer.

"I ain't what you call a choosy feeder," he said bitterly, "but when I pay one big round silver dollar I'm countin' on food that's fit to be et."

"I had a bang-up meal the last time I was here," Donal told him.

"You're talkin' of days that are past." The freighter shook his head sadly. "Them days is no more. Now take this hunk of apple pie. No flour a-tall. Just cement, seasoned with gravel an' rolled out with axle-grease an' filled with wormy apples."

"Nobody asked you to come an' eat here," bellowed an angry voice from the kitchen doorway. "You're too finicky, that's what you are, mister."

The freighter stared coldly at the speaker, a fat man with an unshaven red face and a much-soiled apron tied around his middle. "You got a sign outside that says best meal in town for one dollar. I'm proclaimin' loud your sign is an awful liar."

"You get out of my place," shouted the aproned man. He reached behind him and snatched up a cleaver. "I don't take your loose talk," he yelped, brandishing the meat chopper.

"You're takin' *this*," retorted the freighter. He sprang from his chair, hurled plate and pie at the outraged proprietor.

"That'll cost you another dollar!" howled the restaurant man. "Look what you done . . . broke my plate and messed up the wall!"

"I'll pay you next time I come," promised the freighter with ironic politeness. He grinned at Donal. "Which next time is so far ahaid I won't never ketch up with it." The door slammed behind him.

The proprietor swallowed hard, choked back angry words that were useless now the defamer was gone. He advanced on the remaining customer. "Beef stew is good today," he said encouragingly.

Donal shook his head regretfully. "I'll drop in sometime when it's not beef stew." He turned to the door. It was obvious that Isabel Lee was no longer with the establishment.

"You've let that belly-achin' mule-skinner scare you out," accused the restaurant man resentfully. "I've a mind to set the marshal on him."

Donal temporarized. He wanted to ask him about Isabel. Some sort of pacification was necessary. "A cup of coffee will hit the spot," he said.

The coffee was brought, steaming hot and not too bad. Donal had tasted worse. He smiled genially at the proprietor. "Used to be a girl here."

The fat man nodded, stared sourly at his pie-bespattered wall. Donal tried again. "Where has she gone?"

"Ask me another," grunted the restaurant man. "All I know is she's went."

"Left town?"

"Search me."

The coffee turned to gall in Donal's mouth. He put the cup down and reached for his hat. The proprietor watched him with morose eyes. "Don't come back," he said.

"That's up to me," retorted Donal.

"You won't find me doin' bus'ness. I'm closin' this place." The angry man swore feelingly. "That new hotel dinin' room has took all the trade. No sense for me to try to buck 'em."

Donal waited to hear no more. He followed the freighter into the street, conscious of a strange sensation in the pit of his stomach. Isabel had vanished, and he could think of only two answers that would explain her disappearance. She had left town, or she was now Jim Daker's adopted daughter.

His heart heavy, he made his way to the hotel. Hook Saval was missing from his post behind the desk. Donal elicited the information that Hook had gone back to the Rocking D ranch.

"He wasn't liking it here at the desk," the new clerk explained. "He said it was too much like herding sheep." The clerk shook his head pityingly. He was a round-faced man with oily black hair and a tiny waxed mustache. "Funny notions these old-timers get."

"Hook is an old cowman," Donal rejoined. "But you wouldn't understand."

He went into the dining room, disappointed about Hook Saval. Hook probably could have given him news about Isabel Lee.

A blond waitress greeted him with a professional smile, and after he was seated gave a vocal description of the bill-of-fare. "The roas' beef's all gone," she finished, "an' so's the lamb stew. Plenty steak left."

"Make it steak," smiled Donal. He ventured a question. The waitress shook her head. No, she worked the dining room alone, save for Saturdays and Sundays.

"Always a lot of the boys in from the ranches them days," the waitress said. "More'n I can handle, so the boss gets in a couple of girls to help." She bustled off to the kitchen.

Donal gave his attention to a group of men at a table across the room. He recognized Al DeSang and Judge Soper. The third man, sitting with his back turned, was the town marshal.

Judge Soper suddenly turned his head and looked at him, then to Donal's surprise he got out of his chair and came across the room. "Well, well!" He beamed, held out a pudgy hand. "Glad to see you, Cameron. A pleasure indeed." The judge exhaled a strong aroma of whisky.

"Hello, Judge." Donal sensed there was a reason for this sudden descent on him. "Take a chair."

"Thank you, suh —" Soper lowered himself into a chair.

"My friend, Jim Daker, tells me you have decided to stay with us, suh. Well, well, an enterprising young man, but there's room, suh, room for all of us in this great and glorious territory."

"You warned me not to stay," reminded Donal good-naturedly. "You seem to have changed your mind."

Judge Soper waved a pudgy hand. "It was for your own good, suh. I know Jim Daker's temper. He has violent ways of dealing with nesters, suh."

"I'm not a nester." Donal spoke curtly.

"It's all the same with Daker," smiled the judge. He shook his head gravely. "I still say you are a bold young man. I'll say something more . . . be on your guard, suh. Jim Daker doesn't want you here, and if unpleasant things happen you will know the source."

"Much obliged." Donal's face gave no hint of his thoughts.

Judge Soper flapped his limp hand. "Not at all, suh. It's only fair to warn you." He paused. "By the way, why not drop in at my office this afternoon? We can have a talk. Or are you leaving for the ranch soon?"

"Sorry, but I'm leaving as soon as I finish some business at Cameron's," Donal answered. "Want to get in by sundown."

Soper rose. "Well, young man — it's been a pleasure to see you again. Look me up next time you're in town." He moved off unsteadily.

The visit puzzled Donal. One thing stood out. Soper seemed anxious to make him realize he could expect trouble from Daker.

When he again glanced at the table across the room he saw that Rede Sems had disappeared, and that DeSang himself was approaching, followed by the rotund and somewhat unsteady Soper.

"Hello, Cameron." Desang paused, teeth glinting in a friendly smile. "Drop over and see me at the store sometime. I'd like a chance at the Circle C trade."

"Thanks, DeSang." Donal's tone was noncommittal. "Nothing I want, right now."

DeSang smiled, nodded, and went on his way, overtaking Soper at the door. Donal watched them, vaguely aware of uneasy premonitions. There was something slippery about this smooth-talking DeSang. He shrugged the curious incident aside, finished his dinner and made his way to the hotel porch. There had been a brisk shower, he noticed, with the cattleman's pleased interest in such things. He noticed something else that jerked him to a standstill. The man tying the paint horse to the hitch-rail in front of the Longhorn Saloon walked with a decided limp.

As Donal crossed over for a closer look, the man vanished behind the swing doors of the saloon.

The paint horse drooping at the hitch-rail drew Donal's look. He ran his eyes over the brand. No mistaking that D. Jim Daker's iron.

His gaze lowered to the rain-sprinkled dust. The rider's boots had made clean imprints on the freshly-wet ground. No need for a closer look. The tracks were the same made by the man found lurking under the trellised vines of the Salazar house. The mark of the iron strap on the boot was unmistakable.

Rage took hold of Donal as he stood there. This skulking would-be killer was a Rocking D man, if the brand on the paint horse meant anything. He had been wrong about Jim Daker, wrong in sizing him up as too decent to stoop to a cowardly assassination. Soper was justified in warning him to be on his guard against the owner of the Rocking D.

He moved swiftly to the swing doors and pushed into the saloon. The bar was crowded and he was aware of faces turning for a look at him as he halted inside the door. Far down the long room, a man rose quickly from a chair at a table and made a rush for the rear door. Donal plunged after him, and another man sitting at the same table sprang up and hurled his chair as Donal charged past.

Too late to avoid the spinning chair, Donal tripped, staggered, and brought up sideways against the bar. His gun swung up, menaced the crowd. "I'll kill the next man who tries any more tricks," he warned.

The man who had thrown the chair grinned. "Go ahaid, mister. Only next time don't come bustin' in like a bull on the prod. How was I to know who you was after?"

Donal gave him a sharp look as he hurried past toward the rear door. He would remember that scarred cheek.

He found himself in the passage, heard the door behind him slam shut. A bolt clicked home. He pressed on through the dark windowless passage. A door stood open. He halted, listened for a moment. Light came dimly from a window in the room. No sound, save the clamor of excited voices in the barroom.

His thoughts raced. The man he sought must have gone through the door and was in the room, or he could have made his escape to the outside by means of the window, or another door. In which case he would make for the horse left tied to the hitch-rail.

His straining ears picked up the sound of cautiously-moving feet that suddenly broke into a run. The man was outside and making for his horse.

Donal rushed into the room. The door opening into the alley was locked. He knew it would be useless to go back the way he had come in. Somebody had shut and bolted the door into the barroom. Donal suspected the man with the scarred face.

He made for the window, partially blocked by a pile of liquor cases. He found the catch, slid the window open and climbed out.

The sharp thud of horse's hoofs digging in for a fast start told him he was too late. Dust rolled and billowed, went drifting down the street.

Donal came to a standstill, stared ruefully after the disappearing rider. He had a wild impulse to take one of the horses standing in front of the saloon. There was a chance he might overtake the man. He dropped the idea. He was practically a stranger in the town. No sense in laying himself open to the charge of horse-stealing.

He became aware of Rede Sems approaching from his office. The town marshal halted. "What's wrong, Cameron?" He asked the question without any apparent show of hostility. "You look some heated."

Donal stared at him for a moment. The marshal wore a bandage on one of his hands. "Hello, Sems." Donal pushed his gun into its holster. He felt the least bit foolish. "Seems like I run into trouble every time I come to this cowtown," he dissembled. "First, you get some crazy notion you want to arrest me, and just now, when I amble into the Longhorn for a drink, some fool jasper throws a chair at me because I show signs I want to palaver with the man he's drinking with."

"Seen a feller hightail it away on a paint horse," Sems said. "Was he the jasper you was wanting to hold talk with?"

"Sure he was." Donal was thinking fast. "Need a couple of new hands on the payroll and this man looked like a cow-poke."

"Don't know him," said Sems. "Seen him in town once in a while. If he turns up ag'in I'll pass him the word you'll maybe give him a job with your Circle C."

"Obliged if you would," thanked Donal. He managed a puzzled smile. "He sure acted scary when I started his way. Must have mistook me for some hombre who's out to get him."

"Lots of jaspers act funny that way," commented the town marshal. "You'd be surprised. This Rio Seco country is full of fellers on the dodge."

"Good place to make a quick jump for the border," Donal suggested. "I've an idea I'm lucky I didn't get a chance to put this bashful hombre on my payroll." He was watching the marshal closely.

"Maybe so, Cameron." Sems' eyes narrowed thoughtfully. "I'll keep an eye open for him, in case I should want to clap him in the calaboose. Lots of rustlin' these times. Maybe so this jasper wears the sort of neck you cowmen like to stretch at the end of a rope."

"I'm for law and order," asserted Donal. "I'm leaving rustlers to the law."

The town marshal shrugged skeptically. "Most of 'em don't talk that way."

Donal glanced at the sun, lying on a bank of clouds. "Looks like a real storm. Guess I'll push on for the ranch."

The town marshal hesitated, lowered his eyes in a brief glance at his bandaged hand. "You're a fast man with a gun, Cameron. Never met with a faster draw."

"I'm from a country where a man can't afford to be slow with a gun." Donal's voice was cold. "What about it, Sems?"

The town marshal's hard thin face wore a taut look. He glanced again at his bandage-wrapped hand. "I've said all I'm going to say, Cameron." He turned away abruptly.

The scowl on his young clansman's face lifted Angus Cameron's shaggy brows to question marks. "You're looking sore puzzled, and a wee bit put out, lad," he commented.

"It's nothing," Donal said curtly.

The trader wisely changed the subject. "Marica Torres is in the kitchen. You'll be wanting a word with her."

Marica proved to be considerably younger than her half-sister, and a pleasant-faced, capable-looking woman. Her mother had been a member of the Salazar household in the old days. Her mother had been born on the rancho, she informed Donal, and her mother's father, and his grandfather.

"We have always lived there," Marica said. "My mother died in the terrible raid that took Don Fidel's life." She crossed herself. "It will be like going home," she added simply.

"You will find lots to be done," Donal said.

"It will be work to my heart," Marica assured him. She smiled at the slim youth standing by her side. "This is a good thing that has come to us, Pasqual. Some day you will be chief of vaqueros, like your grandfather and his grandfather."

The boy's head lifted proudly. "I will serve well," he said.

It was arranged that Roderick Dhu would drive them out to the ranch the following day, together with certain small possessions, and a sizeable order that Donal handed to Angus.

The trader checked off the items on the list with a stubby pencil. "A bit heavy on the cartridges, lad, but no a bad notion." His tone was dry. "Plenty of wolves and coyotes, out your way."

# CHAPTER
# NINE

# Encounter in the Mist

A light rain was falling when Donal rode from the stockade corral, hardly more than a drizzle at first, but finally becoming a steady downpour. It was hard to believe that only a few hours earlier the sun had blazed in a sky of flawless blue. Rubio had prophesied rain. He was familiar with the heavy summer rains of New Mexico.

As the horse splashed along the muddy trail he reviewed the several incidents of his brief stay in San Benito. He bitterly regretted his failure to capture the rider of the paint horse. Rede Sems must have known the man.

The town marshal's sudden friendliness puzzled him. It didn't jibe with the man's attempt to kill him. Angus claimed he was a DeSang hireling, and Jim Daker had indignantly denied any complicity with the affair that had resulted so disastrously for Sems. It seemed unlikely he would be disposed to forget his humiliation and rather bore out the trader's assertion that the town marshal took his orders from DeSang.

The thought disturbed Donal. It was possible that DeSang had told Sems to drop the matter. If true, it raised the ugly suspicion that the town marshal's attempted murder must have been at DeSang's instigation in the first place. For some reason DeSang was now inclined to cultivate friendly relations. He had asked for a chance at Circle C's trade.

There seemed no puzzling the thing out to a satisfactory conclusion, nor could Donal find any answer that would explain Judge Soper. He was suspicious of the motive that had brought the lawyer over to his table. Soper had gone out of his way to warn him against Daker. According to Angus, he was tied hand and foot to DeSang and was not to be trusted. Donal had a shrewd idea that Angus believed DeSang responsible for the attack on his freight wagons. They were business rivals, and DeSang would want the lucrative trade that Angus had held for so many years. The man was obviously unscrupulous.

There had been no reason for that visit from Soper, unless the man had been fishing for information about Daker's reaction to the Spanish grant affair. He had laid it on rather thick about Daker and the trouble he would make.

The rain slackened to a fine drizzle, almost a mist that enfolded the landscape in a thick gray mantle. The horse moved along at the same steady pace. Donal made no attempt to hurry the animal. It was impossible to see more than a few yards in any direction. No need for haste. They could easily make the ranch by sundown.

Something clicked in his brain. *Sundown!* That was it! Soper had asked when he would be leaving town, and Donal had told him that he wanted to get back to the ranch by sundown.

He drew the horse to a halt. Perhaps he was crazy to place so sinister a construction upon the judge's seemingly innocent question, but there were many places on that lonely trail where a killer could lie in wait for an unsuspecting traveler.

The horse was impatient to be moving. Donal held him in check. He dared not disregard the little warning bells that signaled caution. If his hunch was correct, enemies lurked in the chaparral.

Somewhere below him a torrent of water was plunging noisily down the stony bed of what an hour before had been a dry wash. Only the clamor of that storm-born brook touched the deep silence.

He sat there in the saddle, rigid, every sense on the alert. He knew from the giant boulder that bulked vaguely in front of him through the mist that he was close to the fork of the trail where it branched west into Aliso Creek Canyon. Rocking D range was over there, and the Aliso Creek fork was a short cut to the Daker ranch house.

He got down from the horse and, removing his slicker, tied it to the saddle. The long oilskin coat would be an encumbrance if need arose for instant action.

Leaving the horse tied to a juniper a few yards below the trail he started cautiously past the big boulder. The fork in the trail would be a likely spot for an ambush. If killers waited in the chaparral they would be looking for a lone rider, not a man on foot who in turn was stalking

**102**

them. And the odds were somewhat evened by the blanketing mist.

A new sound came faintly above the uproar of the arroyo storm waters . . . the dull thud of a horse's hoofs somewhere beyond him in the fog. The sound suddenly hushed. He guessed the rider had halted at the fork for some reason, was perhaps uncertain of his way in that enveloping mist. Presently the hoofbeats went sloshing along the trail and drawing away. Apparently the rider was heading down-trail, instead of taking the left turn toward town.

Dismay took hold of Donal as he stood there, listening to those receding hoofbeats. Unless the lone rider was one of the gang he was almost sure to draw the blasting gunfire of the killers he suspected were concealed somewhere near in the brush. In that veiling mist they would only see the vague shape of a horse and its rider, would believe they had the man they had been sent to destroy under their guns.

To let a probably innocent man ride unsuspectingly into a death trap was unthinkable. He shouted, started running down the slippery trail, drew to a quick halt, his ears shocked by the crashing report of a gun. Somebody screamed . . . a girl's terror-stricken voice . . . Isabel Lee's voice. He could not be mistaken.

Donal was running again in long leaping strides that carried him past the Aliso Creek fork. A vague shape went threshing through the brush. Donal flung a quick shot, saw the scuttling shape collapse with the suddenness of a fleeing rabbit overtaken by a charge of buckshot.

Somewhere in the deep wall of concealing fog another man was breaking frantically through the undergrowth. Donal wasted no time on him. Fear kept him running, fear for the girl. No sound had come from her since that first frightened cry.

Something loomed up in the fog. A horse, lying on its side across the trail.

He gave the dead animal a brief glance, circled it, apprehensive eyes searching the nearby bushes. He came to a standstill, conscious of a vast relief. The girl was still alive, and somewhere close, but fearing to betray her presence. He called her name. "It's all right," he said. "It's all right, Isabel . . . this is Don Cameron . . . you remember Don Cameron?"

A long silence, and then her voice, faint, unsteady, a whisper of sound in the hush of those remote cloud-mantled hills. It touched the straining ears of the anxiously waiting man like the joyful pealing of bells ringing a glad message of good tidings.

"Don! I — I can't believe it! Don — is it really you?"

"It's all right," he said again. "You can believe it, Isabel."

He heard her before he saw her, and suddenly she was coming toward him out of the mist. She halted, looked at him. "I heard you shout," she said. "It *was* you, wasn't it?"

"Yes," Donal replied.

"You knew those men were here?" Her tone was bewildered.

"It doesn't matter, now." He went to her, took her cold, wet hand in his. Her short raincoat was

**104**

mud-spattered, she was wet, brush-scratched, utterly miserable.

"It is very strange," she said. "I was thinking of you — and then I heard your shout." Her mouth quivered. "I couldn't be sure it *was* you. It happened so quickly — the shot — that awful feeling as the horse fell." Her look went to the dead animal in the trail behind Donal. "Why did they try to shoot me?"

"They didn't mean to shoot you," Donal answered. "They were expecting *me*. It was hard to see in the fog. You came along, and then your scream told them of their mistake."

"I think your shout saved me," Isabel said. "I pulled the horse so hard he reared just as the man fired. The bullet hit the horse — instead of me."

"It was a close call." Donal's voice was husky. "Too close."

"I'm completely confused," Isabel said. "How did you know those men were waiting here to shoot you? How did you know I was here? Nobody could see me in this fog."

He saw that she was trembling, on the verge of hysterics.

"Let's sit down," he suggested. "You've had a shock." He put an arm around her.

"I feel like a wet rag," Isabel admitted. "Silly of me."

Donal had reason for drawing her away from the vicinity of the dead horse. One of the killers still lurked somewhere near the scene. The boulder was screened by the branches of a juniper and offered more protection than the open trail.

They sat down, side by side, his arm around her. Her hat had slipped to the back of her head. She pulled it straight, adjusted the elastic under her chin.

"You haven't answered my question." Her voice was steady again and she was not trembling now. His closeness, the reassuring feel of his arm, seemed to soothe her.

"It was a guess, about the men." Donal paused, looked down into her upturned face. "I'd no idea you were here. I heard a horse at the Aliso Creek fork. Didn't dream it was you."

"I was on my way to San Benito," Isabel told him.

"You were headed the wrong way. That's why you were shot at. You were mistaken for me."

"I didn't know I was going in the wrong direction." She smiled ruefully. "I was quite lost when I came to the fork. One turn looks like another in this thick mist." The eyes looking up at him were puzzled. "I still don't understand why you shouted that warning."

"I'd no idea it was you," he repeated. "I did know that anybody headed down trail just then would likely be mistaken for me. That's why I shouted."

She leaned back against his supporting arm, studied him with grave eyes. "You did some quick thinking."

"I didn't stop to do any thinking."

"Lucky for me you didn't." Her voice was warm. "I'd have been where that — that horse is, if you hadn't shouted the moment you did." A faint smile touched her lips. "You have found out how right I was, haven't you?"

"You said I'd run into a lot of trouble if I didn't leave the Rio Seco," he admitted with a grin.

"You must be wondering about me," Isabel said.

"I dropped in at the restaurant. The man wouldn't tell me anything."

"He wouldn't have known I'd gone to the Rocking D. Nobody knew." She was silent for a moment, face turned away from him, fingers toying nervously with the buttons of her raincoat. "I — I couldn't stand it — there."

He was reluctant to question her. It was no time for questions. They were not out of the woods yet. He withdrew his arm, got to his feet. "No sense staying here — if you feel all right."

"I'm quite all right," she assured him quickly. "Only —" Her look went to the dead horse.

"There's a chance I can get hold of another horse," he said grimly.

She seemed to understand. "I — I heard that second shot."

Her coolness encouraged him. No false metal in this girl. No need for a man to hide the truth from her. "I killed one of them," he told her quietly. "His horse won't be far away."

She nodded, made no comment.

"The other man may be somewhere close," Donal went on. "I've been listening . . . haven't heard a sound. I'd have heard him if he'd got his horse and started away from here."

Isabel continued to look at him, her eyes questioning.

"Don't move from this spot," he said. "Anybody looks like anybody else in this heavy fog."

"I understand." She spoke coolly. "I'll keep out of the way — if there is more trouble."

He looked at her intently for a moment, then turned, was lost to view in the mist. Isabel sat very still, her gaze on the dead horse. She repressed a shiver, got up quickly and moved to the other side of the boulder. The sight of the slain animal was more than she could bear. The mist seemed to be closing in more heavily. She could hear nothing in that unearthly stillness. Only the beating of her own heart.

# CHAPTER
# TEN

# Partners in Trouble

The gray mantle of fog had taken on a more somber look. Vagrant puffs of wind, and ominous mutterings of thunder back in the high peaks, foretold another downpour. Despite the unpleasant prospect of being caught in the black night, Donal held his impatience in check. The dead gunman's companion was somewhere close and the safety of the girl was in his keeping.

He crossed the trail and pushed down the slope to where the dead man lay in a grotesque sprawl under a bush. A glint of metal caught his eyes. The desperado's gun. He picked it up. The empty shell in the chamber told the story. The bullet that had killed Isabel's horse had come from this gun. Only a miracle had saved the horse's rider. He was conscious of a grim satisfaction that his own hastily-flung shot had brought swift retribution to the assassin.

He tossed the gun into the bushes and began a careful scrutiny of the ground. He had a hunch the man was making for his horse when overtaken by the bullet.

Two sets of muddy tracks rewarded his search. He followed them cautiously and came in view of a mass of tumbled boulders flanked by a heavy growth of junipers. He halted, studied the place with wary eyes. He smelled danger down there. A careless move might prove fatal.

He could think of only one reason for the failure of the second man to make good his escape. He had lost his bearings in the fog and was having trouble making his way back to the concealed horses.

It was slow work, and the rain-drenched bushes showered him with water. He held on to his patience, crawled on hands and knees until he was below the great mass of boulders that loomed vaguely through the mist.

A cautious look discovered the horses huddled close to a tree. He started toward them quickly, felt the searing breath of a bullet, heard the roar of a nearby gun. Inwardly cursing his momentary carelessness, Donal flung himself flat behind a boulder.

A wisp of smoke, hardly visible against the background of gray mist, curled above the bushes some ten yards below the horses. Donal fired twice, aiming at a point slightly above the ground and directly under the curling smoke. He heard a startled oath, saw a vague shape rise from the bushes and disappear into the fog.

Donal leaped to his feet, flung another shot in the direction taken by the fleeing man. He could hear the quick pounding of feet, the crackle of harsh brush, then other sounds, a long-drawn-out, terrified shout, followed by a series of heavy thuds.

Something of the truth came to Donal. A yawning precipice, unseen in that dense fog, had brought the

**110**

man's headlong flight to a sudden end. He was lying somewhere down there, seriously injured, perhaps dead.

Donal shook off the impulse to investigate. Isabel would have heard the shots. She would be frantic. He could imagine her alarm.

"It's all right," he called. "Isabel — can you hear me?"

Her answering shout reached him. "I hear you, Don." The steadiness of her voice pleased him. The girl's nerves were good.

He called again. "Start up the trail . . . I'll meet you at the fork."

Satisfied that she understood, he went to the horses and loosened the tie-ropes. Both were strong, speedy-looking animals, the sort of horses men like their late riders would insist upon having. He took time to look them over carefully. He was unfamiliar with the brands they wore.

Isabel was waiting at the Aliso Creek fork when he rode into the trail with one horse on a lead-rope. He climbed from the saddle and started to shorten the stirrups. "This brown horse seems gentle," he said over his shoulder.

"The mist is lifting," the girl said. "I could see you coming up the slope."

"More rain," prophesied Donal. He felt her anxious gaze on him, added tersely, "Ran into the other man . . . he lost his nerve . . . went jumping like a jackrabbit down the hill."

She remained silent. He finished the stirrup and moved to the other side of the horse. "I've an idea he took a bad fall." His tone was grim.

"I heard him shout," Isabel said. She hesitated. "He may be dreadfully hurt."

"I'll have a look." He was conscious of a thrill of pride in her. "Means leaving you alone again."

"I'm not afraid."

They rode up the trail and found Donal's horse where he had left it. He shifted over to his own saddle and they returned to the fork with the led horse.

"I'm coming with you," Isabel decided. "I'd rather not wait here on the trail."

He offered no protest, and she followed him down the slope until Donal halted his horse in a small thicket of scraggly junipers. "Here's a good place," he said. "These trees will hide you from the trail."

The rain was beginning to fall. Donal swung down and got his slicker from the saddle. "Better keep dry while you're waiting." He put the slicker over her shoulders and got back to his saddle. "Don't move from here. I won't be gone long."

The wind was freshening, rolling back the mist and bringing the rain in a hard slanting drive across the landscape. It was perceptibly darker. Donal found himself begrudging the delay. He was responsible for the girl's safety. There had been no time for questions, but he guessed she would be wanting to continue on her way to San Benito. It meant he would be obliged to ride back to town with her. To let her go on alone was

**112**

unthinkable. The storm promised dangerous possibilities. The dry washes had a way of turning into raging torrents that were death traps for the unwary traveler.

He reached the bushes below the mass of tumbled boulders and got down from his horse. The precipice over which the man had fallen was not far away, perhaps thirty or forty yards.

The muddy tracks made a half circle around a clump of thorny shrubs, then veered straight down the steep hill. He followed cautiously and in a few moments was standing on a rocky bluff. He peered over, saw what he knew would be lying on the boulders some fifty feet below.

Even from where he stood, Donal could see there was no life in the crumpled body. Pressed as he was for time, he had a desire for a closer look at this man who had been sent to kill him from ambush.

He made his way around the bluff, but a look at the dead man's face told him his trouble was for nothing. He had never seen him before. Nor did a search of his pockets bring anything to light.

Isabel gave him an inquiring look as he rode up. He nodded grimly. She understood.

"It's terrible," she said. "Both of them dead."

"It might have been you, or I — or the two of us," he reminded. "Don't waste your pity on them."

"I know —" Her voice was distressed. "I shouldn't feel this way —"

"They were murderers," he said. "Sooner or later the law would have hung them. We have more important things to think about," he added.

"*You,* to begin with," Isabel rejoined. She started to loosen the fastenings of the oilskin coat. "You'll be soaked to the bone if you don't put on your slicker."

"Won't be the first time, and that slicker stays on you until we get to San Benito."

"You are going the other way," she demurred. "You've done enough for me in one day."

"I'm not letting you ride the trail alone in this storm." His tone was firm. "It's going to be pitch dark long before you could make town."

She saw that further opposition was useless. "I suppose you are right." She spoke meekly. "It *does* look like a bad night. This rain is almost a cloudburst."

It was slow work making progress along the sloppy trail. Donal was more worried than he cared to admit. They would need a lot of luck to get to town without running into trouble. He heard the girl's voice above the splashing hoofs and pelting rain.

"You must be wondering about me."

"I've been making a few guesses," he admitted. He looked at her, was all at once intensely aware of her nearness. The feeling startled him, put a hardness into his voice. "It wasn't difficult to guess why I didn't find you in the restaurant."

She was silent, her face averted, a sudden tenseness in the slight form wrapped in the folds of the slicker.

"It wasn't hard to guess you'd gone to the Rocking D."

"I couldn't stand it in that town any longer."

"Why are you going back?"

"Because I knew I couldn't stand it at the Rocking D. I couldn't!"

His mystification grew. "I don't savvy," he said. "Not that it's any of my business."

They rode on. The last vestige of daylight faded. They moved through a dark and dripping world.

The girl spoke again, slowly: "You've no right to say that to me."

He looked at her, strove to make out the expression on her face, could only see her profile, softly etched against the darkness. "What do you mean?" He asked the question, knowing well enough what she meant.

"You shouldn't say I'm none of your business, not after what you have done for me, and *are* doing this very moment."

He reached out, took her cold, wet hand in his. "All right —" He spoke gently. "I'm making you my business from now on."

He heard her low laugh. "I shouldn't let you, Don. You have enough troubles of your own. Weren't those men planning to kill you?"

He tightened his clasp on her hand. "We're partners in trouble. Let's shake on that, pard."

"You bet, pardner." Her voice was a bit unsteady. She gave his hand a squeeze.

They jogged along, heads lowered against the slanting rain. The slopes were becoming alive with the sound of countless rushing little streams. Donal's anxiety grew. They would know the worst very soon now. Another hundred yards would bring them to the

**115**

bend where the trail dipped steeply to what in ordinary times was the dry bed of a creek.

Isabel was speaking, her horse pressing close alongside. "I have a lot to tell you —" She broke off, and he felt, rather than saw, her startled look. "*Don — listen!*" Alarm sharpened her voice.

The horses swung around a high ridge, and now the roar of rushing waters hit full on their ears. Donal checked his horse. "I was afraid of it." His tone was gloomy. "That dry wash is running bank full."

"You mean we can't cross?" Isabel peered down the steep trail. "It's too dark to see from here."

He was silent. For himself he would not have cared. Isabel complicated things. He was at a loss. Her voice came faintly above the noise of the turbulent waters. "You mean we can't go any farther?"

"You've guessed it," he replied ruefully. "We can't ford that creek tonight, Isabel. We're up against it."

"What in the world can we do?" She was aghast.

"I can take you back to the Rocking D," he suggested after a moment's thought.

"No!" Her voice was so low he heard her with difficulty. "I'm afraid to go back."

"You can't stay out in this storm all night," he said. "I'll have to take you back to the Rocking D. There's no alternative."

Her voice lashed at him fiercely. "I'm not going back to that place."

He could only look at her helplessly. There was no doubting she meant her words. Something had happened at the Rocking D. She feared to go back, had

**116**

hinted she would prefer death in the raging storm waters. Donal was aware of a mounting anger against Jim Daker.

Isabel broke the silence. "You can take me to your own ranch, Don," she said.

He continued to look at her. She reached out, touched his hand. "We're partners in trouble. Those were your words. Be sensible, Don. You must take me to Circle C."

She was right. He knew she was suggesting the only thing left for them to do. "All right." He turned his horse. Isabel followed, and they rode down the trail.

The rain was at their backs and their horses stepped along freely. "The boys are going to have a big surprise," Donal said. "You see — I told them I was going to town for a lady cook."

The girl's laugh rippled. It was apparent her spirits were on the rebound. "Well — I *can* cook. I'm a good cook — and I can try to be a lady."

"Only trouble is I've hired a cook. She'll be out at the ranch tomorrow. A nice middle-aged señora named Marica Torres." His mind was suddenly at ease as he thought of Marica Torres. She solved the problem of Isabel's presence at the ranch.

They passed the Aliso Creek fork. Donal pulled up, looked at the dead horse lying across the trail. "Mr. Daker won't like this," he said.

"Poor thing!" It was obvious that the girl's concern was for the horse and not for Jim Daker.

"Looks like a good saddle." He hesitated. "Hate to see a good saddle go to ruin —"

"It's mine," Isabel told him. "Mr. Daker gave it to me. He gave me the horse, too." Bitterness edged her voice. "He can't accuse me of horse-stealing."

"*Your* saddle!" Donal started to get down. She stopped him. "Please! Let it stay with the horse. I don't want *anything* from Mr. Daker."

Donal made no comment and they rode on. The trail leveled out across the piñon-covered mesa. It was easier traveling for the horses and Donal kept them moving at a fast walk. Ahead of them lay the rugged slopes of Comanche Ridge. The prospect brought a grim look to Donal's face. It was a hard ride in that storm, a grueling test for even a range-toughened rider. He was doubtful of the girl's ability to hold on to her endurance. Nothing else to do but keep moving. He knew of no shelter nearer than the Circle C ranch house.

An exclamation from Isabel broke the silence. "Don! It's not raining so hard!"

He came out of his reverie. "That's right!" The relief in his voice drew a quick look from her. She sensed he had been worrying.

Stars began to glimmer above the ridge. Donal interpreted their message of hope to Isabel. "The storm is heading away from here. We're riding into clear weather."

"I won't be sorry." She reached out a hand, touched his arm. "You were getting worried."

"It began to look like a tough ride over the ridge," he admitted. "Won't be so bad when those clouds break away. There's a moon up there."

**118**

"I wish the moon could be a blazing hot sun," she laughed. "You could do with a good drying out."

"I'm all right. Nothing about me that rain can spoil. A cowman has to take these things."

"A cowman doesn't usually have a helpless, frightened young woman on his hands."

The moon, nearing the full, suddenly pushed from behind the clouds, and Donal saw the girl's face, softly etched in the silvery glow. She was staring straight ahead, and her expression hurt him.

"What has Daker done to you?" he blurted the question.

"Nothing — to *me*." She hesitated. "Mr. Daker has been kind enough, and so has Mrs. Daker."

The opening wedge was in now, cracking her reticence. Donal drove in another. "Then why are you running away from the Rocking D?"

She made no answer. Donal felt a quick shame, an anger at himself for questioning her. "I'm sorry. It is none of my business."

She was suddenly smiling. "But it *is* your business. You said so, back there on the trail. You said you would make me your business from now on."

His good humor returned. "I'm not backing out, if it's all right with you."

"We're partners, Don," she said softly.

Moonlight and shadows touched them fitfully as they rode closely side by side under the clearing sky. Donal refrained from further questions. He was leaving it to her.

"Do you remember the night you came into the restaurant?" She went on, not waiting for his answer. "I warned you against staying in the Rio Seco country. I had my reasons."

"Your father," Donal said. "You told me he was a brave man — but they killed him because he wouldn't leave the Rio Seco."

"Do you remember something else I told you?"

"You said Jim Daker wanted to adopt you because he was sorry for you." He looked at her. "I'd made up my mind you'd given in to him."

"I didn't actually agree I would let him adopt me. Perhaps I wasn't quite fair with him."

"Fair?" He was puzzled.

"I told him I would try it for a few weeks before definitely deciding. He was satisfied, told me that Mrs. Daker would love me like her own child." Isabel's voice took on a regretful note. "I'm sorry — for Mrs. Daker. I liked her."

Donal's bewilderment grew. He couldn't make the thing out. Daker was a rich man. Nothing would have been too good for the girl he wanted to take into his home as a daughter. The Dakers had no children of their own.

"You're thinking I must be crazy, giving up such a chance." Her tone was hard. "Jim Daker's daughter, heiress to his possessions and all that sort of thing."

"You have your reasons," he rejoined. "They must be good reasons."

"I told you I wasn't quite fair with him," Isabel went on. "My *real* reason for pretending to consider letting

**120**

him adopt me would have made him hate me." She faltered. "I — I thought if I went to the Rocking D I might find out things I wanted to know."

He began to get her drift. "Your father — and brother? You thought you might learn the truth — about the raid?"

"Yes." She spoke fiercely. "I want to see the murderers hanged."

He looked at her sharply. "You mean you suspect Daker?"

"Not exactly that." She hesitated. "It's a feeling I have that Mr. Daker knows something about that raid. I think that is the reason why he wanted to adopt me. He was sorry for me."

"It's possible," agreed Donal in a harsh voice. He was thinking of the man who rode a paint horse marked with the iron of the Rocking D. "Did you happen to notice if Daker had a cripple in his outfit?"

"Cripple?" she echoed. "Well, yes, I did. But you've seen him yourself. He was desk clerk at the hotel the night of the Fourth of July dance." She smiled faintly. "Hook is really an old dear. I liked him."

"I don't mean Hook Saval," Donal said. "The man I have in mind would be lame — one leg shorter than the other."

Isabel was sure she had never seen any lame man in the Rocking D outfit while she was at the ranch. "I wouldn't have seen all the men on the payroll," she pointed out. "Lots of them would be out at the cattle camps, working." She looked at Donal inquisitively. "You are having trouble with Daker so soon?"

"I'm not sure that it's Daker," he replied. "I can't pin anything on Daker yet. There's been a man prowling around Circle C. Almost nabbed him in town this afternoon. He was riding a Rocking D horse."

"Oh!" Isabel stared hard at the ears of the brown horse she rode. "Is — is this a Rocking D horse?"

"No, nor the one we turned loose back at the Aliso Creek fork. I don't know the brands."

She seemed relieved. "I hate to think it was Mr. Daker who sent those men to ambush you. I don't like him, and I have reason to believe he knows a lot about what happened to my father and brother, but somehow I don't see him plotting cowardly murders."

Donal's face took on a bleak look. He was not so sure he agreed with her. He was recalling Blue Clover's words. *Jim Daker wouldn't be knowin' all the things that went on . . . He just lets out there's certain folks he don't want 'round . . . He don't bother himself about what happens.*

The trail was lifting up the rocky slopes of Comanche Ridge, so narrow in places they were forced to ride in single file. Presently they were on the summit, resting the horses and looking down on the valley. Donal tried to make a cigarette. His tobacco was too wet. He grimaced, pushed the sack back into his shirt pocket.

"Poor man," sympathized the girl. "But you *would* make me wear your slicker."

122

They both laughed. Their spirits were soaring. It was good to be on top of that mountain ridge, looking down on the long stretch of moonlit valley. Death had stalked them too closely.

Isabel spoke again, hesitantly: "I haven't told you *all* the reasons that made me run away from the Rocking D." She gave him a sidewise look. "Do you remember Lew Trent?"

"Yes." His tone was curt. "Daker's foreman."

"He's another reason — why I couldn't stand it at the ranch."

Donal glowered. "What do you mean?"

"Lew Trent is a dangerous man." Her tone was suddenly vexed. "You're thinking I meant something — not nice."

"Why not?" He spoke gruffly. "I was told Trent wouldn't stand for competition where you were concerned. He would have liked to use a gun on me — that night at the dance."

Isabel was silent for a long moment, her gaze fixed on the floor of the valley far below. A cloud shadow lay across the moonlit landscape, a dark, forbidding thing that for some reason made her think of a monstrous vulture. She repressed a shiver, turned her face to Donal. "I can't help what you think, and anyway it's not the other reason why I couldn't stay at the Rocking D. I mean that Lew Trent knows a lot about what happened to my father and brother . . . I am sure he does." She drew a sharp breath. "I couldn't stay there, seeing him every day, listen to his — his talk — have him touch me."

Donal had not missed the slight stumble. *Trent's love-making*, she meant! He said gently, "I'm mighty glad you got away from there, Isabel."

She gave him a distressed look. "Don't ask me questions about him. It's something that can't be discussed." She paused. "I was lucky this afternoon. He'd gone off to one of the cattle camps, or I wouldn't have got away. He never seemed to take his eyes off me."

"You don't need to say any more." Donal's voice was harsh.

She flared up. "You keep away from Lew Trent as far as I'm concerned. I'm not going to be the cause of trouble between you."

Sudden pity for her held back the retort on his lips. She had been through a lot of hell and was wanting comfort in big doses. He reached out a hand, squeezed hers. "We're partners," he reminded. "Don't forget that, Isabel."

Her long lashes winked ominously, and she said in a tight little voice, "You're a grand partner, Don." Her smile came, shy, contrite. "I'm over it now."

"*Bueno!*" Donal chuckled. "Let's ride. We'll drag Old Sinful from his bunk and have him make us a pot of hot coffee."

"Who is Old Sinful?" she asked as they started the rested horses down the winding trail.

"He's the most cantankerous, best-hearted old scoundrel who ever bossed a chuckwagon."

"He sounds interesting," laughed Isabel.

**124**

"You'll like the Circle C gang," he assured her. "They're not parlor-broke, but they rate one hundred percent in any man's language."

Isabel's face took on a thoughtful look. She shook her head, said slowly, "I won't be at Circle C very long. Only until I can get to San Benito."

"I suppose so." His tone was glum.

"You see, I was planning to go to Angus Cameron, ask him to let me stay at his place until I found a job. I haven't any money, only a few dollars, and I'd feel safer with him."

"You couldn't find a safer place in San Benito," Donal said. His tone was doubtful. "You can't stay in that town. You won't be safe there, not even with Angus. We will leave Daker out of it, if you want. I'm not thinking of him."

"You mean Lew Trent?" She was plainly startled. "I hadn't thought of it that way. I'd be sure to run into him."

"If Trent is guilty of what you suspect, and if he knows you *do* suspect, he won't lose time getting on your trail." Donal paused, added slowly, "There may be other men in San Benito who won't like you to know too much."

She gave him a troubled look. "I've got to go somewhere."

Donal hesitated, said awkwardly, "Nobody need know you are at Circle C. The boys won't say a word. I don't know of a safer place — right now."

"Oh!" She shook her head. "I couldn't —"

"Señora Torres will be there tomorrow," he interrupted. "She will make it all right for you to be staying at Circle C. Nobody could say a word."

She made no answer, but her smile reached out to him, grateful, contented, reassuring him that she had no doubts nor fears.

At last they were down on the floor of the valley. The horses moved into an easy trot. Donal broke the silence. "Circle C," he said contentedly. "Circle C — over there."

Isabel looked, saw the faint glimmer of lamplight. A tiny beckoning star, it seemed to her. She straightened up in her saddle, smiled at her companion. "Sure hope Ol' Sinful fixes up that thar hot coffee pronto, partner," she said.

# CHAPTER
# ELEVEN

# Three Strangers

Tule Creek was running bank full. Rusty Cross reined his horse and speculatively watched a flock of ducks circle the marsh. "Should have brought a shotgun along," he said to his companion.

"I've won me a dollar." Wes Coles wore a satisfied grin.

"How come you won a dollar?" Rusty looked at him suspiciously.

"Had a bet on with Brasca you'd say just what you done said if we run into ducks this mornin'."

"Huh!" The young Circle C foreman was nettled. "What's wrong with talkin' about ducks?"

"Ain't nothin' wrong with talkin' about ducks," drawled Wes. "Only trouble is you don't never get any ducks. You just talk about gettin' 'em."

"Some day I'll fool you," retorted Rusty good-naturedly. "Right now we've got more important business than duck huntin'."

The two men skirted the tules and reached the gorge where the creek drew in between high banks for a tumultuous plunge before it emptied into the west fork of the Rio Seco. They halted their horses.

**127**

"Should hate to ride them falls down the canyon," observed Wes.

"It's been done."

Wes looked skeptical. "Huh. I s'pose you know the feller that done it."

"I know the feller whose dad done it."

"I used to know a hombre whose dad once seen a pink buffalo," scoffed Wes.

"I'm talkin' about Rubio's dad."

"Huh." Wes was impressed. He held Rubio in high esteem. "How come Rubio's dad took a notion to ride them falls?"

"It was the falls, or lose his scalp to a bunch of Comanches."

"Well" — Wes grinned — "mebbe that's one time I'd do the same."

Rusty was scrutinizing the face of the cliff under which they had halted their horses. "No way of gettin' up from here," he said. "Only thing we can do is follow along the bluffs and keep our eyes peeled."

"Should pick up sign easy after the rain," observed Wes as they rode slowly along under the beetling crags. "Ground is good and wet."

A break presently appeared, a narrow gully that some long-ago cloudburst had gouged down the steep side of the rugged slope.

Rusty slid from his saddle. "Been a lot of water down this gully," he said. "If that feller was here his tracks will be washed out by now."

Wes rode on a few yards, halted his horse above the wash. "Plenty tracks this side," he called. "Looks like a couple of fellers has been here and rode off ag'in." He rejoined his companion. "Both of us makin' the climb?" he asked.

"One of us has got to stay with the horses," Rusty decided. "You're elected for the job." He bent down, unbuckled his spurs and hung them over the saddle horn.

"I can climb a lot better than you," grumbled Wes.

"That feller may still be up on the cliffs some place," Rusty conjectured.

"All the more reason for me to go 'stead of you," declared Wes. "I've got two guns that can talk awful fast."

"The dee-bate is closed," announced Rusty. "Keep your eyes and ears open, Wes. No tellin' what'll happen these times." He threw the aggrieved cowboy a good-natured grin and went clambering over the boulders that partially blocked the mouth of the gully.

Wes stood watching until Rusty was lost to view, then with the air of a man who feels he has been grossly mistreated, he picked out a sun-warmed boulder and sat down, fingers reaching in shirt pocket for tobacco and cigarette papers.

His face wore a scowl. There were good reasons why he should have gone, instead of Rusty. He was faster with a gun, and was more experienced in coping with the sort of trouble Rusty might run into up there on the cliffs.

He lit his cigarette and leaned against the slab of rock at his back. The sun felt good. He pulled his hat low over his eyes, drowsily reviewed Bearcat's story of seeing a man on the cliffs the night before. Bearcat wasn't sure about it. Light bad, an' rainin' heavy. Bearcat said he wasn't swearin' a man was up on the cliffs. Might have been one of them long-legged cranes from the marsh . . . Wasn't likely, though . . . Cranes didn't set 'round on high cliffs like eagles did.

Wes flipped his cigarette stub aside. Rusty was some worried when Bearcat come in with his yarn about seein' this hombre up on the cliffs . . . The boss wasn't back from San Benito . . . didn't get in till close on midnight . . . Had a girl with him. Wes didn't know who she was. The boss wasn't sayin' nothin' about her a-tall. The new housekeeper, likely. Rusty said the boss figgered to get a woman over from San Benito. Kind of young, though, an' a doggone good-looker for all she was plumb wore out . . . Was wearin' pants, too, just like a man . . . Could have passed for a kid at first sight. Boss wasn't sayin' nothin' about what had made 'em come in so late. Held up by a washout on the trail, most likely.

Wes closed his eyes, thoughts drowsing on. The boss wasn't likin' Bearcat's yarn about seein' a feller up on the cliffs . . . told Rusty to have a look-see at sunup. The boss wasn't wantin' to go along on account of the girl. Didn't want her to find him gone when she got up. Kind of funny — the way the boss was so anxious about her.

Wes eased his head more comfortably against the rock. His thoughts rambled lazily. Would have been ready to bet old Bearcat he was all wrong about seein' any hombre up on the cliffs . . . he'd told Bearcat he was dreamin' . . . No dream about them tracks above the wash . . . them tracks were sure enough real. A gentle snore came from the cowboy's slightly open mouth.

The two horses, tied to a nearby tree, suddenly lifted their heads in a startled look. It was not the snore from Wes Coles that made them prick up inquisitive ears. They were staring at something several yards beyond the dozing Circle C man. One of them let out a gusty snort.

Wes Coles, whose cat nap had lasted something less than sixty seconds, was instantly wide-awake and on his feet. Dismay widened his eyes.

The guns in the hands of the three men standing near a clump of bushes close to the mouth of the gully lifted menacingly. The odds meant nothing to Wes. He snarled a curse, reached frantically for the .45's in his holsters. A shot rocked the stillness of that remote spot. The Circle C man spun sideways, fell against the boulder, slid with a scraping sound down its rough side and lay motionless on the loose stones of the wash.

The three newcomers stood watching him for a brief space, then, apparently satisfied, the man who had fired the shot spoke to his companions.

"Get the horses. I'll keep watch."

"How about the other feller, Lew?"

Trent's cold gaze went to the speaker, a short, bow-legged man with a scarred cheek. "You heard me, Slash."

The man's lip lifted in an unpleasant smile. "Sure, Lew. It's your show." He followed the other man into the bushes.

Trent's gaze returned to the prostrate form of Wes Coles. He made no move for a closer look. The man was dead. He was sure of it. Instead he went to the horses, untied them and stood waiting with their lead-ropes in his hand.

Slash appeared from the bushes. He pulled at the prickly branches, throwing them aside and making an opening several feet wide. The third man pushed through with three horses on lead-ropes.

Trent called out softly, "Put that brush back, Slash." The scar-faced man said, "Sure. I savvy." He hastily dragged the removed brush back into place and followed the man with the three led horses to where Trent was waiting.

"We'll take these Circle C broncs with us," Trent told them. He handed each man a lead-rope and swung up to his own saddle. "All right. Let's go, boys."

"What about the feller up on the cliffs?" again asked Slash. His tone was truculent. "I've got a stake in this deal, Lew."

"Don't get fool notions you're running this show." Trent spoke quietly. "We're getting away from here while the going's good. The job ain't finished yet and we've no time to lose."

Slash scowled. "Let me tell you somethin'. If that feller up there is Cameron, well — you're sure leavin' dynamite hangin' on our tails."

**132**

"You're loony." Trent's tone was impatient. "I've already told you we attended to Cameron last night. I know where that Brazos four-flusher is, and it's a long way from here."

Slash was only half convinced. "How long is a long ways?" he wanted to know sulkily.

Trent's look went briefly to the limp form lying under the boulder. "As long as *that.*"

"I reckon hell's plenty far," Slash said with a hard laugh.

The three men rode away, followed the stony bed of the wash for several hundred feet, then turned sharply to the southeast and disappeared around the bluffs.

Rusty was up on the rimrock when he heard the shot. He halted. Two more quick shots would mean a signal from Wes Coles. One shot, followed by two quick ones, was always the call for help.

No other sound touched his straining ears. Rusty didn't like it. He didn't like other things his alert eyes were noticing. Fresh tracks on the wet ground, made that morning, since the heavy rain. Other tracks, too, not so fresh, made before the rain. Somebody had found the high cliffs a convenient observation post. A man with a pair of good glasses could see a lot of what went on in the valley. He could even see the Circle C ranch yard — the corrals.

Rusty's alarm grew. Those fresh tracks — that lone crack of a .45! Something was wrong down below. Wes was in trouble!

**133**

The Circle C foreman was already on the run. If he had waited on the rimrock a few minutes he would have seen the three horsemen riding along the stony wash that led away from the little gully.

Caution held his feverish impatience in check as he neared the mouth of the gully. Gun in hand he crawled forward, finally reached a huge boulder that lay across another granite slab. He peered through the wide crack between them. The dead silence appalled him. No sign of Wes Coles . . . the horses gone.

Of a sudden Rusty was moving very fast again, scrambling over the boulders and running with short quick strides across the wash to the prone body of his friend.

His first look reassured him. He gently eased Wes over, stared with some surprise at the wound. A bad wound, but not serious enough to explain why Wes should be so long unconscious. The shock of the bullet could have knocked him down, but the bullet had made a clean passage through the shoulder muscles.

Rusty was puzzled, until his searching eyes saw the gash on the back of the unconscious man's head. He leaned over for a closer look, then stared quickly up at the jagged sides of the big boulder under which Wes was lying.

The foreman let out a relieved sigh. The story was plain. The bullet had made Wes stagger against the boulder and it was the sharp ridge of rock that had knocked him senseless as he fell. The bullet wound, while painful, was not dangerous.

**134**

Rusty jerked off his hat and hurried to the little pool below the granite boulders. He filled the Stetson with cold water and returned to Wes and gently bathed his head. He was delighted to hear the cowboy's voice, weakly indignant.

"What the hell! Tryin' to drown me?"

"You wasn't born to be drowned, Wes," chuckled the relieved Rusty, "nor die of lead poisonin', far as I can see from that hole in your shoulder. No, sir, you ain't born to die respectable, looks like to me."

Wes attempted a feeble scowl. "You're a liar if you claim I'm due to get dangled for stealin' cows." He sat up, winced from the effort to look at his hurt shoulder. "Feel awful dizzy."

"Your own fault for tryin' to beat your brains out on that rock," Rusty said severely. He was busying himself with the bullet wound, washing it clean and fashioning a bandage with his bandana. "I reckon that will hold you till we get to the ranch. The boss has things in his medicine box that'll do a better job." Rusty studied his friend anxiously. "How you feel, feller?"

"Well, leavin' out things like a broke head and a hell of a sore shoulder, I'm feelin' almighty lucky." Wes gazed around, his expression a mixture of bewilderment and dismay. "Don't see our horses, Rusty! Or maybe my eyes ain't behavin' like they should."

"What went on down here, Wes? I was up on the rimrock when I heard the shot. When I got down the horses had gone. Only you — layin' here."

Wes told him about the three strangers. "Looks like they was hidin' in the bushes yonder. We passed up a bet, not taking a look-see in them bushes."

"I'm takin' a look now," Rusty declared.

"I wasn't expectin' them hombres to jump out on me," grumbled Wes. "Couldn't get my guns out fast enough."

"I'm not blaming you," Rusty said gruffly. He picked up the fallen guns, pushed one of them into Coles' holster and placed the other in his outstretched right hand.

Wes grinned, balanced the Colt lovingly. "All right. You mosey along and hunt for sign. Those fellers will be some s'prised if they pop back on me. Reckon they figgered I was dead, leavin' my guns layin' here."

Rusty was gone less than ten minutes. Wes saw him emerge from the bushes, saw him start pulling at the branches. They came away easily, revealed an opening. Rusty wore a thoughtful look on his brown face when he rejoined his companion.

"Hideout back there," he said. "Been used plenty. I've a notion these fellers have been spyin' on us from top of the rimrock. You can see all over the valley from up there. See the ranch yard, with good glasses."

"Sure smells bad," commented Wes gloomily.

"Been keeping their horses back in the hideout," Rusty went on. "It's easy now to figger out about the horses. These stones don't show tracks. They must have rode down the wash a ways and then swung southeast and on around the bluffs. You said you saw tracks over there, Wes."

**136**

"Reckon I didn't look close enough." Wes spoke disgustedly. "It was a smart trick they pulled off, cuttin' 'round by the wash." He stared at Rusty speculatively. "Wonder what their game is?"

"I wish we knew," Rusty replied bitterly. "Only one answer, I reckon. Trouble . . . plenty trouble, and here's you and me most four miles from the house and only shank's mare to ride on."

"I'd figger the house ain't but three miles from here," argued Wes.

"If you could fly it straight like a crow," jeered Rusty. "We've got to circle around the tule swamp."

"I can make it," declared Wes.

"It's a tough walk," reminded Rusty. He looked at his friend dubiously. "You'll have to wait here till we can get you a horse."

"Wait nothin'!" Wes glared at him. "You talk like I was sick."

Rusty grinned. "No call for you to start bellerin' and pawin' dirt. If you say you ain't sick it's all right with me."

"Huh!" It was apparent that Wes was in an irritable mood. "*You'd* sure be plenty sick if you had a hole in your shoulder and the back of your head staved in."

"I sure would," quickly agreed Rusty, diplomatically. "I'd be yellin' my haid off for a doc."

"You're a doggone liar," Wes said. He grinned, got to his feet, scowled fiercely in an attempt to cover the torment the movement caused him. "The hombre that invented walkin' was sure born without good sense. Must have been a sheepherder."

It was a statement he repeated several times with increasing bitterness before they sighted the wagon crawling along the sand flats above the creek.

# CHAPTER
# TWELVE

# A Call For Help

Isabel found Donal in the corral at work on the brown horse with currycomb and brush. For some reason she was pleased.

"He's a good horse," she said. "I owe him many thanks for the lift he gave me last night."

"I should have turned him loose . . . let him find his way home."

Isabel offered no comment. She knew the thought in his mind. The brown horse had earned a good feed, a warm stable.

"I could be charged with horse-stealing if the man who owns him found him in my corral."

"The man who owns him is dead," reminded Isabel. "He fell over the cliff. He might have belonged to the other man, but he's dead, too."

"I don't think those men owned either of the horses," Donal argued. "It's more than an even gamble they were stolen."

"He's such a good horse —" Isabel broke off, stared at the small brand on the left shoulder. "Don!" She spoke excitedly. "That mark . . . it's father's 4L . . . our ranch brand!" She flung her arms about the satiny neck. "Of course! He's Brownie! I used to ride him."

Donal could only look at her. He was too thunderstruck for words.

"I was about to say he's so like a horse I used to ride," Isabel went on. She kept her face pressed against the horse's neck. He saw that she was crying, and he said in a low voice, "Some day we'll find out the truth about that raid on your father's ranch." His voice took on an edge. "I'm beginning to think we won't have to hunt so very far."

Her face came round to him, eyes wet, mouth quivering. "The man who was riding this horse must have been one of them." She drew a sharp breath. "I can't feel sorry, any more, for what happened last night. Those men were murderers."

"Somebody is coming," Donal said sharply. "A wagon!"

The sounds rapidly approached from beyond the concealing line of cottonwood trees. The wagon swung into view. A woman sat on the seat by the driver and there were men crouched behind in the wagon-bed.

Donal muttered a startled exclamation, started hastily toward the corral gate. Rubio must have heard the rattle of wheels. He appeared in the barn door, took one comprehensive look, dropped his pitchfork and ran swiftly toward the approaching wagon.

Roderick Dhu pulled the mules to a standstill. No words were spoken as they removed Wes Coles from the wagon and carried him to the house. Isabel marveled at the swiftness and gentleness of these men.

**140**

The Mexican woman climbed from the high seat. Isabel heard her voice, worried, compassionate. "Thees poor hombre ver' seek."

She realized the woman was speaking to her. "Are you Señora Torres?" She asked the question a bit vaguely. Her mind was on the injured man.

"*Si.* I come work for Señor Cameron. I am Marica Torres." Her large dark eyes held a hint of curiosity as she looked at the girl.

Isabel found herself liking this competent-appearing woman. She smiled. "I'm Isabel Lee. Perhaps you have seen me in San Benito."

"*Si* — at the *cantina.*" Marica seemed puzzled. "The señor no say you at rancho." She shook her head as if impatient at herself. "I go 'elp the señor weeth thees poor hombre. I am ver' good nurse."

Isabel kept pace with her as she went swiftly into the patio. "Marica, what happened to him?"

"I know not'ing. Only thees hombre get shoot. He walk too mooch . . . make heem start bleed *malo.*"

"I want to help," Isabel said.

"*Si,*" answered the Mexican woman with an approving nod. "We queek 'ave thees poor hombre feel all right."

They found Wes Coles on Donal's bed. His shirt had been removed and Donal was examining the wound in the shoulder. He gave the girl a startled look, shook his head.

"I want to help Marica," Isabel told him firmly. "You mustn't send me away. Marica says she is a good nurse."

"*Si.*" Marica smiled reassuringly. "I ver' good nurse, señor. You no need stay. We soon make thees hombre feel mooch good." She began poking into the medicine box, seized a roll of clean white linen. "*Bueno!* Thees make fine bandeege."

Donal knew from the expression on Rusty's face that the foreman had much to tell him. The moments were precious. He gave Marica a grateful look and turned to the door. "All right, Rusty," he said. "We can leave Wes to them."

As the two men hurried away, Marica spoke to the slim dark youth who had helped carry the wounded man from the wagon. "Go with the master, Pasqual," she said in Spanish. "There is trouble on this old Salazar place. You must be another man at the master's side."

Pasqual sped from the room, and Isabel heard the quick sharp beat of boot heels as he ran to overtake his new boss. Marica looked up briefly from the bandage she was preparing. "Always mooch trouble on thees old rancho," she said with a lift of a shoulder. "*Si,* I theenk thees old Salazar rancho 'ave the curse."

Something of the same thought was in Donal's mind as he listened to Rusty's story. Old Sinful hurried up with his buffalo gun. "What's the rumpus?" he asked. "I was back in the trees, stackin' wood, when I seen the wagon comin' like a bat out of hell."

He let out angry snorts as Rusty went on with the tale. "Left you afoot, huh! The mangy skunks!" He gnawed savagely on his plug of tobacco. "Looks like

**142**

Bearcat was right, claimin' he seen a feller up on the rimrock."

"Have you any idea who the men were?" questioned Donal.

"Wes hadn't a chance for a look at 'em," Rusty answered. "The thing happened awful fast. Wes says he went for his guns the moment he got that warnin' from the horses and saw the three fellers come out of the brush. He wasn't wasting time for a look at their faces."

Donal asked another question. "How about those tracks you found on the rimrock?"

Rusty shook his head. "No sign of the lame feller. At least I didn't run across his tracks. He may have been up there before the rain. One thing sure, they're using the rimrock to spy on us."

The faint, far-away report of a rifle shocked their ears. Old Sinful muttered an exclamation. "Somebody shootin'!"

Donal gestured for silence, and they stood there, anxious, every sense alert. Again they heard the distant bark of gunfire, followed after a brief space by two quick shots.

Rusty Cross gave Donal an aghast look, started on the run for the barn. Old Sinful pounded after him. They knew the meaning of those rifle shots. Brasca and Bearcat were in trouble.

Rubio scrambled from the wagon where he was helping Roderick Dhu unload the supplies.

"Throw my saddle on the buckskin," Donal said. "Quick, Rubio!"

Rubio hesitated. "Do I ride weeth you?"

"Somebody must stay with the women," Donal replied. "You and Pasqual will keep watch until we get back."

"*Si.*" Rubio hurried on his way to the barn.

Donal looked at Pasqual. There was a gun in the young Mexican's holster. "Have you a rifle?"

"Yes. In the wagon, señor."

"Get it," Donal said. The boy's alert manner pleased him. He was intelligent, responsive, and his English showed considerable schooling.

Roderick Dhu pulled a carbine from the leather boot attached to the driver's seat. He gave Donal a sober look. "I will ride with you, my brother," he said.

"Thanks, Rod." Donal was listening again to those faraway rifle shots. Their meaning was not to be mistaken. Bearcat and Brasca were calling for help.

Pasqual sprang down from the wagon with his rifle. Donal said curtly, "Give them an answer. Three quick shots, and count five, then three more quick shots. That means we're on the way."

Pasqual's rifle roared three times, then three more shots crashed out. Donal turned to the patio gate. "I'm getting my guns," he said to the Apache. "Rubio will fix you up with a horse, Rod. Tell him I said for him to unhitch your mules and give 'em a feed."

He hurried down the patio walk. Isabel met him in the doorway, an apprehensive look on her face. "Don . . . what's wrong? All that shooting!"

He gave her a brief explanation as she followed him into the house.

"You'll be gone long?"

"No telling." He took down his rifle, examined it carefully. "Rubio and Pasqual will stay with you."

She went to him, looked earnestly into his eyes. "Is it something to do with what happened last night?"

"It's possible." His brows drew down in a frown. "I've an idea that what happened last night to us, and what happened to Wes Coles this morning, and what might be happening to Bearcat and Brasca right now, can all be tied up in the same parcel."

"I hate to think that I'm the cause of more trouble for you. I mean because I'm here in your house." Her tone was unhappy.

"I wouldn't have you anywhere else," Donal said in a low voice. He was conscious of a longing to put his arms around her. Instead he turned abruptly to the door. She made no move to follow. He looked back at her. "How is Wes making it?"

"Señora Torres says he's all right. Just weak from loss of blood. He's worried, though, about those gunshots." She gave him an anxious look.

"Keep him in bed," Donal said. "Don't let him try to follow us."

"The señora is very strong-minded." Isabel's mouth curved in an amused smile. "She'll make him obey."

The stamping of horses' hoofs reached them from the yard, and Old Sinful's strident voice: "All I craves is a chance to git my sights on the skunk as bushwhacked Wes Coles. I'll sure blow the gizzard out of that crawlin' sidewinder." And Rusty's dry, bitter voice, "Skunks and

**145**

rattlers don't wear gizzards, but I'm ridin' the same notion."

Donal took another step toward the door, looked back again at the girl, standing slim and straight where he had left her. She was pale, unsmiling, but the eyes that met his look were steady and unafraid. He said softly, "*Adios.*" And then was moving with quick, long strides toward the gate.

Isabel watched for a moment. She drew a sharp breath, went out quickly to the corridor and ran down the path.

Perhaps fifteen minutes had passed since they had unloaded Wes Coles and carried him into the house. And now Donal was riding away on a big buckskin horse, and with him rode Rusty Cross, and Old Sinful with his long Sharps buffalo gun, and the slim young Apache who had been driving the wagon — all of them heavily armed and grim of face.

Isabel watched until the green cottonwood trees hid them from view. She was wondering about something she had seen in Donal's eyes when he looked back at her from the doorway. The thought of that look quickened her heart, brought a tender light to her own eyes.

Rubio approached from the bunkhouse. He carried a rifle, and his weathered brown face was very serious.

"*El Señor* say you no go far from *casa*," the Mexican said to her gravely.

"I won't leave the garden," she promised.

"*Gracias.*" Rubio smiled, and went to help Pasqual who was unhitching the mules from the wagon.

**146**

Isabel walked slowly back to the house. Sounds came to her from beyond the cottonwood trees. The thud of horses' hoofs, fading into the distance.

# CHAPTER
# THIRTEEN

# Bearcat Makes Gun-Talk

The lone rider drew Brasca's eyes as a magnet pulls at a piece of steel filing. He checked his own horse, stared under furrowed brows at the stranger sky-lined on the ridge a little less than a quarter of a mile distant. Too far away to identify without glasses.

The narrow valley ran east and west, between low hills sparsely covered with piñon trees. Numerous gullies broke down from the rugged slopes, and looking north across the valley Brasca could see Bearcat working on the split-rail fence Donal wanted thrown across the mouth of one of the smaller of these ravines. When the fence was completed the place would be a good corral for working cattle at the roundups.

Handling an ax was a task none of the Circle C men enjoyed. It was arduous, sweaty work, splitting logs and setting up the posts. The men took turns at the job. Each did his daily stint, and as there would be no need for the corral until fall roundup they took their time.

Brasca's look went back to the unknown horseman on the ridge. His uneasiness grew. He was suspicious of strangers unless they were quick to prove honest intentions. And this particular intruder was showing no desire to explain his presence on Circle C range, a lack of courtesy that aroused Brasca's indignation.

He reflectively made a cigarette, still holding his gaze on the motionless horse and its rider. The thing puzzled him. No sense in the way the feller just set there on his bronc . . . Hadn't made a move in five minutes . . . Looked like he was figgerin' to attract attention.

The perplexed Brasca scowled, thumbnailed a match and lit his cigarette. Sure almighty queer, the way the jasper was behavin' . . . Didn't make sense . . . A cow thief wouldn't be showin' hisself so plain.

His troubled look went to the herd leisurely grazing near the bottleneck at the east end of the valley. The grass was plentiful and the cattle were keeping well bunched. No need for them to travel far for water. Every little hollow held a pool, and anyway, with all that wet grass to get their tongues around, the cows had no need to hunt for water. Nor would they be tempted to wander on through the gap. Nothing but lava beds the other side of the pass.

It was apparent that Bearcat had noticed the mysterious stranger. He got on his horse. "Who's the feller?" His tone was belligerent.

"Search me," grumbled Brasca. "Been settin' his saddle long enough for his bronc to sprout roots. He's got me guessin'."

"Let's go see," Bearcat said curtly. He muttered an annoyed exclamation. "Left my rifle back there at the corral!"

They had ridden hardly a hundred yards when the lone horseman vanished below the ridge.

"Ain't wantin' us to get too close!" Brasca jerked his rifle from its sheath and spurred his horse into a dead run up the long slope.

Bearcat, loudly lamenting his own forgotten rifle, reached for the .45 in his holster and raced after his companion.

They surged over the ridge in time to glimpse their shy visitor disappearing into the brush-choked mouth of a ravine. Their suspicions now at white heat, the two Circle C men rode in furious pursuit.

No sign of horse and rider met their searching eyes when the ravine was reached. They pulled their horses to a standstill and exchanged disgusted looks.

"He's some place close," growled Bearcat. "He wouldn't have rode far up this gully. Too much brush."

They stared about disappointedly. Tumbled masses of boulders and steep brush-tangled slopes between which flowed a shallow stream of water over a stony bed.

"He must have followed up the creek," argued Brasca. "A horse could just about squeeze between them two boulders. I'm bettin' that's where our jasper went."

"You've lost your bet, mister."

The threat in the unseen speaker's voice was not to be ignored. Brasca and Bearcat were too wise to do more than look with shocked eyes at the rifle barrel poking through the shiny green leaves of a madrone bush.

**150**

"You fell for the play awful easy," said the man concealed behind the rifle. "Followed the bait like a pair of coyote pups."

The Circle C men held their silence, but their eyes were active, saw with growing dismay that they were indeed trapped. Four other rifles menaced them from behind bushes and boulders.

The man concealed in the greenery of the madrone spoke again: "Climb from your saddles. It's your own fault if there's trouble."

Brasca and Bearcat were in no mind for more trouble. Not with *all* the cards stacked against them. They got down from their horses. Booted feet crunched the stones behind them, hands reached out, took Brasca's rifle, plucked the Colt from his holster and the .45 dangling from Bearcat's fingers. The Circle C cowboys exchanged dismayed looks.

The leader's toneless voice addressed them again. "Spread yourselves face down on the ground. Don't try to get a look at us. It's up to you if you don't want trouble."

Bearcat attempted a weak protest. "These stones is awful hard and bumpy to belly down on. Ain't you got a softer bed for us?"

"You're lucky it ain't a pile of stones on *top* of you," retorted the unseen man. "We're in a hurry," he added with an oath.

The two Circle C men reluctantly laid themselves prone on the ground, faces down, and in a few moments were securely bound hand and foot, and bandanas drawn tightly over their eyes.

It was all swiftly done, and without further talk. It was apparent that these men were in haste to be on their way.

Brasca rolled over on his back as the clattering hoofs drew away from the ravine. "Awful nice folks, huh?" He wiggled his bound wrists tentatively. "Kind of shy and bashful. Wasn't wantin' us to see their faces."

"Some day I'll meet up with the gent that done all the talkin'," Bearcat said bitterly. "I won't be needin' to know his face. All I want is to hear his voice. Ain't forgettin' that voice if I live to be a hunderd."

"You can buy chips for me on that bet." Brasca squirmed closer to his companion. "First job is to get rid of these blinders they tied over our eyes. Hold still for a minute while I get my teeth clamped good on yours."

He found a loose end of the bandana bound over Bearcat's face, took hold with his teeth and ripped it open.

"Easy with them choppers," grumbled Bearcat. "I still got use for that nose I wear."

"Excuse me," ironically apologized Brasca. "I thought it was your ear I was nibblin' at." He chuckled. "You got a awful nose, Bearcat."

"My nose suits me," growled Bearcat. "Get your grinders workin' ag'in. Can most see with my left eye already."

In a few moments he announced that his eyes were uncovered. "I can do a better job on you, young feller, now that I can see where to get my teeth on your blinders."

152

A brief minute's work left Brasca relieved of the offending bandage. He blinked his freed eyes. "You look like something out of a circus, with them bits of red silk flappin' 'round your face," he said with a wry grin.

"Nothin' you say can make me laugh." Bearcat shook his head dolefully. "Them buzzards have took our horses. I'm feelin' small enough to crawl in a lizard hole, lettin' the boss down like we done."

"You don't feel worser'n me," Brasca declared. He did some more squirming and turned his back to his companion. "See if you can wrastle that knot loose with your teeth," he added.

Bearcat set to work on the rope that bound Brasca's wrists. It required several minutes to loosen the knot enough for Brasca to wriggle his hands free. In a few more moments both men were on their feet.

Brasca shut the blade of his clasp-knife and stared around gloomily. "Took our guns along with the horses." His tone was wrathful.

The two men stared at each other. No words were needed between them. They knew the answer to the affair that had left them on foot and unarmed.

"Let's get movin'," Bearcat said harshly. "Can't do no good standin' here."

They made their way out of the ravine and scrambled up to the ridge overlooking the valley. What they saw brought them to a dismayed standstill.

"There they go!" Brasca spoke hoarsely. "Every damn cow we got! Hell's fire, Bearcat! Circle C is sure busted for keeps!"

153

The older man gave him a grim look. "I've knowed the boss some longer'n you have," he said. His gaze went back to the closely-bunched cattle being harried through the distant gap at the eastern end of the valley. "Let me tell you something about Don Cameron. It's when he's takin' a lickin' that he gets up and fights best."

"I'm hatin' like poison to face him," muttered the inconsolable Brasca.

"Same with me," growled Bearcat. "We got to face him, though, and the quicker the better." His voice brightened. "Good thing I left my rifle back at the corral. Come on, Brasca! Let's get down to the corral and make gun-talk. Maybe they'll hear us at the house."

# CHAPTER
# FOURTEEN

# Disaster

The rustlers held the advantage of a good running start, and a waning afternoon. Despite the furiously-pressed chase, darkness found the trail lost in a maze of canyons that flanked the rugged slopes of the Comanches. Further pursuit was worse than hopeless.

Gloom rode with Circle C as the outfit headed back for the ranch house. Overhead, the night sky was a blazing splendor of stars, but there was no bright star of hope to cheer the desolated hearts of these men. Despairing lines grooved their tired faces. The whole affair was too shocking, left them without words.

Talk was useless. Only quick action could save Circle C from ruin, and here they were, jogging homeward, every thudding hoofbeat widening the distance between them and the cattle they had brought up the long and perilous trail from the Brazos.

The ranch lights broke through the darkness, like stars winking from the black rim of the world. Two moving shapes materialized into Old Sinful and Roderick Dhu who had surrendered their horses to Bearcat and Brasca and made their way back on foot to the ranch. Obtaining fresh horses, they were hurrying to overtake their comrades.

In grim silence the pair joined the gloomy little procession. No need for them to ask questions.

They rode into the ranch yard and swung down from their saddles. Brasca began to unburden his soul.

"Why ain't you sayin' something, boss? Why ain't you sayin' what you think of Brasca and me?" The cowboy's tone was bitter.

"Not your fault," Donal said curtly. "These things can happen to any of us." He disappeared into the barn with his tired horse.

Brasca's gaze followed him. Donal would have been startled could he have seen the adoration in the man's eyes. "I'd sure ride the trail to hell and back with *him*," Brasca said softly. "We goes and acts like a couple of damn fools and he just won't say a word of blame."

"You cain't feel worse than I do," fumed Rusty Cross. "Not after what that bunch of wolves done to Wes and me. It's my notion this outfit needs a nurse." He forced a rueful smile.

Bearcat and Old Sinful nodded grim assent. "We just ain't growed up yet," declared the boss of the chuckwagon. "Mebbe it's my fault for not mixin' gunpowder in my biscuit dough. We've gone awful soft."

Rubio made a hasty appearance with a lighted lantern. The señora had a hot meal waiting in the kitchen, he informed the weary cowboys.

**156**

Old Sinful expressed his deep satisfaction. "Been a sight o' Sundays sense I et vittles I can cuss another cook for spoilin'."

"Cussin' ain't ree-fined manners when the cook is a feemale," crustily reproved Bearcat.

"I ain't takin' lesson from *you* about how a gent behaves," retorted Old Sinful. "You watch your *own* step."

Donal and Roderick Dhu attended to their horses and made their way under the starlight to the patio. The young Apache wore a solemn look. He halted as they pushed through the gate. "The blow has been struck, my brother," he said gravely. "It is a hard blow."

Donal gave him a slow smile. "I can take it, Rod. I can take the worst they've got."

"We do not know where to strike back," worried the Apache. "We do not know where to seek out these white devils who strike in the dark."

"No need for you to get mixed up in this business," Donal said. "You leave the *we* out of it, Rod."

"I said *we* because I am your friend and brother," rejoined Roderick Dhu. "I am an Indian, and I am a Cameron." The dark mask of his face lighted. "A strong brew, Angus says, and it makes a big *we* between us."

The harassed owner of Circle C was silent for a long moment. Sounds came from the bunkhouse, the rattle of tin basins, the splashing of water, a low murmur of voices. Loyal to the core, those men, and even more cut to the heart than their boss by the stunning blow that had befallen Circle C. His fight was their fight too. Every last man of them would cheerfully go through hell with him. It was the code of their hardy, untamed breed.

Speech at that moment was difficult for him. He said simply, "Thanks, Rod," and he moved on toward the house, where a girl stood framed in the lamplight that flowed through the open door. The Apache watched him for a moment, then went slowly across the wild tangle of garden to the kitchen.

Donal met Isabel's eager look with a shake of his head. Disappointment drew a quick shadow over her face. He said briefly, "Too late," and then, "How is Wes making out?"

She was watching him intently, dismay deepening in her eyes. "Too late?" Distress unsteadied her voice. "You mean —"

He nodded. "They've just about cleaned me out."

"You — you couldn't overtake them?"

"Those canyons all look alike in the dark." He shrugged. "We hadn't a chance."

The weariness in his voice drew her pity. She put a hand on his arm. "I could cry, but crying won't do any good."

"No," he said, "crying won't do any good." Grim amusement touched his voice. "We're not the crying kind."

He could feel the tense press of her fingers on his arm as she stood there, looking up at him, her eyes bright with unshed tears, an oddly fierce brightness that seemed to flash fire.

"We're the *fighting* kind," she said with a quick flow of returning confidence in him — in herself. "We'll fight — and *fight*."

**158**

"You once told me it would be useless to stay here — and fight."

"I've changed my mind." She gave him the same bitter little smile he remembered from that afternoon of their first meeting in the restaurant. "You want to get your cattle back on the range, and I want to find and punish the man responsible for the murder of my father and brother." She drew a quick breath. "So we are going to stick it out, and fight — and — and kill — if we must."

Donal thought of the man his bullet had found in the piñon scrub. They had roped the body to the horse and sent it back to those who had hired him to kill, a grim message from Circle C. He thought of the ambush set for him at the Aliso Creek fork, and he thought of Rede Sems, and the man with the scarred face, and the lame man who twice had lain in wait for him. And back in his mind, as he thought of all these men, were vague faces of other men, Lew Trent, Jim Daker — and Al DeSang. A grotesque procession of faces that seemed to peer at him through a red mist.

"I've had to kill two of them already," he said soberly.

"They were trying to kill you. You have done the world a service." Isabel paused, added in a low voice, "I wouldn't be here now, alive, talking to you, if you hadn't shot fast and straight."

"It's bad business at the best." His tone was gloomy. "This Rio Seco country will never amount to anything until we get the law here."

"You will bring the law, and we'll spell it with a capital L," Isabel declared confidently.

Her vehement faith in him was the tonic he needed just then. He gave her a pleased smile, looked at her more attentively. She was wearing a crisp pink and white print dress.

His puzzled expression seemed to amuse her. She laughed. "You're wondering where this dress came from, aren't you? It's out of Marica's funny old leather trunk. I had to have *something* fresh to put on."

"Looks nice," he said.

"A little large for me, but it will do until I get to San Benito."

He looked at her thoughtfully. "No need for you to hurry away, now that Marica is here."

She fingered the print dress nervously. "I hate adding to your troubles."

"We're not going into that again," he said almost gruffly. He switched the subject to Wes Coles.

"He is doing nicely," Isabel informed him. She smiled faintly. "Marica threatened to tie him to the bed if he didn't mind her. He was determined to follow you."

"I'll have a look at him."

"Wes thinks it is all his fault."

"Nobody's fault." Donal's face darkened. "This thing has been working up for days. What happened last night was part of it."

"They planned your murder," Isabel said, the hard brightness back in her eyes. "You were too clever for them."

**160**

"It was all part of the plan," Donal went on; "those two men were sent to get me, leave me lying dead in the trail. The rest of the gang were all set to pull off the raid. They'd been scouting the place from the bluffs, probably had their glasses on us for days. Rusty and Wes ran into them this morning, came close to spoiling their game."

"Somebody is using brains," speculated the girl with a worried shake of her head. "They haven't missed a thing."

"There was one bet that paid no money," Donal said with a bleak smile. "They got the cattle, but they didn't get me."

"They won't stop trying." Her voice was unsteady. "They won't stop trying, Don. The thought frightens me."

Her concern sent a glow through him. He smiled, shook his head. "It's my turn at trying things."

"You don't know where to turn," she pointed out in a troubled voice. "You can only make guesses."

His look went to the lighted windows of the big kitchen across the patio. Old Sinful's strident voice was making itself heard above the clatter of pans and dishes. "These here biscuits is sure light enough to make wings for angels."

Isabel said quickly, "Don — you must be starving!" She gave him a concerned look.

"No hurry." He fished in his shirt pocket, drew out tobacco-sack and papers. "What's your guess, Isabel?"

She was silent for a moment, long dark lashes lowered, and he saw the color leave her face. He said quietly, "You're thinking of Jim Daker. You're thinking that he's the man whose brains are back of this thing, and all the other things that have been making a hell out of the Rio Seco country."

Her eyes lifted, and he was struck anew by the lovely amber lights in their brown depths. "I don't know, Don —" Her hand lifted to her hair, touched a loosened wisp into place. "I hate to think it of Mr. Daker."

"I've got to find out for sure," he said. "I've thought of Daker, and I've thought of DeSang."

"DeSang?" She was astonished.

"Angus Cameron told me it was DeSang who brought Rede Sems to San Benito and made him town marshal." Donal put a match to his cigarette. "You know what happened the morning after the dance."

"Sems tried to kill you. Yes — I saw —"

"He was obeying somebody's orders," Donal said. "Daker's — or DeSang's. I'd like to know which one." He smiled thinly. "Daker claims he'd nothing to do with it."

She stared at him perplexedly. "Mr. DeSang was always polite to me." She hesitated. "Somehow, I don't see him as that kind of man."

"He's a smooth article," Donal said dryly. "He doesn't show his hand."

"I don't like him," confessed the girl. "He was always very nice to me when he came into the restaurant." She made a face. "He'd leave a silver dollar under his plate —"

**162**

They both laughed, and she said, "Mr. Daker used to tip me, too, only he was different. He'd put a dollar in my hand and pat me in a fatherly way, tell me to buy something pretty." She paused, brows puckered thoughtfully. "Mr. Daker is different in every way from Mr. DeSang. He doesn't beat about the bush, just shouts out what's on his mind. You can take it or leave it. That's why it is so hard for me to think of him plotting such dreadful things."

"You ran away from him," reminded Donal.

She bent her head, and the lamplight laid warm glints on golden-brown hair. "I told you why I couldn't stay at the Rocking D."

"Daker is Lew Trent's boss." Donal's voice was hard. "Daker must have known what Trent was up to. He didn't interfere."

"There's a lot he may not know about Lew Trent." She hesitated. "I don't like to think Mr. Daker even suspects what I suspect — about Lew Trent."

"I'm not so sure he doesn't." Donal was thinking of a paint horse that wore the Rocking D brand. Its rider had made two attempts on his life. It was possible the lame man was a horse thief, but hardly probable that he would show himself in San Benito with an animal so readily identified. There could be only one answer. The lame man was a member of the Rocking D outfit. Isabel had declared she had not seen a man of his description while at the ranch, but that was no proof the slippery little gunman was not on Jim Daker's payroll.

163

Isabel was watching him with troubled eyes. "I shouldn't try to have any ideas about it," she said timidly. "You know a lot more than I do. I can only make wild guesses."

"I asked you for your ideas. We're both in this."

"I'll say one thing more. I hate to even think of Lew Trent, but he got very boastful one time, said enough for me to begin to wonder how deeply he might be involved" — she faltered — "in what happened to my father and brother."

"Daker will be just as deeply involved," Donal said harshly. "If Trent had any part in that raid on your father's ranch, Daker knows it. There's no other answer."

Isabel looked at him intently, saw that his face was a hard mask. Instinctively she divined the purpose in him. "You're not going to the Rocking D?" Panic made her voice almost shrill.

"I've got to start somewhere."

"If you are right about Mr. Daker, you'll be killed," she protested passionately. "You won't have a chance — you and your few men against so many."

He only looked at her, his eyes implacable. She tried again. "You will be doing only just what they want and expect you to do. Ride into a trap from which there will be no escape. It will be the end of you in the Rio Seco — the end of Circle C."

"I came to this man's country to make a ranch," he said. "I'm not going to let a bunch of crooks scare me out." His face hardened.

**164**

She saw there was no dissuading him. "I think I hate this country!" Her voice broke.

He seemed disturbed, stood staring at her, then moved close to the wide hearth and flipped his cigarette stub into the fire that was blazing there. He still wore his spurs and they rasped and jingled as he walked across the hard adobe floor.

Isabel thought of long-gone Salazars as she looked at him standing there, his back to the blazing log, so tall and so proudly strong. They too had dragged their spurs across the hard mud floor of this ancient room. Bold, indomitable *rancheros* with the frontier in their blood. Don Cameron belonged to this man's country. She heard herself saying contritely, "I'm sorry —"

A slow smile broke the stern set of his face, and he went to her and took her hands in his. "It's a good country, and — and it hurt, to have you say you hate it."

"I didn't mean it —" She was almost tearful. "*Really* I didn't, Don."

"I don't know just why I should want you to like it the way *I* do." There was a wondering note in his voice. "But I *do*."

She withdrew her hands, a soft color in her cheeks. "You said we were partners —" She was a bit breathless. "I suppose partners should like the same things."

He seemed about to say more, but saw that her look had gone to the door, and he saw Rusty Cross hesitating there.

"I was figgerin' to have a look at Wes," the foreman said with a bashful sidewise glance at the girl.

"Wes is getting along splendidly," Isabel assured him. She liked this efficient-looking Circle C man.

Rusty was skeptical. "The señorita said the maverick was kind of on the prod and all set to bust out of the corral."

"I've already done busted out," announced a defiant voice. Wes Coles grinned at them from the corridor door. His damaged arm was in a sling and he wore a bandage around his head. "Nothin' wrong with me a-tall," he asserted.

"I've a mind to put hobbles on you," Rusty said severely.

"You just try it," chuckled Wes. His face sobered. "Boss, I been doin' some thinkin' about them fellers that jumped me."

Isabel interrupted him. "You really must eat something," she said to Donal.

"I'll take a cup of cawfee with you, boss," promptly offered Wes. He grinned at them. "Maybe a couple of them biscuits I heard Old Sinful yowlin' about. Got me all hungry, hearin' him rave."

"If he ain't already et all the señora could drag out of the oven," chuckled Rusty. "He was still goin' strong when I left him settin' there at the table." The foreman smacked his lips. "Wouldn't mind another piece of her apple pie my own self."

The three men trooped out to the corridor. Isabel watched them from the doorway until they

**166**

disappeared into the kitchen, then went thoughtfully to her room.

She made no attempt to light the lamp, but walked directly to the door that opened on the corridor, and stood there, looking across the patio at the lighted windows of the kitchen. An indescribably tender smile curved her lips as she watched.

# CHAPTER
# FIFTEEN

# A Powwow

Donal sat at the head of the kitchen table, a massive piece of furniture stoutly fashioned from ax-hewn oak timbers and richly darkened from generations of use in this ancient *casa* of the Salazars.

"You can blame the señora if you founder yourself on them biscuit," solemnly warned Old Sinful. "She's too good, boss. A feller just cain't stop reachin' for 'em. Take a look at Bearcat! He ain't in no shape to fork a saddle. He's sure weak when it comes to apple pie."

"I shouldn't have et them last two hunks," Bearcat admitted. "Trouble is we ain't used to *real* good cookin' like the señora's."

Old Sinful glared at him wrathfully. Only the presence of the beaming señora held him from resenting the implied insult with loud and bitter words.

Rusty Cross made haste to seize the conversational reins. "What's on your mind, Wes? About them fellers that jumped you at the bluffs this morning."

"Well" — Wes put down his coffee cup — "I cain't say for sure . . . didn't have much time for a good look, but it sticks in my mind that I've seen one of 'em some place. Just cain't remember where."

Donal's gaze traveled around the table to the intent faces. With the exception of Rubio they were all there, the entire roster of the Circle C payroll: Bearcat, Old Sinful, Brasca, and, opposite to them, Wes Coles, Rusty Cross, and one other who was not a member of the outfit, but his sworn friend and brother, Roderick Dhu. Pasqual Torres was there, too, helping his mother, his dark eyes bright as he covertly watched the array of grim faces grouped around the table.

Donal spoke to him. "Tell Rubio we want him here, Pasqual."

The Mexican dropped his dish towel and sped away. Donal's look went to Wes Coles. "What makes you think you've seen one of them before?"

The cowboy wrinkled his brows, rubbed his sore head thoughtfully. "I been wrastlin' with the picture all day. Like I already told you, I heard the broncs snort and went for my guns . . . only managed to get a flash look when the bullet knocked me over ag'in the boulder. I wasn't knowin' nothin' after that . . . not till Rusty came sousin' me with water." Wes scowled, gestured hopelessly. "I reckon I'm still some loco from that knock on my haid. Don't seem able to get that feller's face in my mind, what I seen of it."

"I'm not blaming you," Donal said. "I'm not blaming any of you."

Spurred boot heels scraped uneasily under the table, a sound that warmed Donal's heart. These men were ready to ride the moment he said the word. They had taken time to eat, because to eat when they could was a wise precaution. But they still wore their spurs and their guns. No trouble for him to read their minds.

He put their thoughts into a blunt statement. "You boys think I'm taking this thing too easily," he said. "You think we should be out there, combing the Comanche hills." He sent a questioning look around the table.

Rusty answered for them. "I reckon that's hittin' the mark plumb center." His tone was defiant.

Donal looked around at their intent faces, and then, "We can't beat out a prairie fire with feather dusters, and that is about all we'll be trying to do, if we go chasing blind into the hills."

"How come you figger it that way?" asked Wes Coles, scowling into his coffee cup.

"We're up against brains." Donal spoke quietly. "We've got to fight brains — *with brains*."

Rubio and Pasqual hurried into the room. The older Mexican's harshly-lined face wore an apprehensive look. "You 'ave sen' for me, Pasqual say."

Donal nodded. "I wanted all of you for a powwow." He looked at Pasqual. "You too, now you're on the Circle C payroll." He paused, hard, unsmiling gaze going from face to face. "You all know how things are since Circle C moved into this Rio Seco country."

"Well" — Bearcat smiled bleakly — "I'd say we've been told plenty that we ain't what you'd call welcome here."

"I was warned in San Benito to move on," Donal continued. "We've been dodging hot lead ever since, and we don't know who is back of it."

**170**

"Jim Daker," Rusty said bluntly. "It was Daker who jumped you in San Benito, and it was Daker who come next day with his outfit and tried to run us off."

Wes Coles' head lifted with a jerk. "That's it!" he exclaimed. "That's the time I seen the feller!" He frowned at their intent faces.

"What feller?" snapped Rusty.

"The feller that shot me. I've been tellin' you I'd seen him some place."

"Are you trying to tell us it was Jim Daker?" asked Donal sharply.

The cowboy shook his bandaged head. "No . . . not him. One of the jaspers with him." He wrinkled his brows. "I'd stake a year's pay I'm right."

"Daker had most a dozen fellers along with him," grumbled Rusty.

"Might have been Lew Trent," guessed Donal. "The big hard-faced man that Rusty had words with. Was he the man, Wes?"

Wes rubbed his sore head ruefully. "Cain't say for sure he was the feller. All I'm claimin' is that one of the three skunks that jumped me this mornin' was along with Daker's outfit the time we called their bluff."

Donal's voice broke the silence that followed. "We're due to pay the Rocking D a call — if Wes is right."

"Sure I'm right," asserted the cowboy.

"I'm not asking any man to come along if he doesn't want to come." Donal's look flickered over their faces. "It won't be a polite call."

Their grim, mirthless smiles answered him, said more than words.

# CHAPTER
# SIXTEEN

# A Parley

Isabel stood watching from the unlighted doorway of her room. The cigarette's fitful glow made her think of a firefly flitting there in the blackness under the chinaberry tree.

The men had gone to the bunkhouse beyond the high adobe walls that enclosed the patio. Isabel could hear the subdued voices of Marica and Pasqual, and the clatter of pans and dishes. All was darkness in the patio, save for the soft lamplight in the kitchen window — and the firefly glow of Donal Cameron's cigarette.

He must have picked out the vague shape of her in the pink and white dress that had come from Marica's old leather trunk. She heard the rustle of fallen leaves underfoot as he left the bench under the chinaberry tree, the sharper sound of boot heels on the flagstoned walk, and then she saw the tall outline of him approaching the corridor.

"I thought you'd gone to bed," he said.

"It's not late." Isabel stepped into the corridor from her open door. "The moon is just tipping the hills, and that makes it about ten o'clock."

He snubbed out his cigarette and leaned against one of the peeled-log beams that supported the corridor roof. He still wore his gun-belt, the girl noticed.

"We're riding at sunup," he told her briefly.

"I guessed as much." Her tone was grave, and of a sudden a shaft of moonlight slanted down through the trees, delicately etched the upturned profile. "You mean the — Rocking D?"

"Yes." His voice was harsh.

"I've already told you what I think." Isabel gestured hopelessly. "It's a dreadful risk, Don, against so many."

"We're used to risks in the cattle business." His expression softened as he looked at her, and again he fought off the impulse to draw her into his arms. He said more gently, "The cattle business is one gamble from start to finish. The weather, the market — rustlers. If it's not one thing it's another. A man afraid of risks has no place in the cattle business."

She saw that he was attempting to lead her away from the subject uppermost in her mind. "You want to confuse me," she reproached. "I'm not talking about the cattle business." And then, abruptly, "What makes you think it was Mr. Daker who raided Circle C this afternoon?"

"Wes Coles claims the man who shot him was along with Daker when he paid us a little visit the other day."

"Wes might be mistaken."

Donal shook his head. "I've been fitting a lot of pieces together. They make a pattern that points to Daker."

She stood silent, her eyes downcast, her heart in a turmoil of rebellion against the mad thing he proposed to do. If he were right about Jim Daker it was all the more dangerous to confront him in his own back yard. The Rocking D outnumbered Circle C ten to one at the least. The meeting would end in a massacre. Jim Daker would be immune from any trouble with the law. He'd claim that Circle C had deliberately attacked the Rocking D outfit on Rocking D soil. There would be no Circle C men left alive to dispute his story.

Moonlight filtered through the trees, laid a delicate fretwork of lights and shadows across the patio. From somewhere nearby a coyote barked sharply, was suddenly silent. Donal's head lifted, and the girl saw his profile, harshly tense against the moonlight.

"What is it?" she asked him.

"That coyote," he muttered. "Didn't finish his yipping."

"What of it?"

"Something scared him." His hand lifted in a gesture for silence. "Listen —"

They stood there straining their ears and finally Isabel let out her breath. "I don't hear a thing. Only the wind in the trees and Marica in the kitchen." She broke off as his face turned in a look at her. "You *do* hear something?"

He nodded. "Horses —"

Alarm filled her eyes as she now caught the faint thud of approaching hoofs. A shape appeared at the patio gate, came up the flagged walk on soundless feet.

**174**

Isabel recognized Angus Cameron's adoped Apache son. His look covered her briefly, went to Donal.

"Jim Daker," he said softly.

Donal stared at him, too thunderstruck for speech. It seemed incredible.

"I was lying on my blanket in the wagon," the Indian went on. "I heard the horses crossing the dry bed of the creek below the cottonwoods."

Donal found his voice. "How do you know it's Daker?"

"I scouted through the trees for a look," Rod answered. "They had halted their horses at the fork and seemed to be talking things over. I heard Daker's voice." The Apache hesitated, gestured at Isabel. "He spoke her name."

There was a brief silence, broken by a loud shout from the bunkhouse. Others were now aware of the approaching horsemen.

"He is looking for me," Isabel spoke in a frightened whisper.

"It's up to you," Donal said. "Do you want him to find you here?"

She shook her head. "No, *no!*" Fear made her voice unnaturally thin. "Don — I'm afraid —"

"Keep out of sight," he said.

"The men —" she began.

He cut her off. "I've already warned them to keep mum about you. Daker won't get anything from them." He looked at Roderick Dhu. "How many riders with Daker?"

"That is the queer part of it." The Indian's tone was puzzled. "Only Hook Saval —"

Donal and Isabel exchanged astonished looks. Both were struck by the same thought. If Jim Daker was responsible for the afternoon's raid on Circle C he would not have dared to show himself at the ranch in so strange a manner.

Loud shouts from the corral jerked Donal from his momentary trance. He said sharply to the girl, "Get back into the house and keep out of sight."

She went quickly into the room and closed the door, stood listening to the uproar in the yard. Jim Daker must have lost his senses. The Circle C men were in a dangerous mood. Daker stood in imminent peril of being swung from the nearest cottonwood tree handy for the purpose. Only Don Cameron could save the Rocking D man from a shocking death.

Isabel was not at all sure what Don would do about it. Daker had sworn to run Don out of the Rio Seco country, and there was every reason to believe that he was back of the raid that had stripped Circle C to the bone.

Astonishment was plain in Jim Daker's eyes as he gazed at the grim-faced men who had swarmed from the bunkhouse. No mistaking the menace of those drawn guns, the hard and angry looks.

"You've got a nerve," Rusty Cross said to him.

Hook Saval answered for the obviously bewildered rancher, "You boys seem some hostile. What's the idee?"

**176**

"You'll get the idea quick enough," retorted Bearcat. His look went significantly to the big cottonwood tree over the horse-trough. "We hang cow thieves where I come from."

"You're crazy!" Hook's tone was mildly peevish. "Looks like you ain't knowin' who we are."

"Rocking D, ain't you?"

"Sure am," admitted Hook.

"That's enough for us to swing you 'longside of Daker," declared Bearcat.

Donal pushed into the group, the Indian at his heels. Daker broke his silence. "What's this bunch of yours hellin' about, Cameron?" His voice crackled with indignation.

"You should know the answer, Daker."

"Talk sense," snapped the owner of the Rocking D.

Donal's look traveled slowly over the implacable faces of his men. They believed Daker guilty. He had only to say the word and justice would be done on these two. The rude, hard justice of the remote frontier.

He found the thought revolting.

Daker was speaking again. "I didn't come here looking for trouble, if that is what you mean."

"You've saved us a long ride," Donal told him. "We were heading for your place at sunup." He looked curiously at Hook Saval who gave him a nod of recognition.

"Somethin' awful wrong here, son," the old man said acidly. "Bein' called a low-down cow thief don't set good in my craw." He glared angrily at Bearcat.

**177**

Hook's genuine indignation resolved Donal's doubts. He had liked the veteran range man from the moment of their meeting in the hotel. Hook Saval was honest, and no rustler, nor would he work for a man who violated the code of all good cowmen. It came to Donal that he was all wrong about Jim Daker. The pieces he had put together made a meaningless pattern. Jim Daker was not guilty, or Hook would not be on his payroll.

He became aware that they were all watching him intently, the faces of the Circle C men grimly expectant as they waited for the accusation against the Rocking D.

He made his decision. "Put up your guns, boys," he said in a flat, toneless voice. "We're on the wrong track."

Old Sinful dropped an angry ejaculation. Donal's face darkened. "You heard me!" He holstered his gun, gave Hook Saval a tight-lipped smile. "Our mistake, Hook. Circle C was rustled clean this afternoon and we're a bit on the prod."

There was a silence, and then Daker said in a stifled voice, "That right, Cameron?" He paused, shook his head like an angry bull. "Why would you blame it on me?"

"You warned me away from the Rio Seco," reminded Donal. "I've heard tales of what happened to other men who didn't move on when you told them to get out."

"I don't rustle another man's cows," Daker said stormily. "I'm no cow thief! I hate a cow thief!"

"It's said you look the other way when it happens to a man you don't want for a neighbor." There was a lash in Donal's voice that made Daker jerk up his head sharply. "You want to hog the range for yourself. That's the talk I hear."

"Talk!" Daker frowned. "I don't mind a decent man settling in this country, but I'm not standing for low-down nesters who think they can build up herds at my expense." He snorted angrily. "When I run a man out of this country it's because he's a no-good cow thief."

"You tried to run *me* out," again reminded Donal. "You rode over with your outfit the day we pulled in." He spoke bitterly. "You'd have shot us down if we hadn't been too quick for you."

Daker's face took on a troubled look. He said slowly, "My mistake, Cameron. I'd been running cattle on this Salazar range so long it seemed like it was mine. I thought you were horning in on my territory. You showed me where I was wrong and I let the thing drop."

"I'd like to believe that."

"I'm not disputing your rights here." Daker spoke gloomily. "I'm not claiming you're a nester."

"Tell him about that hideout at the bluffs," Donal said to Wes Coles.

Wes told his story briefly. Daker listened, heavy brows drawn down in a worried frown.

"I don't know a thing about it," he asserted. "It looks bad, but I've nothing to do with it."

"I'd swear the feller that shot me was with you the time you come to run us off," insisted Wes.

Daker's expression was skeptical, and Donal said slowly, "I'm laying all the cards on the table. You can see for yourself how the thing looks. Wes believes he was shot by one of your men. An hour or two later, Brasca and Bearcat were trapped in a gully. The men who trapped them were careful not to let their faces be seen, which proves they feared recognition. None of our boys have been in town yet. Too busy. Nobody around here the boys would recognize except the men who were with you the other day. Brasca and Bearcat were left tied up and blindfolded and their horses were stolen. The thing was carefully planned, spies staked out on the bluffs, watching our movements, the time set to make pursuit hopeless in the dark. Somebody used brains, Daker."

"Has a bad smell, son," admitted Hook Saval. "I don't blame you boys for havin' a touch of trigger-itch when you seen us comin'." He grinned amiably at Bearcat who attempted a ferocious scowl that ended in an answering grin.

Daker made no comment. It was obvious that he was deeply perplexed.

"How does it smell to you?" Donal asked him.

"Hook said it," tersely answered the owner of the Rocking D. Harsh lines creased his big-boned face. He shifted uneasily in his saddle.

"There's a lot more you won't like. Did you tell Rede Sems to run me out of town?"

**180**

"No." Daker spoke resentfully. "I told you at the time I had nothing to do with that play Sems pulled off."

"We'll let it pass," Donal said. "I'll put another question. Have you a lame man in your outfit? The one I have in mind wears an iron strap on his right bootheel. Has a short leg that makes him lame."

"I reckon he means Gimpy Drane," muttered Hook.

"He'd maybe have a paint horse in his string," Donal suggested.

"That's him," nodded Hook. His eyes narrowed in a curiously speculative look at the circle of intent faces.

"What about him?" Daker's tone was uneasy. "When did you run into Gimpy?"

"He's the man who tried to kill me the evening we got in with the herd," replied Donal. "He got away from us, but he left tracks." His voice hardened. "It's mighty queer, Daker . . . one of your own men lying in wait to kill me."

"You're crazy! Why would Gimpy be trying to bushwhack you?"

"I thought *you* could answer that one," countered Donal. "He tried it again, a day or two later. Another man with him. They laid for Wes Coles and Brasca in the chaparral. Killed Coles' horse. Gimpy got away, but we sent his friend's body home roped to his own saddle."

"Don't know a thing about it," Daker again asserted. His eyes had a tormented look in them. "If there'd been a Rocking D man killed I'd have heard of it."

"I was in town yesterday," Donal went on. "I saw Gimpy with a paint horse. The horse wore your brand. You can't blame me for thinking things."

"I don't keep killers on my payroll," Daker said violently.

"I tried to nab him in the Longhorn. A man with a scarred face interfered and Gimpy made his getaway."

Hook Saval muttered an ejaculation. "Sounds like Slash Driver."

"Who is Slash Driver?" asked Donal.

"DeSang's cattle boss . . . runs DeSang's DS spread."

"I see." Donal looked thoughtful. "Well, I'll know the man if I see him again." His look went back to Daker. "Rede Sems could have stopped Gimpy for me, but he didn't. He claimed he didn't know this lame man. Why did Sems lie about it, Daker? Was it because he knew Gimpy was on your payroll?"

"That settles it." Daker spoke in a relieved tone. "Proves your man wasn't Gimpy, or Sems would have said so. He knows Gimpy." His hand lifted in a fierce gesture. "Let me tell you something, Cameron. I was mighty upset when you exploded your story of the Salazar grant under my nose. You can bet I didn't waste time getting my lawyer after the records. He told me you had me licked. It was bad medicine, but I swallowed it down and let the matter drop." Daker's voice deepened with sincerity. "Believe it or not, if any man's hand is against you it's not mine."

Donal wanted desperately to believe him. He said earnestly, "If it's not you, Daker, who is it?"

**182**

Hook Saval interrupted him. "Listen, son. I've worked for Jim Daker a lot of years and I know him awful well. Jim don't lie." His weathered face wrinkled with the intensity of his emotions. "We don't know who stole your cows, and we don't know nothin' about this bushwhackin' bus'ness."

"That's gospel truth," vehemently affirmed Daker. He paused, gaze fixed intently on Donal. "I'm looking for a girl, Cameron. I'm about crazy with fear for her. Is she here?"

"What girl?" Donal managed a covert glance at his men, saw from their poker expressions that Isabel's secret was safe with them.

"You'll remember her. You saw her the time I met you in the restaurant. She ain't a girl a man would forget easily."

"You mean the little waitress?" Donal shook his head. "I was in town yesterday and looked her up. The restaurant man said she'd quit . . . didn't know where she'd gone."

Dismay looked from Daker's eyes, his big shoulders sagged dejectedly. Donal felt sorry for him, but Isabel's secret was not his to betray. She believed that Daker was in some way responsible for the ruthless killing of her father and brother. He was convinced now that she was mistaken. Nevertheless he was determined not to divulge the truth of her whereabouts. It would be up to Isabel to do that. Also there was the matter of Lew Trent. Isabel felt she had good reason to distrust and fear the Rocking D foreman.

"We've been looking all over for her," Daker said wearily. His big hands clenched hard over saddle horn. "Found her horse near the Aliso Creek fork — dead in the trail." His voice went husky. "Cameron, it looks as if she'd been kidnaped."

"Were you thinking I had kidnaped her?" asked Donal stiffly.

"The signs point to it," Daker answered.

"Dead hombre layin' in the brush," laconically interjected Hook.

"Only one answer to it," Daker went on in the same husky voice. "She's been kidnaped." His deep-set eyes glittered under heavy brows in a hard look around at the circle of attentive faces. "I'm killing the man who's got her hid."

There was a pregnant silence, broken by Old Sinful's belligerent voice. "How come you git the notion to hunt sign on Circle C?"

"Her dead horse was headed down trail." Daker's look fastened on Donal. "Rede Sems told me you'd pulled out of San Benito just before the storm broke. Angus Cameron told me the same."

"That was right," Donal admitted, uneasily aware of Hook Saval's curiously intent gaze.

"Hook and I did some thinking about it," continued Daker. "We figured there was a chance it was you who killed the man we found in the brush. You might have run into him just when he shot her horse. You killed him . . . brought the girl on to the ranch here."

**184**

The reasoning was too close for Donal's comfort. He said dryly, "I get your point, Daker. Wish I could say your guess was good."

Daker looked at him gloomily for a moment, and then, "I'd give a lot to find her. She — she's my adopted daughter, Cameron."

Old Sinful made an unfortunate break. "Seems almighty queer the gal'd run out on you," he said.

Daker pounced on him. "What makes you say that?" He glared suspiciously at the speaker.

Old Sinful ejected a stream of tobacco juice. "Was just thinkin' out loud."

"I don't like your talk." Daker spoke wrathfully. "The girl didn't run out on me. She's been kidnaped. I can give her everything a girl wants. Why in hell should she run away?"

"Search me," Old Sinful said laconically.

Hook Saval slanted him a sharp look, then again fastened his curiously probing gaze on Donal. "Not much use for us to stick 'round here," he said gruffly to Daker.

The cattleman nodded. "Might as well get started back to the ranch," he agreed in a dull voice. He hesitated, added awkwardly, "Sorry about your cows, Cameron. I'll spread the word for you."

"Thanks, Daker —" Something moved Donal to offer his hand. "I'm mighty glad to have you for a friend."

Daker leaned from his saddle and gripped the proffered hand. "Same with me, Cameron. Liked your style from the start. Liked the way you handled Rede

**185**

Sems. You've the guts this man's country needs." He faced his horse around to the yard gate.

Hook Saval swung his own horse close to Donal, leaned toward him. "Too bad, son, you couldn't tell Jim we was right figgerin' you mebbe run into the girl up on the trail." He nodded, a hint of a wintry smile touching his lips, and rode on through the gate.

Bearcat overheard the softly-spoken words and sent a belligerent look after the disappearing Rocking D man. "The same as called you a liar," he exclaimed wrathfully.

Donal shrugged his shoulders. He knew Hook had not been deceived. Hook had guessed the truth about Isabel. The old man was shrewd.

Rusty Cross spoke unhappily. "What about the cows? If Daker didn't steal 'em who did?"

Donal considered their anxious faces. He was thinking that he needed some advice. There were things he wanted to know, and Angus Cameron was the man who could tell him. He wanted to know more about Al DeSang and the tie-up between him and Rede Sems. And there was the puzzling and alcoholic Judge Soper more and more claiming his attention — and the scar-faced man who Hook had surmised might be Slash Driver, the foreman of DeSang's DS outfit and evidently a friend of the clubfoot man who rode a Rocking D horse.

Rusty was watching him intently. He broke the silence. "You've got something, Don?"

"I don't know for sure." Donal spoke thoughtfully. "It's a hunch, Rusty, and I've a mind to play it out."

**186**

# CHAPTER
# SEVENTEEN

# Wanted for Murder

Rede Sems stood on the porch of the Daker House, gaze idling up and down the street. Feet wide apart, hat tipped over his eyes against the early morning sun, he leisurely made a cigarette, chewing meditatively the while on a toothpick with the air of a man who had just done ample justice to a good breakfast.

The swing doors of the Longhorn Saloon slammed open and Judge Soper stepped out. He paused for a moment to button his black Prince Albert against the wind, and, this accomplished, started across the street, still muddy from the recent heavy rain.

"Worse than a hog wallow," he complained as he mounted the hotel porch with noisy stamps to shake off the clinging mud. "It's time somebody did a little work on this street."

"I'm only the town marshal," Sems said. He put a match to his cigarette, a hint of a sneer in his eyes as he looked at the rotund lawyer. "Been having your mornin' snort, huh?"

"You could do with an eye-opener once in a while yourself, Rede," testily retorted Soper.

"Meanin' just what?" Sems asked.

The impact of his unwinking stare seemed to disconcert Soper. His ruddy face under the wide-brimmed black hat changed color. "Nothing, Rede . . . nothing at all." He rubbed his freshly-trimmed goatee with pudgy fingers and glanced into the lobby. "Sounds like Al coming downstairs." He hastened on through the door.

Sems stared at the glowing tip of his cigarette. It was apparent that he was thinking unpleasant things of Judge Soper. The hand holding the cigarette was swathed in a white bandage with the fingers protruding. The town marshal lifted the cigarette back to his lips and keeping the hand close to his eyes he carefully scrutinized the fingers, wiggling them and bending the hand back and forth at the wrist. The experiment seemed to please him. He smiled thinly, dropped the hand and returned his attention to the street.

Three horsemen were approaching. They rode at a slow trot, passed Billy Winch's livery barn, and Al DeSang's new store, and drew rein in front of the hotel as the town marshal stepped down from the porch, hand raised in a signal for them to halt.

"Hello, Cameron." Sems spoke civilly, but his face wore no welcoming smile. "I'd like a word with you."

"Sure." Donal flicked a warning glance at his two companions. Rusty and Wes knew all he could tell them about the deadly little gunman and they were watching him with lively and wary interest. "What's on your mind?"

**188**

"Couple of fellers killed night before last." Sems slid a casual look at the arm Wes Coles wore in a sling. "Was wonderin' if you'd heard."

"Heard what?"

"About 'em bein' killed." Sems spoke patiently.

"Where were they killed?"

"On the ridge trail, near the Aliso Creek fork. You were on that trail the night of the killin'."

"Sure I was," admitted Donal. "A tough night . . . rained pitchforks, and then the fog came down. A man could hardly see a hand before his face." He paused, wrinkled his brows. "At that, a killing up on the ridge trail is out of your bailiwick, isn't it, Sems? It's a job for the sheriff."

"I'd like a straight answer," the marshal said unsmilingly.

"Were these men friends of yours?" Donal spoke softly.

"That's neither here nor there, Cameron. There's been a killin' done." Sems looked pointedly at Wes Coles' bandaged arm. "Was you on the trail that night, feller?"

"Was never quick at answerin' questions that's nobody's bus'ness." Wes grinned at his companions. This snake-eyed star-packer wouldn't get anything out of *him*.

Sems regarded him attentively. "What for you got your arm in a sling?"

"Just a notion." Wes spoke solemnly. "The boss will tell you I get lazy spells . . . just cain't stand to lift both arms at once. Right now I'm feelin' that way . . . got to

**189**

have one of my arms held up for me." He looked sadly at Rusty. "Ain't that the truth?"

Rusty nodded gravely. "Wes is sure the laziest hombre ever forked a saddle," he confirmed. "We brought him to town to have a doc look him over. We'd figger it was maybe the foot and mouth disease, only his jaw don't seem troubled none. He can still talk plenty."

Sems reddened, shifted his attention back to Donal. "Let me tell you something, Cameron. Get out of this town quick as you can, and *keep* out. San Benito ain't healthy for you and your outfit."

"Thanks for the tip, Sems. I'll bear it in mind." Donal flicked a glance at the town marshal's bandaged hand. "You said the same the first time we met."

"Yes —" Sems lifted the bandaged hand, stared at it curiously. "I ain't forgettin', Cameron." His eyes swept up in an oddly challenging look. "I'm saying it again, for more reasons than you know. It's a good tip, Cameron." He turned away abruptly.

"One queer jasper," muttered Rusty as the trio rode up the street. "Cain't make him out."

"He's poison," asserted Wes, and added with a chuckle, "I sure got him peeved. Did you see the way he got red in the face?"

Donal offered no comment. It was obvious Sems suspected the truth regarding the fate that had overtaken the two men sent to waylay him on the trail. The town marshal was under no illusions as to what had happened, a fact that made his half-hearted questioning all the more baffling.

**190**

The man puzzled him. He had apparently gone out of his way to warn him against a danger that had no concern with his own private feud against the owner of Circle C. There had been a curious expression in his eyes when he looked at his bandaged hand. Not a yearning for revenge, but rather a wondering amazement, a conflict of emotions pulling him this way and that.

Rusty's voice broke into his reflections. "There's a doc's shingle."

Donal checked his horse, stared for a moment at the sign in the window. "Dr. Edward Polk," he read aloud. "All right, Wes. Ask him to take a look at your shoulder. You go with him, Rusty."

"Sure," agreed the foreman. He glanced back at the Longhorn Saloon. "I'll buy you a drink when the doc gets finished with you," he encouraged.

"I'll be needin' a drink," muttered Wes gloomily. "I'll be needin' *two* drinks when the doc is done cleanin' that bullet hole."

"No drinks," Donal said firmly. "You boys come on to the store first. When you drop in at the Longhorn I want to be along."

"Don't make me wait too long," grinned Wes.

"You're in town for two reasons," Donal continued. "We want the doctor to fix your arm up, and we want to see if you can spot the man who shot you. Keep your eyes peeled, Wes, especially when we drop in at the Longhorn."

"Ain't sure I'll know him," doubted Wes.

"It's a long shot," admitted Donal. He continued up the street to the Trading Post.

Angus Cameron himself stood in the doorway. "Ride in to the corral, lad, and give your horse a feed."

Donal made his way through the alley to the corral where an old Mexican took his horse.

"A couple more of us coming along soon," Donal told him.

The Mexican promised a hospitable welcome for them and Donal returned to the store. He found Angus at his desk in the rear of the long room.

"You're back in town soon, lad." The trader looked at him inquisitively over his pipe. "Rod has no got in with the wagon yet."

"He's on the way," Donal informed him. "He started for town when we pulled out from the ranch. He'll be along in a couple of hours."

"Aye" — Angus nodded — "a good ten miles longer by the wagon road." He puffed at his pipe, eyes very bright under their shag of grizzled brows. "You've a grim look to you, lad. I can fair smell fire and brimstone."

"You hit the mark close, Angus." Donal's tone was rueful. "Somebody has played hell with Circle C." He gave the trader a brief account of the raid.

"Daker," guessed Angus. He puffed furiously on his pipe. "Daker will no let you get away with the Salazar range."

"I don't think it is Daker."

Something in the young cattleman's voice drew a sharp look from the veteran frontiersman. He frowned, nodded thoughtfully. "I've a notion of what's on your mind, but it won't be easy to prove."

"I'd have got wise sooner," Donal said. "All this Daker talk put me on the wrong track."

Angus nodded again, his expression grim. "Aye, it's a wolf you're after, and that wouldn't be Jim Daker, who is more grizzly bear than wolf."

"A pack of wolves." Donal's voice took on a hard, implacable note. "I'm hunting them down, Angus. They won't find holes deep enough to get away from me."

The trader stared at him from narrowed eyes that sent out tiny gleams. He removed his pipe, tamped the blackened bowl with a horny forefinger, said slowly, "You can count on me, lad, and there are others in the Rio Seco who'll ride the wolf trail with you."

"Meaning who?"

"Well — there is Blue Clover. He's taken a rare liking to you, and" — Angus frowned — "and if what you say about Jim Daker is true, why Jim's Rocking D should want to be in on the kill."

Donal's expression was doubtful. He was thinking of the Rocking D's foreman. Angus said in a puzzled tone, "What's settled your mind about Jim Daker? It's long been the talk that he is a ruthless man."

"He paid Circle C a visit last night," Donal replied. "We had a heart-to-heart talk. I charged him with a lot of things that have happened since Circle C moved into the Rio Seco. He convinced me I've been wrong about him."

Angus showed no undue signs of astonishment. "I was thinkin' Jim would be over your way. He stopped in at the store, him and Hook Saval." The trader paused, keen eyes studying the younger man's noncommittal face. "Jim was in a rare dither about Isabel Lee. Found her horse dead in the trail close by the Aliso Creek fork, but no sign of the lass. He was fair wild with grief."

"She's with Marica Torres," Donal told him with a faint smile. "She is safe, Angus."

"At the ranch, you'll be meaning?" Angus arched grizzled brows. "You set Jim's mind at rest about her?"

"No. I didn't tell him. There are reasons why we don't want him to know Isabel is at the ranch." Donal paused, added quietly, "Don't let it go any further, Angus."

"I'm no the one to talk," rejoined the trader curtly, and then, frankly curious, "It's a puzzler, how the lass got over to your place."

Donal gave him an account of the attempt to ambush him on the storm-bound trail — the meeting with Isabel.

"God was riding with you the night," Angus said solemnly. " 'Twould have gone hard for the lass, save for your quick thinking — and courage." He got to his feet, held out his hand. "Donal, lad, as one Cameron to another, I'm proud of you."

"Call it luck," Donal said with a grin. "A few minutes later, or sooner, and we'd have missed each other in that fog. Those killers might have got me before Isabel reached the fork."

Two young women entered the store, stood smiling at the trader. Donal recognized one of them as the pretty Lucy Clover. Angus got out of his chair and went

**194**

to them, his rugged face wreathed in a welcoming smile.

"Blue has come in for the barbed wire you ordered for him," explained Mrs. Clover. "He's back in the corral, putting up the team for a feed. Molly and I thought we'd come along and get some things we need," she added with a glance at the well-stocked shelves. "We're making some dresses."

"I've some new goods that will please your eyes," Angus assured her. "Percale, gingham, calico — and some verra pretty muslin, if you're looking for something extra nice." He beckoned to the man behind the counter. "Tommy — show them the new stock we got in last week."

"Thank you, Mr. Cameron." Mrs. Clover's blue eyes filled with quick interest as she looked at the tall man standing by the desk. "It's the other Mr. Cameron, isn't it?" She gave Donal a shy smile of pleased recognition.

He approached the group and Mrs. Clover introduced him to her sister, Molly Ransome, who was quite as pretty as herself.

"Blue will be along in a few minutes," Lucy Clover told him. "He'll be awfully glad to see you." She turned to the counter and began examining the bolts of cloth Tommy was arranging.

Angus watched them for a moment, his expression thoughtful. "A word with you," he said to Donal, mysteriously.

They went back to the desk. Angus began refilling his pipe from a doeskin pouch. "It's about the lassie. She wouldn't be having much in the way of clothes with her, I'm thinking."

"Only the clothes she was wearing that night," answered Donal.

"Aye, she'd be wearing her riding skirt —"

"She was wearing pants," Donal interrupted with an amused look. "Overalls, she'd managed to get hold of."

Angus frowned. "Pants are no seemly for a lass to wear. It's no respectable."

"She hadn't much choice. She was running away and she felt she would attract less attention, especially in the dark."

"There's truth in that," agreed the trader. "Nevertheless, we cannot permit her to keep on wearing pants. It will no be decent."

"Marica has lent her some things," Donal assured him.

Angus wagged his head reprovingly. "It's no laughing matter for the lass." He looked at Lucy and her sister who were making little contented sounds over the display of pink-sprigged muslin. Donal guessed his thought. He shook his head warningly. "Be careful, Angus. Isabel doesn't want it known where she is."

"I'm no fool," frowned the trader. He walked away, and Donal saw him draw Mrs. Blue aside.

In a few moments he was back, a satisfied look on his face. "Lucy says she'll pick out such garments as a girl will need. I told her the same size she wears herself will fit. Isabel is very close to her in height and weight." He read the question in Donal's eyes. "Have no fear, lad. I no mentioned names."

**196**

"Thanks, Angus, and if you will enclose a note with the things it will save me the trouble of explaining."

The trader's eyes twinkled. "Aye," he assented dryly. "I'll do the same, and she will understand the thought was me own." He lowered himself into his desk chair and picked up a stubby pencil.

Blue Clover came in. His frank, sunburned face lighted as he saw Donal. "*Buenos dias!* When did you get in?"

The two men shook hands, and Donal said soberly, "I want to have a talk with you, Blue."

The young rancher gave him a keen look. "Sure, Don . . . anytime you say." He grinned cheerfully at the trader. "Hello, Angus. My wire get in?"

"Been here three days past," Angus replied. He folded the sheet of paper and tucked it in an envelope. "Tommy!" he called.

The clerk hurried up and Angus handed him the envelope. "Pin this to the bundle of things Mrs. Clover is having made up for me, and double wrap the bundle in canvas for tying to a saddle."

Blue Clover watched the departing clerk with puzzled eyes, then looked inquiringly at Angus. "Just a wee bit job Lucy is doing for me," the trader told him with a bland smile. "Sit you down, Blue. There are a lot of things Don wants to know and maybe you can give him a bit of help."

"Sure," assented Blue again. He pulled out tobacco and cigarette papers, looked quizzically at the Circle C man. "What's wrong?"

"Rustlers," Donal said laconically. "You warned me, Blue. My own fault for not being more careful."

"I'd no say that," disagreed Angus. "You're up against a verra smart gang by the looks of things."

Clover looked doubtful. "I don't know that I want to get mixed up in it, Don." He sent a glance at his wife. "Lucy knows how I feel about not wantin' to get mixed up in things that ain't my business."

"That's all right, Blue," hastily interrupted Donal. "I can savvy how you feel about it. I've no business dragging you into this."

The Little Bend rancher shook his head. "I ain't finished. Lucy don't want me to look at it the way I do . . . says she won't stand for me not doing what's right for fear of harm to her."

"Such talk is to her good credit," declared Angus approvingly. "A right brave lass."

"You bet your boots," agreed Blue with a pleased smile. "It all boils down to this, Don . . . I'm with you in this fight."

"I sized you up for that kind of man," Donal said simply. His eyes narrowed thoughtfully. "You said the other day that both Daker and DeSang claim they're losing cows to rustlers."

"That's the talk I hear." Blue shrugged. "Al DeSang does the loudest hollerin'."

"What's your idea about DeSang?" asked Donal.

"He could have me arrested for what I think of him," Clover said dryly.

"He's a friend of Daker's," Donal pointed out. "I'm told they're partners in the store."

Angus grunted. "I would no say Jim is a real partner in the store with DeSang. Jim put money into the business, but that is as far as it goes. DeSang has likely paid him off by now."

Donal stared thoughtfully at the sunlit doorway. Rusty and Wes were tying their horses to the long hitch-rail outside. His look swung back to Angus. "Daker wouldn't back DeSang with money if he didn't believe in him."

"Jim is an easy mark, for all the bigness and bluffness of him," Angus said contemptuously. "he is no match at all for a sly schemer like Al DeSang."

"He could have put money into *your* business if he wanted an investment."

"I use no man's money in my business." The old trader snorted. "It's like this with Daker: He listened to DeSang's smooth talk about being cock o' the walk in these parts. He built the new Daker House and he backed DeSang's store, thinking my customers would flock to him like silly sheep. He was to be all things in this town of San Benito, the mighty Jim Daker, benevolent lord and despot of the Rio Seco." The trader's shaggy brows bristled. "Jim is fair daft and swollen with pride. He is in no condition to see the pitfalls DeSang is setting for his downfall."

Rusty and Wes approached through the cool dimness of the big store with brief interested looks at the young women.

"We're having a powwow," Donal told them. He glanced at Wes. "What's the good word?"

The cowboy shook his head gloomily. "The doc claims I won't be usin' my arm much for a couple of weeks."

"Touch of blood poisonin'," Rusty said. "The doc wants him to take it easy." His eyes strayed down the store to the young women at the counter. "Nothin' to worry about," he added abstractedly.

Donal saw the look, winked at Blue Clover. "He's wondering which one is the sister I was telling him about."

Ruddy reddened. "You're a liar —" He attempted an offended glare. "Was only wonderin' who they are."

Clover chuckled. "Lucy, come on over," he called. "You and Molly. Got a feller here all curious about you."

Mrs. Clover and her sister came tripping up and introductions were made. Molly Ransome, slim and dark-haired, appraised the red-headed Circle C foreman with friendly eyes. "We've been hearing a lot about the Circle C," she smiled.

"I hope that what you've heard ain't all to the bad, ma'am," answered Rusty. He looked at her with frankly approving eyes.

Miss Ransome tossed her dark head. "I'm not telling," she retorted.

Wes Coles grinned. "We're one tough outfit, ma'am, and Rusty here, why he's so tough and onery he has to have gunpowder in his cawfee 'stead of sugar."

Rusty glared at him indignantly. "Don't you go believing this no-count cow-prodder, Miss Ransome."

**200**

"Well" — Molly seemed doubtful — "I'll think it over, Mr. Cross." She wrinkled a small pert nose. "You'll have to take sugar, though, when you come over to *our* house. I won't let you have gunpowder in your coffee."

"You just try me," chuckled the delighted Rusty. "You cain't make it too soon. I got a big hanker to prove somebody is all of him a liar." He fixed Wes with a stern look.

Molly smiled at them impartially.

"I'd sure like to be there, too," Wes brazenly announced. "I ain't believin' him unless I see him take sugar with my own eyes."

"You can both come," graciously assented Mrs. Clover's pretty sister. "Any time you like." She flashed a provocative smile at Rusty and followed Lucy back to the counter.

A man suddenly pushed in through the doorway. Other men followed close on his heels. The first man — he wore a deputy sheriff's star — spoke in a harsh voice. "I'm lookin' for Don Cameron . . . wanted for murder."

# CHAPTER
# EIGHTEEN

# Rede Sems Draws Again

Angus said quickly, "Let me do the talking, lad." He got out of his chair, stern gaze fixed on the men clustered inside the door. "What is your business in my place?"

"You heard me," retorted the man. "Don't try to make a monkey out of the law, mister." His hard eyes roved over the faces of the men grouped near the desk. "I know you, Clover, so I reckon Don Cameron is one of the other fellers. If he don't speak up I'm arrestin' all three of 'em."

"Not so fast," interrupted the old trader quietly. "Since when have you been wearing a deputy's star?"

"Keep your nose out of this," warned the man.

Angus held his ground. "You're Jed Stiles," he said. "You're a worthless loafer and no deputy sheriff. Get out of my store. Dinna ye ken there are ladies present?" The trader's eyes blazed.

"I ain't makin' trouble if Don Cameron will come along peaceable," Stiles said gruffly.

At a significant look from Donal, Blue Clover spoke to his wife. She nodded, started for the door that led into the rear of the store. Molly followed, her eyes big with apprehension as she looked at Rusty's hard mask of a face.

"Get out of my store," repeated Angus. "You're no deputy sheriff."

"I'll show you," blustered Stiles. He was a tall, hulking-shouldered man with small restless eyes set in a fleshy, mottled face that was bisected by an untidy drooping mustache. A mean and formidable-looking person as he stood there, feet planted wide apart, hand resting on gun-butt. "Don't blame me if blood runs in this damn store."

"Ye scum!" Angus was finding it hard to keep a leash on his temper.

Donal interrupted him, and moved quickly between the two men. "Did Soper put you up to this?" he asked sharply.

Stiles insolently looked him up and down. "Are you Don Cameron?" His gun flashed up. "Reckon you're him, all right. Take it easy, mister, or I'll drop you cold."

The guns in the hands of the four men flanking him covered Blue Clover and the two Circle C men. Tommy stood frozen behind the counter, his face aghast. Stiles motioned to him. "Get back to the others," he ordered. "Keep your hands up, brother, or you won't never reach that desk."

"Was it Soper?" asked Donal again.

Stiles ignored the question. "I'm takin' you to jail for that killin' on the ridge trail," he said. His loose mouth twisted in a sneer. "Don't guarantee the jail will hold you long. Them fellers you killed have plenty friends. Won't be my fault if they take you out and swing you."

"You're crazy," Donal said contemptuously.

"Are you comin' peaceable?" It was plain that Stiles was deliberately working up his rage. His small mean eyes took on a murderous glitter. "Save your talk for the judge."

"What jail will you take the lad to?" queried Angus quietly. "Rede Sems runs the jail in this town. Why is Rede Sems no here with you?"

"This is county bus'ness," retorted Stiles. "I'm takin' this jasper to the county jail."

"I'm no thinkin' it's the truth you speak." The trader's voice showed his dire misgivings. "You're a pack of wolves and plan to kill him in cold blood."

The sly fleeting grins on their faces were proof that Angus had correctly divined the purpose of these men. He sent a helpless look at Blue Clover, at Rusty Cross and Wes Coles. They stood like men turned to stone. The slightest movement toward holstered guns would mean instant death for Donal. They could only watch with hot, angry eyes, hold their straining hands in tight leash.

Donal knew there was only one answer. He must go with this satanic brood of killers. Any other course at that moment would turn the place into a shambles. It would be a massacre, with himself and

204

his friends the victims. He made one more desperate attempt.

"Get Rede Sems here," he said. "I'll go with Sems."

Stiles guffawed. "Ain't needin' Rede Sems for this job." His weasel eyes gleamed. "If Sems is smart he'll keep his nose out of this."

"You're wrong, Stiles," broke in a curt voice from the porch. "Maybe I ain't awful smart, but I'm too smart for you."

The faces of Stiles and the four ruffians with him swung as if on a single pivot to meet the unwinking stare of the small man framed in the wide doorway. He stood in a half crouch, a gun in each hand.

"I should kill you, Stiles," the grim little town marshal went on. "Why don't you start something, you mangy coyote?" The shadow of a mirthless smile flickered across his mask of a face. "My horns is out and they're damn sharp."

Stiles seemed to have difficulty with his breath. His head turned slowly in a look at the men back in the dimness of the store. He saw more guns leveled at him, saw Donal's cold smile, the triumphant grins of Blue Clover and the Circle C men.

Slowly, very carefully, he lowered his own gun, slid it into its holster. His companions followed suit. They were fairly caught between two fires. Fear was stark in their eyes. They were whipped.

"Take off that star you're wearin'." The town marshal's tone was acid.

"You'll be sorry for this, Sems," Stiles said hoarsely. "You'll git hell —"

"Shut your mouth!" flared Sems. He sent a curious look at Donal. "I'd as soon kill you as not, Stiles — if you make another peep."

Stiles fumbled at the star pinned to his shirt. His hand shook.

"The man claimed he was a deputy sheriff," Angus said angrily.

Sems shrugged, held out his hand and caught the shiny bit of tin as Stiles tossed it. "I'm taking your guns." His own weapons continued to menace the crestfallen men. "One of you fellers get 'em for me."

Rusty and Blue made haste to remove the guns which they threw on the counter.

"First time I heard *you* was a deputy," sneered Sems.

"You ain't heard the last of this," muttered Stiles.

"From *you* I have," rejoined the marshal. "You and your bunch are forkin' saddles now and immediate." Sems' voice took on the thin edge of razor steel. "Don't show your faces in this town again. I'm shooting on sight." He darted another of his enigmatic glances at Donal, and added softly, "I won't be missing my shots — not this time."

He drove them out of the store like a pack of curs, and they trooped down the street to their horses, sullen-eyed, wordless, and obviously in terror of the frozen-faced little man at their backs.

"'Twas touch and go," Angus Cameron said solemnly. Wonder deepened his voice. "I would no have thought it of that tight-lipped little man. 'Twas but the other day he would have shot you down in the street."

"I can't make him out," admitted Donal.

"Aweel" — Angus looked down his big nose — "the man paid a debt to you this day. 'Twas a trick Stiles was up to. A cold-blooded plot to take you off some place and murder you."

Mrs. Clover and her sister reappeared, both of them big-eyed with excitement. Blue said, "It's all over, Lucy. You can finish your shopping."

"You all look so — so fierce," Molly Ransome declared with a sidewise glance at the gun in Rusty's hand. He flushed, pushed the weapon into its holster. "We heard it all," she added, widening her eyes at Donal. "You don't seem a bit worried, Mr. Cameron — and those men trying to kill you."

"You run along," Blue told her a bit gruffly, at which Rusty gave him the beginnings of a scowl. Molly followed her sister back to Tommy and the bolts of finery spread on the counter. She flashed Rusty a demure look as she passed him. His half scowl had not been lost on her.

Wes Coles was watching Stiles and his companions ride away. "Here comes Sems," he called over his shoulder. "I reckon he wants to collect them guns he took from them."

The town marshal was wanting more than the confiscated guns. He was wanting a word in private with Don Cameron, he said as he gathered up the weapons from the counter.

Donal accompanied him outside. Sems went down the porch steps, walked a few yards toward his office, halted and looked at Donal with hard, angry eyes. "I warned you to get out of this town."

"It's my town," rejoined Donal. "I come and go as I please."

"You make me sick," grumbled the town marshal. He stared frowningly at the toes of his boots, seemed at a loss for words.

"I don't know why you did it, Sems," began Donal, "but I'm grateful."

Sems gestured impatiently. "I can't be johnny-on-the-spot *all* the time. That's why I want you to keep out of this town."

"I don't see why *you* should worry. You tried to kill me yourself the first time I was in this town." Donal stared at Sems with perplexed eyes. "You've got me puzzled. I can't make you out."

Sems lifted his eyes, and there was pain in their slaty depths. "I'm what folks call a killer, but I've been damn sorry for that gunplay. I was told you was one yourself and was out to get me. I'm knowin' different. You could have killed me, but you held your fire, offered me an even break, and after what I'd done."

"Who told you that lie about me?" asked Donal in a hard voice.

"That's my business," Sems said curtly. "I'm 'tendin' to it myself."

"I've been expecting you to try it again," Donal told him with a thin smile. "Why haven't you tried again, Sems?"

Sems considered with intent eyes. "Maybe it's because I'm a damn fool, or again maybe it's because I like your guts." A faint, inscrutable smile flickered

**208**

across his face. "Take your choice, Cameron." He hesitated, added softly, "Why don't you scout 'round in the Comanche hills sometime? DeSang's DS is over that way." He jerked a curt nod and went on toward his office.

# CHAPTER
# NINETEEN

# Wolf Bait

The trader gave Donal a shrewd look when he returned. He smiled grimly. "You've been having a few words with Rede Sems," and then worriedly, "Can you trust the man?"

"*Quien sabe.*" Donal shrugged. "He may be playing both ends against the middle."

"He's DeSang's man," reminded Angus dryly. "Don't you forget that fact, lad."

"I'm not forgetting." Donal looked at him thoughtfully. "Speaking of DeSang, you said the other day that you could name the man responsible for the raid on your freight wagons."

"I did no say his name was DeSang," Angus replied cautiously.

Donal smiled. "Let it pass. But you did say there were more ways than one to trap a wolf, and that is what you called DeSang."

"Aye," admitted Angus slowly, "aye — he is a wolf, and a wary one at that. He'll no be caught with the sprinkling of salt on his tail."

"What do you know about him?" Donal spoke bluntly. "I want every detail you have on him, Angus."

"I've done a bit of ferretin' around," Angus confessed. "Aye, I know conseederable about the man. 'Twas no hard, for he's left a trail behind him, a bad name and a lot of bad notes."

"Bad notes? What do you mean?"

"I've been picking up plenty of them here and there," Angus said with a crafty smile. "DeSang had a way of raising good money for which he'd give the innocent and trusting lender his unsecured note of hand. A smooth man, DeSang, with his talk and affable ways."

"I've seen him," Donal commented dryly.

"You'll understand, then, what I mean." Angus puffed hard on his pipe. "'Tis such a man who is all the more dangerous, a wolf in sheep's bonny dress like in the fairy tale."

"I'm wondering about these unpaid notes," prodded Donal.

"Aye, close to twenty thousand dollars of the paper, and all of it good in court if the man can be made to pay, which is improbable if not impossible."

"What was your idea, picking up these worthless notes?"

"They cost me but a wee bit, a few cents on the dollar." Angus chuckled. "I've a weakness for a long shot, lad, and 'twas in my head that maybe these notes might make good wolf bait."

Donal's eyes narrowed thoughtfully. "I'd hate to be on the wrong side of you," he said. "Sooner or later you always trap your wolf."

"Aye." The trader's smile was bland. " 'Tis the same with you, lad. Only you like action, patience not being one of your virtues."

"I can't afford to wait," Donal said gloomily. "I'm ruined, if I don't track down the man who stole my herd." He got out of his chair. "Sems gave me a tip, Angus. He was a bit vague about it, and I don't quite savvy his game, but I'm riding into the Comanche hills for a look at DeSang's range."

"If what you suspect is true, you will be riding into dangerous country," warned the old frontiersman gravely.

"I'll take Rusty with me." Donal paused, and his look strayed to a canvas-wrapped bundle on the floor. "Wes can take that stuff back to the ranch."

"You'll be starting for the Comanches when you leave here?" queried Angus.

"Within the hour, just as quick as Blue Clover can give me the layout of the country over there."

"Blue can do that," Angus assured him. "He knows the Comanche hills like his own back yard." The trader paused, added musingly, "The way your herd was run off reminds me of Ed Landers."

"Never heard of him."

"He's gone now. Left the Rio Seco for good."

"What happened to him?"

"His herd was rustled, but he'd money left, enough for a fresh start. Al DeSang sold him a bunch of two- and three-year-olds, a couple of hundred. They went the same way as the first herd." Angus wagged his head. "Ed knew he was licked . . . loaded wife and bairns into

212

his wagons and got out. DeSang's DS now has his bit of range," he added dryly.

Donal sat silent for several moments. "You're trying to tell me something," he finally commented.

"'Twas spread around that Jim Daker was responsible for Ed's bad luck." Angus arched his grizzled brows. "'Twas well known that Jim no liked nesters, which Ed Landers was in a way of speaking. Jim claimed the most of 'em were born cow thieves and he'd no tolerate 'em in the Rio Seco."

"Was Landers that kind?"

"Ed was an honest man," asserted Angus. "But he'd no the brains, nor the heart, to fight villainy." He shot Donal a keen look. "You have both, lad, and it will take the same to win this fight."

"I'll give it all I've got," muttered the young man. He sat for a while longer, brows furrowed in deep thought. Both Soper and DeSang had thrown out strong hints that if trouble came to him it would be from Jim Daker. He was to look out for Daker.

Angus was watching him closely. "You're doing some hard thinking, lad?"

Donal looked up and his eyes were cold and hard. "I'm beginning to understand a lot of things that have had me puzzled." He got to his feet. "I see daylight ahead, Angus."

Rusty Cross wore a satisfied expression as he rode stirrup to stirrup with his boss up the street. Donal gave him a shrewd look. "You and Molly seemed to hit it off."

Rusty's smile widened. "She's a peach!"

"Watch out, or she'll get a rope on you."

"I'm feedin' out of her hand right now," drawled the Circle C foreman. He chuckled contentedly. "Just as quick as we get done hangin' a few rustlers I aim to ramble over to Blue's place for a taste of her apple pie. Molly claims she cain't be beat for her apple pie."

A man hailed them as they drew abreast of the San Benito General Merchandise Store. Donal recognized Al DeSang and Judge Soper, standing on the porch.

"Just a moment, Cameron!" DeSang hurried into the street.

The Circle C men halted their horses. "What do you want?" Donal's tone was curt.

"I've been hearing about that trouble you had at the Trading Post." DeSang's smooth voice showed concern. "An outrage, if there ever was one."

"Didn't amount to much," smiled Donal. His face showed no hint of his surprise.

"Had all the looks of an attempt to kidnap you," asserted DeSang. "This Stiles was a rank impostor."

"Absolutely," hiccoughed Judge Soper from the high porch. He was having difficulty with his tongue and his round, prominent eyes blinked owlishly. "An outrashas per-performansh." He teetered unsteadily, wind whipping his Prince Albert. "Thish town needs new peash offisher."

Donal was watching DeSang with wary eyes, trying to read the purpose behind the man's affable mask.

"Mighty sorry to hear about that raid on your place," DeSang continued sympathetically. "This rustling gives

**214**

the Rio Seco a bad name." He shook his head regretfully. "Tough luck, Cameron. Let me know if there is anything I can do."

"Thanks." Donal's face showed no hint of his lively interest in DeSang's words. With an effort he restrained the question on the tip of his tongue. DeSang had made a slip, admitting knowledge of the raid.

"We cattlemen must get together," declared DeSang. He stroked his heavy black mustache musingly. "About time we hang a few of these cow thieves." His eyes lifted in a swift probing look. "Any idea who rustled you?"

Rusty saved Donal the trouble of answering. He said harshly, "If we knew that much we'd be on their trails right now."

"That's right." DeSang flicked him a careless glance, then looked at Wes Coles who rode up with the canvas-wrapped bundle tied to his saddle. DeSang showed quick interest in the bandaged arm. "Are you the man who was shot? Sems said something about it."

Wes grimaced. "The doc claims it was a bullet that somehow got into my shoulder."

"Did you see the man who shot you?"

"I ain't in court," retorted Wes irritably. "Never was good at answering nosey questions."

"Wes was shot from ambush," hurriedly put in Donal. "He had no chance for a look."

Something like suspicion lurked briefly in DeSang's black eyes. Donal was sorry he had spoken so quickly. This soft-spoken man was smart. "Wes gets peeved to be asked about that gunplay," he added with an amused chuckle in an attempt to cover up his indiscretion. "He was caught napping and doesn't like to own to it."

Perhaps it was a subtle warning in Donal's voice, or it may have been his own intuition. Wes put on a good imitation of injured feelings. "Seems like I ain't goin' never to hear the last of it," he grumbled. "I'm sure sick of bein' jeered at for sleepin' on the job."

"You didn't see the man, then?" persisted DeSang.

"I was just tellin' you I didn't," snapped Wes.

Relief crossed DeSang's face like a flicker of light. He nodded sympathetically and looked at Donal. "What are your plans, Cameron?"

"That's a question." Donal forced a careless smile. "It's good-bye to the cow business, unless I can get hold of another stake."

"That's too bad," commiserated DeSang. He hesitated, glanced at Judge Soper who had sought the steadying influence of the wall at his back. "We should help our friend, don't you think, Judge?"

"It would be a conshiderate deed," responded Judge Soper with a wave of his hand. "Mishter Cameron disherve conshideration."

DeSang appeared to be thinking. His face brightened. "See here, Cameron . . . my range is a bit overstocked. Maybe I can help you out . . . say a few hundred head."

"That means money," Donal said with a wry smile.

DeSang made a swift mental calculation. "Four hundred head, say, at an average of twenty-five dollars. Two- and three-year-old stuff and a few unbranded calves thrown in."

"Ten thousand dollars more or less," Donal said. "That's money, DeSang." He stared thoughtfully into space, brows furrowed. "You give me an idea at that."

"Let's hear it." DeSang's smile was genial.

"I'm heading back for a talk with Angus Cameron," Donal said with a show of excitement.

"I get you." DeSang nodded. "His note is good with me any time."

Donal gave him a steady look. "I think I can do better than that. We won't need *his* note."

"All the better," laughed DeSang. "You can't beat cash when it comes to a deal."

Donal's face wore an inscrutable smile as he swung his horse. "I'll let you know. I'd want to go over to your range and look the stuff over."

"Any time you say," agreed the other man.

"Sometime next week," Donal decided. "I mean if Angus comes up to scratch with me."

Flanked on either side by Rusty and Wes, he rode back to the Trading Post. The two Circle C men wore mystified looks.

"You've got me guessin'," muttered Rusty.

"Me too." Wes scowled. "I sure no savvy the play. I only savvy that I ain't likin' that jasper a-tall."

They stared curiously at the stern-set face of the man who rode between them. He said nothing until they reached the hitch-rail in front of the Trading Post.

He stepped down from his saddle. "I'll only be a few minutes," he told them. "Wait here for me, boys." A hard smile touched his lips. "DeSang seemed to know all about the Circle C being rustled, which is strange, because we've told nobody save Angus and Clover."

"I'll say it's strange," muttered Rusty.

"Doggone strange!" echoed Wes.

Donal left them mulling over the curious incident and made his way to the big desk in the far end of the store. Angus greeted him with a surprised lift of shaggy brows.

Donal's eyes twinkled. "I'm buying some of your wolf bait," he said. "I'll want about ten thousand dollars' worth."

The old trader's weathered face creased in a slow smile. He nodded. "I take it that DeSang wants to sell you some cows. Is that the idea, lad?"

"It is." Donal's eyes were hard.

"So it is wolf bait you need," purred the old Scot. "Aye, lad, it is yours at five cents on the dollar and ready for you any time."

"I told him I'd want to look the stuff over sometime next week." Donal laughed softly. "He doesn't know I'm heading for the DS today."

"The brains are working," murmured Angus with a low chuckle.

Donal grinned, turned on his heel. The trader leaned his weight back in the big chair, puffed furiously on his pipe. Hoofbeats faded into the distance. Angus tapped the ashes from his pipe. "Tommy," he called to the clerk, "tell Roderick Dhu I'm wanting him quick as he gets in with the wagon. I've a job for him to do."

# CHAPTER
# TWENTY

# The Altered Brand

Blue smoke lifted lazily above the cabin half hidden in the willows near the creek. A man sat on an upturned box near the door, leisurely splitting chunks of wood with a hatchet. The sound of the blows reached up to the two men crouched on the high bluffs.

"The cook," guessed Rusty Cross. He eased up to a sitting position and rubbed a leg. "Horses in the corral, but nobody 'round but him."

"I wish we could have got here sooner," Donal said. "We'd have known which way the others went."

"Be gone all day most likely," surmised Rusty. He rubbed his other leg. "These rocks get to feelin' awful hard. Cold last night, too. A slicker don't make much of a bedroll."

Donal was watching the scene below with speculative eyes. The early morning air was brilliant, typical of mid-June in New Mexico. Lazy cloud fragments touched the higher peaks across the valley, and far in the north the high skyline held a thin silvery curtain of rain. Overhead bent a vast arch of matchless blue.

"I bet we could get a cup of coffee down there," suggested Rusty. "I could stand a cup of coffee."

Donal sat back on his heels. "We've seen all we can from up here," he said, and got to his feet.

The two men moved cautiously away and finally worked down to the small clearing where they had left their horses.

"I'd hate to be caught up here in the dark," Rusty said. "This place is the devil's own back yard. A feller could step into nowhere and drop a thousand feet." He got into his saddle and looked inquiringly at his chief.

"We're going to pay a call on that camp cook," Donal informed him.

"I admire the idea," chuckled the foreman. "I can almost taste that coffee now. Ham and eggs would go well, too."

"We're going after more than a pot of coffee."

"Sure," grunted Rusty, unabashed. "Just the same it won't hurt us to do a little foragin'. Only got a couple of them sandwiches left that Angus had his Mexican woman fix for us. No tellin' how much longer we'll be foolin' 'round here."

A good half hour brought them to the mouth of a deep, high-walled canyon from which the creek meandered across the flats. The sound of the hatchet no longer broke the stillness of that remote spot, but the thin spiral of smoke lifting above the willows beyond the bend of the creek told them they were close to the cabin.

"He won't likely welcome us with open arms," observed Rusty. He stared at the curling smoke. "He'll hear us coming, have his gun on us when we break through the willows."

**220**

"We'll take him from both sides," Donal decided. "I'll pick up that trail we noticed, where it fords the creek. You can get in behind the shack, have him covered when I ride up."

"Give me fifteen minutes' start," Rusty said. "I'll have to leave my horse hid in the brakes and make a sneak back of the corral where them hides were hanging." He rode away at a slow walk and disappeared into the willows.

Donal rode off to the right, followed the meanderings of the creek until within a few yards of the trail where it dipped down to the ford. He drew the horse to a standstill behind a clump of stunted trees.

A small opening allowed him a partial view of the cabin, and on beyond, to the hides strung along the corral fence. His eyes narrowed. He had a keen desire for a closer look at those hides.

The minutes dragged. No sound touched his ears, save an occasional stamp of hoofs from the horse corral beyond his view. Apparently the cook had retired inside the shack, his morning chores done, and was probably amusing himself with a game of solitaire, or had stretched out in his bunk with a cigarette.

Of a sudden a movement in a clump of tall weeds caught his alert gaze. He continued to watch, saw Rusty slip around the corral fence and drop behind the hides.

Donal loosened the gun in his holster and turned his horse into the trail. He rode leisurely, let his body sag in the saddle like a man weary from a long ride, hat tipped low over watchful eyes.

They splashed into the shallow stream. He let the horse sip a few mouthfuls, spoke loudly as if in impatient admonition. "Get along, feller!"

His ears caught a faint stirring in the cabin, then a hasty thud of feet, followed by a deep silence. He guessed that the man inside was observing him. He ventured a shout. "Hello there!"

The man appeared, stood framed in the doorway, rifle in hand. "What you want, stranger?" His tone was belligerent. "If it's grub, you won't git none."

Donal let a friendly grin spread over his face. "Looks like I've got my trails mixed, or am I headed right for the Little Bend?"

Suspicion stared from the man's eyes, and there was no answering smile on his unshaven face. He lifted the rifle with a menacing gesture. "Don't come no closer, stranger."

Donal checked the horse, gave the man a surprised look. "What's eatin' you?" he grumbled. "No savvy why you act hostile."

"We don't like strangers in this camp," the man said gruffly. "In fact, mister, this camp is plumb unhealthy for folks that come nosin' 'round."

"I've been out in the hills all night," Donal said truthfully. "Picked up your smoke and headed this way all set for a cup of coffee and cakes."

The man was staring at him intently, startled recognition in his eyes. He laid his cheek against rifle stock, squinted down the barrel. "You're a liar," he said curtly. "Climb down from your saddle — and watch your hands."

222

"If that's the way you feel about it," grumbled Donal. Out of the corner of his eye he glimpsed Rusty cautiously moving into sight from behind the cowhides. "Friendly as a porcupine, that's you." Slowly, and taking care to keep his hands in sight, he got down from the horse. "You're loco, I reckon," he added with a show of indignation.

"Keep your hands up," ordered the man. "Yeah, I'm loco like a fox, that's why I ain't fooled none, Mister Nosey Cameron." He leered triumphantly. "So you went and lost your way, huh? That's a good one." His voice took on a snarl. "Get down on your belly, you mangy spy, and keep your nose in the dirt. I'm taking that gun you wear."

Rusty was standing within twenty feet of the man by now. Donal took another look at the menacing rifle. Anything was better than letting a nervous trigger-finger send a heavy .44 bullet crashing into him, and Rusty was at a disadvantage as long as the man's rifle covered Donal.

"Get down flat like I said." The cook's tone was impatient. "I ain't wastin' time nor takin' chances."

Without further parley, Donal eased himself face down on the ground. The man lowered his rifle and started toward him. Donal heard Rusty's low, bitter voice. He lifted his head for a look, saw the cook come to a sudden standstill. Rusty spoke again: "Drop your gun!"

The rifle slid from the cook's hands and he slowly craned his head and stared at the speaker. Donal sprang to his feet and seized the fallen Winchester. The

**223**

cook rolled dazed eyes at him. "I was only foolin'," he muttered. "At that you cain't blame me for actin' careful."

"Your acting is too good," drawled Donal. "Where's the rest of your outfit?"

The cook hesitated, licked dry lips. "I wouldn't be knowing which way they went," he finally answered.

"You're a liar," snapped Rusty. He poked his gun hard against the man's ribs. "If you were fooling, we ain't."

The cook breathed heavily. "There was some talk about they was headin' for Sheep Springs," he stammered.

"Trailing a herd that way?" questioned Donal.

"Waal" — the cook hesitated, rolled nervous eyes at Rusty's gun — "I reckon they was pushing some cows to the Springs. Ain't swearin' to it."

The Circle C men exchanged significant looks. Donal went to the open cabin door and glanced inside. The place was empty. He saw a coil of rope hanging from a nail. He took it down and went back to the others.

"Did you see those cows your outfit was trailing to Sheep Springs?" he asked the cook.

"The cows wasn't close to camp no time." The cook spoke sullenly. "I didn't get to look at 'em."

"When will the outfit be back?"

"Sundown, I reckon . . . mebbe some later."

"Might be a good idea for us to have that coffee," suggested Rusty. "I'm sure empty."

**224**

"I'll fix you some breakfast," offered the cook. "Got in a new side o' bacon . . . made me a fresh batch o' bread this mornin'."

"You'll look prettier tied up," Donal said dryly. He gestured for the man to precede them into the cabin.

"He'll look good in his bunk," Rusty chuckled as they swiftly and securely tied the prisoner's wrists and ankles with pieces of rope cut from the coil Donal had found.

They rolled the trussed cook into his bunk and set to work on the breakfast.

"I'll get the bacon fryin' while you fix the coffee," Rusty suggested.

"I'm hopin' the stuff poisons you," muttered their prisoner.

The Circle C foreman grinned at him cheerfully. "You sure have bad manners, talking that-a-ways to your guests," he reproved.

The cook subsided, watched with sullen eyes while his two unwelcome visitors ate their hastily-prepared breakfast. Donal kicked back his stool and stood looking at the bound man, fingers busy with paper and tobacco. "Who bosses this outfit for DeSang?" he finally asked.

"Slash Driver," replied the cook. He added an oath. "He'll fix you for this bus'ness."

"Do you know Lew Trent?"

"I ain't sayin'." A curious pallor spread over the cook's face.

"Does Trent come around here? Have you seen him lately?"

The prisoner's lips tightened obstinately.

"Acts like the mention of Trent's name most scares him to death," commented Rusty. He drained his coffee cup and got to his feet.

"Just a moment." Donal's expression was thoughtful. He was recalling Hook Saval's words about the scar-faced man who had helped the lame man escape from him in the Longhorn. *Sounds like Slash Driver.*

The cook was speaking sulkily. "What you fellers goin' to do with me?"

Donal looked at him for a moment. "What does your boss, this Slash Driver, look like? Has he a scar on his face — a knife slash?"

"Yeah — I reckon he has."

"Hook said he was DeSang's foreman," reminded Rusty. His face darkened. "This jasper says the same, and putting two and two together I'd say he's the man you run into in the Longhorn."

"That's what I was thinking." Donal's look went to the door. "Let's take a look at those hides, Rusty."

One by one they made a careful inspection of the hides, finally pulled down two from the fence rail. Donal sat on his heels, forefinger tracing the brand burned deep on one of the hides. "Smart work." His tone was admiring. "A nice DS for all the world to see."

"DeSang's iron," muttered Rusty. "Let's turn her over for a look-see on the inside."

They flipped the big hide over, stared with hard eyes at the scars on the under side. Rusty made a clucking sound with his tongue. "Rocking D, sure as you're born."

226

"Smart work," Donal said again. "A running-iron did the job, Rusty. See, here's your Rocking D." Using a sharp-pointed stick he traced a D on the ground. "And here's how they turned it into a DS." — He drew a curving line from the right point of the rocker, ran it through the center of the D and curved it over the top in a rocker similar to the one at the bottom. The result was a perfect S superimposed on the D.

Rusty swore softly. "Jim Daker himself wouldn't guess what they done to his Rocking D," he said admiringly. "Some brand-blottin'."

"Foolproof, all right," agreed Donal. "Nobody would know the truth, looking at it on a live animal. But a branding iron burns deep and a skinned hide will show the original scars. They stand out like a sore thumb against the new ones. And the running-iron wouldn't burn as deep as the branding iron that made the Rocking D. These old scars under the hide don't lie."

"They can sure prove that the man who done it is a brand-blottin' cow thief," growled Rusty. He fished in his shirt pocket for tobacco-sack and papers. "Daker's going to keel over dead with surprise when he gets a look at these hides." The foreman's eyes had a hot glow in them. "I'd like to have a peep at those cows they've trailed over to Sheep Springs."

"We will." Donal's tone was grim. "We won't try it alone, Rusty. We'll need help for *that* job."

"Lew Trent is mixed up in the dirty business all right," guessed Rusty. "That cook was scared to death when you asked him about Trent."

Donal nodded, his eyes hard. "DeSang is the brains," he said. "Trent is the field man."

"He's a damn rustler," grunted Rusty. He scowled. "I reckon he could tell us a lot, huh, Don?"

"We'll have to ask him." Donal was staring at the incriminating hides. "He's in with DeSang hand and foot . . . stealing from the man who trusts him."

Neither of them noticed the two horsemen watching from the edge of the willow brakes. The riders dismounted, started a stealthy advance, keeping the cabin between them and the men they stalked.

Donal stooped, began to fold up the hide at his feet. "Get one of those horses from the corral," he said to Rusty. "I saw a pack-saddle lying near the gate."

Rusty turned, came to a frozen standstill as he saw the two strangers now within fifteen yards of the corral. His gasp brought Donal to his feet, hand reaching for his gun. One of the men spoke. "Don't try it, Cameron."

Donal slowly turned and looked. The authority of those two menacing rifles was not to be questioned. Wordless for the moment, he lifted his hands.

The man who had spoken came up quickly and removed their guns. "Think you're smart," he sneered. He kicked at the hide contemptuously. "You won't get the chance to show these in any court, Cameron."

"You're pretty good with a running-iron, Trent. We've been admiring your work." Donal spoke coolly.

"You won't have a chance to tell anybody about it," Lew Trent retorted. He turned to his companion. "Get a rope, Gimpy."

The man hurried off to the cabin. He had a bad limp. The Circle C men exchanged looks.

"Yeah" — Trent was watching them closely — "he's the man you asked Daker about. I had to fire him off the Rocking D payroll, but he's still on *my* payroll." He gave them a tight-lipped smile. "I'd let him kill you now, Cameron, but first I'm finding out what you know about the Lee girl."

"You double-crossin' snake," Rusty said.

Gimpy reappeared, a rope on his arm and a furious cook at his heels. "Found Denver hawg-tied in his bunk," the lame man said with a grin.

"I'll fry the skunks in their own grease!" howled the cook. He was beside himself with rage.

The Circle C men were quickly made fast. Denver took pleasure in drawing the knots tight around Donal's wrists.

"I'm purty slick at trussin' a hawg my own self," he chortled.

The prisoners were marched into the cabin and through the kitchen to an inner room. Bunks lined the log walls of this room which was about twenty feet long and fifteen across. A plank table stood on the dirt floor and odds and ends of saddle gear littered the place which was ventilated by two small openings set shoulder-high in the walls. Cowhide flaps hung over these openings and the room was dark, and stuffy with stale tobacco smoke and the smells of sweaty, unwashed men.

"Stinks in here," complained Trent. "Pull the flaps up, Denver, and then go fix some breakfast for us."

The cook pushed the strips of cowhide aside, letting in light and air, and with a leer at the prisoners he returned to his kitchen.

Donal was not feeling any too good about the situation. Trent was a dangerous man. His secret was no longer a secret, which made him all the more dangerous. He would not hesitate to destroy the men who could unmask him.

Trent broke the silence. "What else do you know, Cameron?" He leaned his rifle against the table, began to build a cigarette. Gimpy stood with his back to the closed door, a Colt .45 in his hand and watchful gaze on the prisoners. "What do you say we talk this thing over and do a little bargaining?"

"What do you mean?" Donal's tone was cautious. He sensed that Trent was not at all sure of his own position.

"Well — this thing don't need to go any further, not as long as nobody else knows — what *you* know."

Donal guessed the man was trying to find out if there were others who knew the truth. Jim Daker for instance. Once Trent was convinced the two Circle C men alone possessed the secret their doom was sealed. He said, still cautious, "You've got us in a tight hole, Trent. We'd be fools not to dicker with you, but I'm not sure it would do you any good."

Trent stared at him, a hint of doubt and fear in his eyes. He was obviously disturbed. Suddenly he gestured savagely. "Was it that damn fool Soper who put you wise? I want the truth."

230

"Figure it out for yourself." Donal was feeling more sure of his ground. Trent was worried. "You must be crazy, thinking you could keep on making a fool of Jim Daker." He was watching the other man closely.

"Must have been the girl got suspicious," muttered Trent half to himself. "I was a fool all right, talking to her so free."

"I didn't say it was the girl who told me anything," Donal said.

"Where is she?"

Donal shrugged his shoulders. "Let me tell you something, Trent. You're in bad and if you're smart you'll get out of the Rio Seco while the going is good. Turn us loose and you and your killer climb your saddles. We won't stop you."

"Like hell you wouldn't," sneered the Rocking D man. His expression was ugly. "I've too much at stake, and I ain't licked."

"Daker won't waste time when he gets his hands on you," warned Donal. "You know what he does to cow thieves."

"He'll stretch your neck double quick," Rusty said with relish. "Stealin' him blind, and you his trusted foreman."

Gimpy muttered an oath, limped toward the Circle C foreman menacingly. Trent's look stopped him. The lame man scowled. "I'd like to bash his teeth down his lyin' throat, and the other feller too. They'd mebbe tell us what we want to know. Let me rough 'em up, boss."

231

Trent shook his head. "No sense going off half cock," he said gruffly.

"What you figger to do with 'em?" demanded Gimpy irritably.

"We can do a lot of things," Trent replied. "Not here at the camp. Can't tell but what they've got friends headed this way."

"I savvy." Gimpy looked at the prisoners reflectively. "There's places in the Pot Holes where fellers can get lost so nobody can *ever* find 'em."

Denver poked his head through the door. "Come an' git it," he announced laconically. He came into the room. "I can keep a gun on these jaspers while you go eat."

Trent moved to the door, pulled it open and looked over his shoulder at the prisoners. "You can do some thinking," he said. "I'm giving you a chance to tell who else knows the truth. I want to know if Daker is on to me, savvy?" He paused, added significantly, "You won't do any talking in the Pot Holes."

Gimpy followed him out. Donal noticed that the door hung crookedly and would not stay open unless propped. His pulse stirred as he stared at it. This door that would not stay open offered interesting possibilities. For the moment, at least, they were alone with only the cook to guard them.

# CHAPTER
# TWENTY-ONE

# The Camp Cook Talks

Denver watched them with vicious satisfaction on his stupid face, feet braced wide apart while he made himself a cigarette. He caught Rusty's longing look at the gun he had placed on the table within quick reach. He grinned maliciously. "No chance, mister, not with the knots I put in that rope. You cain't bust loose this side of hell."

The Circle C foreman discreetly held his tongue. It was apparent that the cook had been resorting to a bottle.

Donal got up from the stool and moved casually to one of the windows.

"You keep away from there," warned Denver. "Don't go makin' trouble for yourself."

"No need for you to worry," smiled Donal. "A man can't squeeze through that hole with his hands tied behind his back."

"You're sure speakin' the truth," grinned the cook. He put a match to his cigarette.

Donal turned from the window, moved along the wall and came to the door. Denver said nothing. No chance for escape through the door, not with Trent and

Gimpy in the kitchen. He continued to watch complacently. Only a fool would try to go through that door with Trent and Gimpy on the other side. And anyway the prisoner's hands were tied. He'd have a lot of trouble pulling that door open.

Rusty caught Donal's significant look and sensed that something was up. His muscles tensed, and after a moment he saw Donal glance at the table. Trent's rifle still leaned against it at the end nearest the door. On the opposite end of the table lay Denver's .45, ready for the cook's reaching hand.

Donal's gaze roved around the room, fastened on a saddle lying in the corner beyond his bound companion. "That looks like your saddle," he said to Rusty. "The one stolen with your horse the other day."

Rusty looked, and so did the cook, and Rusty said wrathfully, "Sure is my saddle, and the other yonder is that Cheyenne that was stole from Wes." Out of the corner of his eye he saw Donal lean cautiously back against the door. In that fleeting instant he slid the heavy bolt.

The unsuspecting cook was enjoying Rusty's sulphurous comments. "You won't be needin' your saddle ag'in," he told the indignant Circle C man. "You'll only be forkin' a horse one more time and after you get to the Pot Holes you won't be worryin' none about saddles nor nothin'." Denver shook with unholy mirth.

Donal left the bolted door and passed the other window and the cook. He looked longingly at the man's cigarette. "How about a smoke?" He came to a standstill close to the cook's shoulder and sent a warning glance to Rusty on the opposite side of the table. The foreman nodded, his eyes hot and eager.

"Smoke, huh?" Denver hesitated, pulled a flask from his pocket and took a long drink. He set the flask on the table and grinned at Donal. "Cravin' a smoke?" he repeated. He fished tobacco-sack and papers from another pocket and began making a cigarette. "Reckon there's no harm in lettin' you have a smoke."

Donal edged closer, kept on talking in a low voice. "That's mighty white of you, Denver . . . I sure do crave a whiff."

Unnoticed by the absorbed cook, Rusty was on his feet and turning his back to the rifle that leaned against the table. His bound hands fastened over the gun and holding it across his back he soundlessly edged around the table toward the unsuspecting Denver.

"Here you are, mister." The cook stuck the cigarette between Donal's lips and rasped a match into flame against trouser leg. He shivered, stifled a gasp, stood very still, the burning match in the fingers of his raised hand.

"One little sound out of you and I'm squeezing trigger," warned Rusty. He stood sideways behind the cook, the rifle in his bound hands pressed hard against the man's spine. Horror glazed Denver's eyes. He seemed unable to breathe.

Donal turned his back to him. "Get that rope off," he whispered.

**235**

Urged on by a prod from the rifle, Denver untied the thongs. Donal swung around and set to work on Rusty's wrists.

Hardly five minutes had elapsed. It seemed like an eternity to Donal as he feverishly released Rusty's wrists from the rope. He could hear the subdued rumbling of voices in the kitchen, the clatter of tin coffee cups. Trent would be impatient to be finished with the business and any moment might find him at the door.

As the rope fell from Rusty's wrists, Donal snatched up the .45 from the table and held it against Denver's head. No word was spoken. Rusty brought the rifle down to his side, leaned it against the table and reached for the fallen rope. In a moment the cook's arms were lashed tightly behind his back. Rusty seized the other cord and tied the man's ankles. He stepped back, looked around questingly, saw the red bandana hanging from Denver's hip pocket. He snatched it, stuffed it into the cook's mouth and fastened it securely.

Donal pushed the gun into his holster, and lifting the helpless man bodily they carried him to the bunk and rolled him underneath the blankets.

Footsteps sounded in the kitchen, then Trent's voice. "The damn door's stuck!"

Donal drew the .45 from his holster and motioned for Rusty to make for the nearest window. Rusty grabbed the Winchester and started climbing through the opening. It was a tight squeeze for him.

Donal kept his gaze fixed on the door. He heard Gimpy's thin, raspy voice: "The draw-bar must have slipped into the catch." His voice rose to an angry shout: "Denver — the door's stuck! Open up!"

Rusty squeezed through and dropped outside. Donal started to follow, but evidently aroused by Denver's strange silence, the two men in the kitchen began a violent attack on the frail door. It burst open and Gimpy plunged headlong into the room. Trent, more cautious, halted outside the broken framework.

Donal was halfway through the window when the lame man's bullet crashed into the log wall just above his head. He swung his gun across his chest and fired, saw Gimpy, still running toward him, pitch forward on his face.

Trent was jerking at his gun. Donal had no time to free his leg from the window. He fired again, saw Trent wheel and dash back into the kitchen.

He pulled free from the window and started toward the wrecked door. Somebody yelled, Rusty's voice, and there was the heavy thud of pounding feet, the crashing report of a rifle.

The Circle C foreman stood near the corner of the cabin, smoking Winchester in lowered hands and hard gaze on the man slowly picking himself up from the ground.

"He ain't hurt," Rusty said as Donal made a breathless appearance from the kitchen door. "He was tryin' to get to his horse back in the brakes yonder. Changed his mind when I took that shot at him."

Trent faced them sullenly. He had tripped on a grass root and taken a hard fall. Blood welled from a long cut on his cheek. He lifted an arm and wiped it with his shirt sleeve. "How in hell did you bust loose?" he asked.

"Denver hasn't much sense," answered Donal. He smiled frostily. "Your mistake, Trent. We've got more savvy than you guessed."

The Rocking D foreman's face was ghastly. "I should have hunted you down that time at the dance," he said. "I should have killed you that night, Cameron."

"You tried, didn't you? Or was it DeSang who told Sems to kill me?"

Trent was visibly startled. "What do you know about De-Sang?" His voice was hoarse.

"I'm learning fast," Donal said grimly.

Rusty found another rope and in a few moments the prisoner's arms were lashed behind his back.

"How about the other jasper?" queried Rusty.

"He won't need tying up," Donal told him laconically. "Get their horses over from the brakes," he added.

Rusty hurried away and Donal gestured at the cabin door. "We'll step inside and have a look at your friend, Trent."

He herded the dazed prisoner through the kitchen and into the back room. The lame man sprawled on the floor where Donal's bullet had caught him between the eyes. Trent's menacing look went to the bound and gagged man lying in the bunk. "You damn fool," he said bitterly.

Donal loosed the cook's ankle ropes and removed the gag. Denver crawled from the bunk. He was in a dejected frame of mind. "I did it apurpose," he said

**238**

hoarsely to Donal. "I knew what you was up to and fixed it for you to make the break. You should let me get away from here, mister."

"I'm taking you to a nice safe place, Denver," smiled Donal. "It depends on you what happens after that."

"Anythin' you want, boss," earnestly declared the frightened cook. Hope glimmered in his mean eyes. "I'm sure glad you plugged Gimpy. He was a killin' snake . . . never knowed when he was fixin' to knife me."

Trent cursed him, but Denver's courage was reviving. "You ain't scarin' me none," he sneered. "You're a killin' wolf that's took a dose of poison. You're done for proper."

Rusty came in, a satisfied look on his face. "We'll take those saddles they stole from us," he announced. "We can load 'em on the pack-horse along with the hides." The foreman broke off, stared wonderingly at Denver seated at the table with a pencil between his fingers. "What's goin' on here?"

"Denver is writing a little farewell note," Donal told him gravely. His eyes twinkled.

The cook laid the pencil down. "She's done, boss," he said, and held out a piece of brown wrapping paper.

Donal read the scrawl aloud, grim amusement in his voice.

Gimpy got plenty ugley and he run into som hot led. he wuz a dam killer anny ways and i am gittin outer this dam place so you dont git no chanse to swing me for me killin the dam snake

Rusty Cross chuckled. "Smart work," he said admiringly. "You've got a head on your shoulders, Don." He turned to the door. "I'll go pack those saddles and hides." Donal's voice halted him.

"Those saddles stay here. We don't take anything except Trent and Denver. The DS outfit won't know we've been here or what has happened. They'll find a dead man, and Denver gone, leaving this note."

"I savvy." Rusty grinned. "It's a smart idea at that." With a regretful glance at the saddles he went off to pack the hides.

Trent was a man who took defeat hard. His heavy shoulders sagged and he had lost the jaunty insolence that always marked his bearing. His eyes held a feverish brightness as he spoke. "Are you taking us to San Benito?"

Donal sensed his vague hope. There would be a chance for him in San Benito. Al DeSang was top dog in that sordid little cowtown. Hireling killers jumped to do his bidding. Trent knew he would not be in the toils long if Donal was fool enough to take him to San Benito.

"I've another place in mind," Donal told him. "You won't get bail where I'm taking you, Trent."

"You're loco," muttered Trent. "You can't do this to me. I've got friends."

"Did you ever hear of Mark Lee?" Donal put the question softly.

"You mean the girl's father?" Trent's eyes took on a stony look. "Yeah, I knew him. Used to run a small bunch of cattle west of the river."

"Perhaps you know a few more things about him," prodded Donal. "Perhaps you know what became of those cattle when Lee and his son were murdered."

"What are you driving at?" Fear put a hoarse rasp in Trent's voice.

"You're going to find out before I'm done with you," answered Donal. He shot another question. "What did you do with my Circle C cows, Trent?"

"You can go to hell with your questions," sneered the man.

"What's your connection with DeSang?" Donal was relentless. "You're part owner with him in the DS, isn't that right?"

"Think it out for yourself." Trent spoke sulkily.

"That's what I'm doing, and I'm doing pretty well, don't you think?"

Rusty's voice reached through the door. "All set to ride, Don." He came into the room, looked at Denver's unbound hands and picked up the tie-rope.

"I'll go peaceable," protested the cook. "No call to tie me up."

"You bet you'll go peaceable." Rusty retied Denver's wrists. "You'll have to sit awful quiet in the saddle, Denver. That wall-eyed bronc of Gimpy's looks some mean." He chuckled. "Cain't help but laugh at the way this thing has turned out. That DS bunch won't guess we've been here. They'll figger that Denver has killed Gimpy and hightailed it on Gimp's horse."

"Is that my gun in your waistband?" asked Donal. "Where did you find it?"

241

Rusty handed over the Colt. "Found it layin' where Trent throwed it near the hides."

Donal pushed the gun into his holster and returned his attention to Trent. "One more question. We've looked over quite a bunch of cattle as we came in, all of them wearing the DS iron, but not all of them earmarked the same."

"That's right," agreed Rusty. "Some of 'em were V-notched in both ears."

Trent shrugged his heavy shoulders. "You can keep on asking questions till hell freezes."

"I can tell you about them earmarks," offered Denver with a malicious sidewise glance at Trent. "Them cows is all DS stock, born and raised on the range, which ain't true of the others wearin' different crops."

"Meanin' the others is rustled stock?" bluntly asked Rusty.

"I ain't sayin'," Denver answered cautiously. "I'm only camp cook and don't you go callin' me a rustler."

"You've said enough," commented Donal dryly. He gave Denver a thoughtful look.

"I could tell you more." Denver's eyes took on a sly gleam. "I could maybe tell you about them cows Slash Driver is pushin' over to Sheep Springs."

"We're listening," encouraged Donal.

"Keep your fool mouth shut, Denver," muttered Trent furiously.

"I ain't cravin' to swing," Denver said sullenly. "Not if I can help it." He gave the Circle C men a crafty grin.

242

"We'll do what we can for you," agreed Donal. "What about those cows Slash Driver has taken over to Sheep Springs?"

"Waal" — the cook hesitated, doubt and fear in his mean eyes as he glanced at Trent — "I'd say from what I seen of the brands on their hides they was Circle C cows."

"You damn fool!" Trent said again, savagely. His face was ashen.

Donal and Rusty stared at him, their eyes hard. The Rocking D man's lips twisted in a crooked smile of bravado.

"All right." Donal gestured for the prisoners to move toward the door. "Let's ride."

"Ain't you goin' to turn me loose?" Denver's voice was panicky.

"You're too valuable to be running around loose," Donal told him. "We're keeping you in a safe place, Denver."

Sundown found them riding into the ranch yard. Donal headed the procession, with Trent and Denver strung out behind him, their horses on lead-ropes and their hands tied to saddle horns. Rusty followed with the pack-horse loaded with the two cowhides.

Rubio's excited shout brought Brasca and Wes on the run from the bunkhouse where they were washing up for supper.

"We fetched home a couple of little playmates for you," the foreman told them with a satisfied grin.

Bearcat hurried over from the barn, stared with popping eyes at the prisoners. "Looks like you've been on the warpath," he commented enviously. "Wish I'd been along . . . doggone the luck."

Trent's hands were freed from the saddle horn and he slid from his horse. Wes looked at him searchingly, muttered a startled exclamation. "Where did you pick him up? He's the feller that shot me."

"I shouldn't wonder," Donal said.

"Sure he is," asserted Wes. "I remember him now. He was along when old Daker come over that first time. I said it was one of the fellers I'd seen with Daker."

"What do you say, Trent?" Donal spoke grimly.

"He's a liar!" Trent's face was pale. "I was miles away from the bluffs that morning."

A deep silence followed his denial, and Trent knew as he looked at their bleak faces that he had made a ghastly mistake.

It was Rusty Cross who broke that ominous silence. "Nobody said anything about the bluffs. How come you know that Wes was at the bluffs when he was shot?"

Bearcat was swearing softly. "Let's string him up," he rumbled. "He's said plenty to make a hangin'."

"Stole our horses," complained Wes bitterly. "I wouldn't have lost that saddle for five hundred dollars. Won that saddle at Cheyenne when I got first prize for best ridin'."

"We seen your saddle this morning," Rusty informed him. "There was reasons why we couldn't bring it along, and mine too. But we know where they are and you can bet we'll get 'em back."

Wes brightened at this bit of welcome news. He let out a delighted whoop, then anxiously, "You mean you got track of the cows, Rusty?"

"We know where they are," Rusty replied. He seemed reluctant to say more. "It's up to the boss when we go after them."

Brasca stared menacingly at the prisoners. "Was it these jaspers done the stealin'? There's plenty trees handy."

"I ain't no rustler," protested Denver in a terrified voice. "You ain't hangin' *me*."

"You'd look awful good danglin' at the end of a rope," Bearcat said with a hard smile.

Donal had been having a brief conference with Rubio. He overheard the remark. "We're going to the court with this case, Bearcat." He gave Trent a cold glance. "I've an idea that one of these men will hang in due time, but right now we're keeping them both in a safe place."

"The old *carcel*, huh?" grunted Rusty.

They exchanged satisfied looks. The long unused dungeon of the Salazars was a grim place, with its manacles and rusted leg-irons.

Rubio led the way through the trees, past the great *casa*, to a low, squat building. Trent halted when he saw the place. "You're not putting me in that rat hole!"

"Mebbe you'd rather swing," slyly suggested Bearcat, loath to give up the idea. He hated rustlers and believed in short and sharp justice.

Trent saw the point and reluctantly went inside. The adobe walls were more than three feet thick and pierced with small openings in which were set stout iron bars. Iron chains hung from the walls of the two cells, proof that the Salazar dons were stern jailors.

The prisoners were searched for knives and locked up in separate cells. Rubio, who was to be jailor, promised fresh straw for bedding.

Donal peered through the grating of Trent's cell door. "I'm not keeping you any longer than I need," he told the sullen Rocking D man. "Rubio will see to it that you have plenty to eat." His voice took on a stern note. "You can't get out of this place, Trent. We're guarding you day and night."

"You have no right to lock me up like this!" shouted Trent. "You're not the law!"

"I'm putting the law into the Rio Seco country," rejoined Donal. "When you go to the county jail you'll have company. I've started something, and I'm seeing it through to the finish."

"You're up against more than you know," Trent said hoarsely. "You can't buck Al DeSang."

Donal left him abruptly. Anger blazed in his eyes, and a tremendous, uncompromising purpose. He made his way through the trees and entered the patio by the small side gate. Isabel was standing under the chinaberry tree. She turned quickly as she heard his step, stood looking at him.

Suddenly they were moving toward each other and he saw that her face looked very pale in that fast-deepening twilight. He was conscious too of his hammering heart at the sight of this slim girl who had been waiting for him to return to her.

She came to a standstill, grave face lifted in a long inquiring look. "They say you have brought some men back with you — *prisoners*."

"We've had quite a day of it," he admitted.

"You have been gone so long," Isabel said, and then, "Wes brought me some things from the store." She gave him a faint smile, touched the trim white skirt she wore. "Marica and I have been busy sewing. It was nice of you to think of such things when you have so much on your mind."

"It was Angus Cameron's idea," hastily disclaimed Donal. "I had to tell him you were here, Isabel."

"Did you see Mr. Daker?" She asked the question hesitatingly. "I've been worrying about him, after what you told me."

"He wasn't in town, and if I'd seen him I wouldn't have told him — not then." Donal paused, added slowly, "I'd tell him *now*."

Her eyes widened, and she was silent for a long moment as though analyzing his words. "*Donal!*" Excitement took her breath. "You mean —" She went close to him, tried to read his expression. "It's getting so dark I can hardly see your face, but something in your voice tells me you mean that one of those men is *Lew Trent*."

"He's where he can't harm you," Donal said, and he added grimly, "I think we've got the man who murdered your father and brother."

She made a little sound, drew back from him, stood there, slim body taut, her face like a pale light in that growing darkness, and he saw that she was crying softly.

247

# CHAPTER
# TWENTY-TWO

# Sems Turns In His Star

San Benito lay baking under the fierce noonday sun when a group of horsemen rode into the dusty street. There was something formidable about these riders. Grim, silent, watchful, they drifted past the Daker House.

Jim Daker stood on the hotel porch with Hook Saval. "Cameron has quite an outfit with him," he observed. "Wonder what's up?"

"He's mebbe headin' for the Panoche," speculated Hook. "Shouldn't be s'prised but what he's had word that his cows is over that way. Panoche's handy to the border an' sure one rustlin' hell-hole."

"Blue Clover is with them," muttered Daker, his expression thoughtful.

"Blue savvies the Panoche country. I reckon that's why Don is takin' him along. Harry True an' Bert Clements is with 'em, and Jack Grayson an' Curly Peters." Hook's gaze followed the riders, thoughtfully.

Daker nodded. The names were well known to him. All cowmen with small ranches. He had no quarrel with them. "They're good men," he said. "Young Cameron has a nose for picking good men."

248

"He's a smart hombre," agreed Hook. "I'm backin' his play any time. It's my notion he's goin' to be poison to these skulkin' rustlers."

"Suits me," Daker said grumpily. "We've been hit hard the last two years, Hook. Worse than I suspected. I was looking over the tally sheets and the figures gave me a headache. I wouldn't have believed them, but they were Lew's own figures."

"Somethin' rotten hid in the old straw pile," muttered Hook. He wagged his head. "Mighty queer about Lew. He ain't showed up in two days."

"He went looking for the girl," Daker said. "Lew knew I was all broke up about her. Lew's hard, but he's a good man. He knows how I feel about that girl."

Hook stared up the street, a curious gleam in his eyes. He remarked casually, "Nary one of 'em even stopped off for a drink at the Longhorn. They sure look like they mean bus'ness." He speculatively gnawed off a chew of tobacco. "Headed straight for the Tradin' Post."

Daker bestirred himself. "I want to see Don Cameron before he gets out of town. Come on, Hook."

The two men started down the porch steps, halted as a voice hailed them.

"What do you want, Al?" Daker's tone was curt. "I'm in a hurry. Want to catch young Cameron before he gets out of town. He just rode in with quite an outfit."

DeSang came on across the street. "Plenty of time, Jim. I know what brings Cameron to town. He's heading for my DS to pick up some stuff he's bought from me. He was over there yesterday, picking out a few

**249**

hundred two- and three-year-olds I told him he could have."

Daker's face showed surprise. "I didn't know he could find cash for a deal like that."

DeSang gestured carelessly. "Old Angus is backing him. Guess he's over there to get the cash now. I'm to meet him at Soper's office. The judge has the papers all ready for the deal. I'm looking for Slash Driver to get in any moment with the tally sheets." DeSang paused, added casually, "I was wanting to ask if Lew Trent is in with you. I left word at the Longhorn I wanted to see him, but he hasn't shown up yet."

"Don't know where Lew is," replied Daker. His tone showed worry. "He went off a couple of days ago and hasn't come back. Some trouble at one of the camps, I reckon."

DeSang nodded. "Nothing important . . . was only planning to have him help me get up a dance. This town needs livening up. A dance brings the boys in from all over."

Two riders approached up the street and drew rein in front of the Longhorn Saloon. Hook watched them for a moment. "Slash has just rode up," he drawled. "Reckon he's lookin' for something to cut the dust from his throat."

DeSang took himself off toward the vibrating swing doors. Hook's frowning gaze followed him. "Never did like that smooth-talkin' cuss," he said. "Don't savvy how come you got to be pardners with him in his store."

250

"DeSang's all right." Daker gave him an annoyed look, but made no further comment. Hook had been with him a long time and had earned his right of frank criticism. The old cowboy was a friend as well as an employee.

Rede Sems stood in the doorway of his office. His thin hard face seemed more sinister than usual. He jerked the Rocking D men his brief nod and swung abruptly on his heel as if anxious to avoid conversation.

"Acts like he's got somethin' on his mind," remarked Hook. He grinned. "He's one sidewinder, if you ask me."

"Keeps order in this town," Daker said.

"All depends on what you call order," observed Hook dryly. "There's some mighty tough hombres hang 'round the Longhorn."

"They mind their own business," rejoined Daker.

"You bet they do. It's all accordin' what their bus'ness *is*." Hook scowled. "They don't never say . . . just come into town an' set 'round playin' cards in the Longhorn an' all of a sudden they're gone. When they get back they don't say nothin' of what's took 'em away. Sure they mind their own bus'ness, but we ain't knowin' *what* their bus'ness is."

"You talk too much and want to know too much," grumbled his boss. "You're old enough to mind *your* own business, Hook."

The rebuke left Hook unperturbed. "Mebbe so, Jim. Doesn't hurt none to be kind of inquirin' once in a while. I reckon that's the trouble with you, always settin' so high in your saddle an' never seein' nothin'.

**251**

Some day your horse will stick his foot in a hole an' you'll go sky-hootin'."

The town marshal was again framed in his office doorway, gaze riveted on the two Rocking D men. He watched until they were mounting to the high porch of the store, then faced to the opposite direction and stared at the frock-coated little man crossing over from the Daker House to the saloon. Judge Soper was on his way for the wherewithal that would put a good bite on his always substantial midday meal.

The town marshal's slaty eyes took on a cold light as he watched the judge push through the swing doors. He looked down at the low-slung guns on either hip, dropped hands to butts, eased them tentatively in their leather sheaths and made his way leisurely along the boardwalk in the direction of the saloon.

Al DeSang and Slash Driver sat at a table in the far corner, a whisky bottle between them. The DS foreman's face was creased with a broad smile. "Cameron, never knowed me a-tall," he chortled. "I was settin' over in that chair yonder the time he come bustin' in after Gimpy Drane. I stuck out my foot and tripped him, but he was so damn anxious to lay his hands on Gimpy he wasn't takin' time off for a good look at me." Slash touched his scarred cheek reflectively. "He'd sure have recognized me yesterday when he come over to look at the cows."

"A lucky break," smiled DeSang. "Might have spoiled the deal if he'd recognized you. Cameron's smart. He'd have smelled a rat."

"He ain't smart," sneered the DS foreman. He shook his head regretfully. "I ain't so sure we didn't pass up a good bet. Only one other feller with him. We could have handled 'em easy."

"Time enough for that." DeSang spoke softly. "Won't be long now." He narrowed his eyes at the whisky glass in his hand. "That Salazar grant is getting awfully close to us, Slash. At that I was a fool to let Cameron get the jump on me there."

"Old Daker will be hog-wild," chortled the scar-faced man.

"Daker's a fool for all his big talk," DeSang said. His black eyes took on an ugly glint. "He'll go the same way as Don Cameron when I'm ready to deal with him."

"You're a devil." Slash Driver's tone was admiring. "You and Lew Trent both. Never seen a play more smooth and when there's a howl it's Jim Daker gets the blame. Jim Daker — the schemin' old range-hog."

DeSang gave him an angry look. "Don't talk so loud, and if you can't drink whisky without getting loose with your tongue, the whisky's out."

"Sure," muttered the foreman. He looked at the other man uneasily.

DeSang considered him for a moment. "You brought the tally sheets?"

"Got 'em in my pocket. Tote up to four hundred and seventy head." Slash frowned. "Kind of queer, the way Cameron picked the stuff. Wouldn't look at anything that didn't carry the V notch in the ears — both ears."

"That's all our own DS stuff," DeSang said quickly. "Born and raised on the range . . . all of them white-faces."

"You sent word for me to let him take his pick," reminded Slash sulkily.

DeSang was silent, face dark with annoyance. He was mentally agreeing with his foreman that the thing *was* queer. Cameron couldn't possibly have known the significance of those V-notched ears. It must have been sheer chance. Just the same it gave him a bad turn, sent a shadow of doubt over him.

With an impatient gesture he dismissed the curious incident from his mind. Uncanny, but of no importance. It was not possible for Cameron to have any suspicions.

"Doesn't cut any ice," he said to the glowering DS foreman. "They won't be wearing the Circle C mark on their hides long enough to do any harm." His mustache lifted in a sly smile. "You see why I didn't want any trouble when Cameron was out there with you. I'm getting ten thousand from him today." He laughed softly. "Old Angus Cameron is loaning him the cash and that means Angus will be left holding the bag when we're finished with Circle C."

"I was sayin' you're a devil," grinned Slash. His face sobered. "Ain't got 'round to telling you about some queer business happened at the camp. Denver, he's the cook, killed Gimpy Drane and lit out for parts unknown. Left this note layin' on the table, and Gimpy sprawled in a heap on the floor with a bullet hole between the eyes."

DeSang reached across the table for the piece of brown wrapping paper and carefully studied the penciled scrawl.

"Denver must have gone loco," grumbled Slash Driver. "We got in at sundown from Sheep Springs and found him gone and Gimpy layin' there dead as a doornail."

"Doesn't make sense," muttered DeSang.

"It sure don't," agreed Slash. "I'd like to get my hands on him." He scowled into his whisky glass. "Took Gimpy's horse and got away from there. I guess he knew Lew Trent would sure blow his light out for what he done to Gimpy."

"Lew must have sent Gimpy over to the camp with some word for you," speculated DeSang. He frowned worriedly. "I'd like to know what's keeping Lew. He was to be in town yesterday. Hasn't turned up."

"We looked Gimpy over careful," Slash told him. "Didn't find nothin' on him. His gun was layin' on the floor, one shot fired." The foreman tipped the whisky glass to his lips. "Gimpy was a bad actor," he went on, putting down the emptied glass. "It's an even bet he got peeved with Denver and drawed on him. No tellin' what happened."

"Lew won't like it," DeSang said. "Lew thought a lot of that little lame killer."

Slash Driver leered. "Gimpy has done plenty of killin' for Lew all right."

"Shut up," snapped the other man. "No more drinks for you while you're in town. You're too flip with names." DeSang got out of his chair, his frowning gaze on Judge Soper who was in heated conversation with the barman. The judge faced around and glared indignantly at DeSang. "I've been insulted," he spluttered thickly. "I demand, suh, to know why you have in-inshtructed thish man not to sherve me my likker. Damnable outrashe!"

DeSang drew the judge aside. "We've got a business deal on, Soper. I don't want you getting drunk, not until we've fixed up this deal with Cameron. Have sense, man."

Soper blinked, frowned heavily as though deliberating some weighty matter. "Thash so." He nodded importantly. "See you at my office, DeSang." He moved unsteadily toward the swing doors, came to a standstill as Rede Sems pushed into the barroom. The town marshal gave him a look with eyes that blazed with contempt and made his way straight to DeSang.

"I've had enough," Rede Sems said curtly. He unpinned the star from his shirt and tossed it on the bar.

DeSang's face darkened. "Men don't quit my payroll." He spoke softly. "And when I fire a man you know what that means."

"Yes," replied Sems, "I know how you fire a man." His wary look went briefly to Slash Driver watching from his table. "When you fire a man he don't live long enough to do any talking." His thin lips twisted in a sneer. "You don't fire me that way, DeSang. I carry good insurance against *your* kind of pay-checks." He patted the low-slung guns. "You nor any killer on your payroll ain't got the guts to try it."

256

"You're crazy," retorted DeSang. He smiled placatingly. "What's got into you, Sems? You can be town marshal in this town as long as you want the job."

"I've got some savvy," Rede Sems said. "I ain't fooled none. You've got me marked to be fired because I run Stiles and his crowd out of town the day they pulled that play on Don Cameron."

"You're wrong," smiled DeSang. "I told Cameron myself that you did right." His tone grew impatient. "What's eating you?"

"Plenty," said Sems. "You've got me fooled the same way you've got Don Cameron fooled. Savvy?" He gave the other man a thin smile.

"What do you mean?" Something like fear flickered in DeSang's eyes.

"Think it out for yourself," sneered the little gunman. He swung abruptly on his heel and made for the door, then whirled with the swiftness of a cat, both guns in his hands as he fell into a crouch.

Slash Driver, half out of his chair and tugging at his forty-five, sank back, a silly grin on his scarred face. Sems looked at him intently for a moment. "You won't try it again," he said quietly. The swing doors closed behind him.

# CHAPTER
# TWENTY-THREE

# A Boomerang

There was mirth in old Angus Cameron's deep-set eyes as he handed a large brown envelope to Donal. "I'd like to see his face when you settle with him." The trader chuckled. "Aye, 'tis poison bait that will give him a bellyache and drive him to madness."

Donal tucked the brown envelope away. "Four hundred and seventy head, Angus," he said contentedly. "No rustled cow in the lot. Slash Driver was inclined to baulk, but DeSang had sent word I was to have my pick." The young cattleman's smile was hard. "I picked 'em all right. Only took stuff that carried his private earmark. Nobody can come back at me and claim I bought stolen cows."

"You've got the good head on your shoulders," Angus said in a satisfied voice. "Slash Driver did no suspect you recognized him, I take it."

Donal shook his head. "He'll know different pretty soon. He's to meet me at Soper's office with the tally sheet."

"I see you've come prepared for trouble." Angus looked approvingly at the group of half score men outside on the porch.

"The DS outfit is holding the cattle at Lava Gap, ready for us to take over."

"DeSang will try to stop you," prophesied Angus.

"We'll have those cattle through the gap before the DS men know what has happened." Donal spoke confidently. "DeSang won't have a chance to send them word to stop us. We'll see to that." His face darkened. "I'm only taking back what he's stolen from me, and when those cattle are on my range I'm going to pull off a showdown that will blast him out of the Rio Seco. DeSang is headed for jail, or worse."

"It's a big order, lad, and will need proof."

"Those hides will be proof enough to make Jim Daker see red," Donal asserted. "He'll be riding with us, Angus."

Daker pushed through the cluster of men at the door, giving curt nods to the ranchers he knew.

"DeSang tells me he's sold you a bunch of cows," he said to Donal. "A man would think you expected trouble judging from the size of your outfit," he added with a wintry smile.

"I've been learning things since I moved into the Rio Seco." A purposely enigmatic statement. Donal looked at the big cowman thoughtfully, wondered how much he dared tell him. Nothing at all, just yet. Daker was an impulsive man. He would go berserk when he learned the story of the altered brand on those hides. No amount of persuasion would keep him from immediately denouncing DeSang to his face. Donal's carefully laid plans would be ruined. He wanted possession of those V-notched cattle before anything happened to DeSang.

**259**

Also it was quite possible that Daker would refuse to believe the story of the hides. He trusted Lew Trent. It would be hard for Daker to believe his foreman guilty until he had seen those altered brands with his own eyes.

"I'm wanting a talk with you," Daker was saying. He looked ill, his face unshaved and haggard.

Hook Saval said slowly, his eyes intent on the young Circle C man, "Jim's just plain loco about the girl. We cain't find no track of her a-tall."

Donal sensed the unspoken plea in Hook's words, his voice. Hook knew the truth about Isabel. He wanted Donal to put Daker out of his misery. Hook could do the same if he chose, but he obviously distrusted his own understanding of the affair. He was leaving it to Donal to tell Daker of the girl's whereabouts.

"Something has happened to her," Daker said somberly. "I'm afraid she's *dead*."

Donal hesitated. He wanted to tell him the truth, but the immediate results would be disastrous. Daker would be furious with him, and he'd no time to bother with Daker at this moment. "It's possible she doesn't want to be found — just yet," he suggested. "Have you thought of that angle?"

Daker gestured impatiently. "Hook's been giving me the same fool talk. No sense to it. Why would she run off and hide from me? I can give her anything a girl wants and she knows it."

"You can't always tell what a girl will do." Donal paused, gave Hook a curious look that drew a quick gleam from the Rocking D man's eyes. "I'll make you a

**260**

proposition," he said to Daker. "You get the best men of your outfit together and meet me at Circle C tomorrow. We'll be in from the drive by then. We'll find her, Daker. She's somewhere around, and we'll find her."

Daker's face brightened, and Hook said quickly, "Sounds good, Jim. Let's get back to the ranch and git the boys organized like Don says."

Daker seemed dubious. "Lew is off some place. Hasn't been back for two days. We'd need him along."

"I'm not sure that we do." Donal shrugged. "For all you know Lew Trent is the reason that made her run away. She doesn't like Trent."

"You seem to know a lot," flared Daker. He stared at Donal suspiciously. "When did she get to talk to you about Lew?"

"I was at that Fourth of July dance," parried Donal. "I could see how it was between her and Trent. She was afraid of him. You can take it for a guess on my part," he added dryly.

"A crazy guess," growled Daker. "She'd have no call to be scared of Lew." He paused, came to a decision. "All right, Cameron. We'll see you at your place tomorrow."

"I'll have something to show you," Donal said in a curious tone.

"Huh?" Daker was puzzled. "Show me something?"

"It will keep," Donal said with a grim smile.

Hook Saval hesitated as he turned to follow Daker outside. "I savvy, son. Leave it to me. I know every puncher on the payroll. We'll have fellers along you can trust."

Angus stared after the two Rocking D men thoughtfully. "You didn't tell him about the hides?"

"Would have messed things up right now," Donal replied. "He wouldn't have believed me anyway."

"Aye, he's a stubborn man. He sees nothing but what is set before his eyes."

"Those hides are going to hang some murderers."

"Aye," muttered the trader. "'Tis the mark of death they put on those hides — death for themselves."

He stood at the door, watched the eleven horsemen ride off in the direction of Soper's office. His look went to Roderick Dhu, also watching from the alley. "Rod," he said, "keep your eyes and ears verra sharp the day and night. I'll want to know everything DeSang does. It is verra serious."

"I can hear the fall of a leaf in the dark," the Apache youth answered gravely. "Where DeSang goes, my eyes will follow."

"You're a good lad," Angus said with a warmth uncommon in him. He stood there between the massive doorposts, in his eyes the far-away look of one whose thoughts are back in the past. White men, and red, in mortal combat. The crash of guns, and horsemen charging the Indian camp, sabers flashing — the wailing of the fleeing squaws, the savage cries of painted warriors as they fought and fled — and fell. The young squaw, lying half concealed under a greasewood bush, a dark-skinned baby held against her breast. She was dead.

**262**

Angus had often wondered at the impulse that had prompted him to take the Indian woman's baby away with him. It was an impulse he had never regretted.

He spoke again, a gruff tenderness in his voice. "Rod, you can hold your own with any man. I'm proud of you, lad. You're a credit to the Camerons."

"You taught me the things a man should know," Roderick Dhu said simply. He was staring at something in the street. "Rede Sems is on his horse, and he has his blanket roll and a water canteen." The Indian's voice took on a surprised note. "He does not wear his star!"

"That is a strange thing," muttered Angus. He went out on the porch, watched the disappearing rider with a puzzled frown.

"He knows it is time to leave this town." Roderick Dhu gave his foster-father a shrewd look.

"I'm thinking you are right," Angus said grimly. His gaze went back to the horsemen clustered in front of the San Benito General Merchandise Store. Only two of the riders followed Donal into Judge Soper's office, a small frame building adjoining the store.

Al DeSang looked up with a somewhat sour smile as the three men entered. He was fingering a shiny star lying on Soper's desk. "I've kicked Sems out," he said, answering the question in Donal's eyes. "He's yellow . . . hadn't the nerve to throw Stiles and his gang in jail the other day when they tried to kidnap you."

Donal's face betrayed no hint of his lively interest in the news that Sems was no longer the town marshal. "He's a queer bird," he said noncommittally.

**263**

"He's a skunk," growled Slash Driver from his chair on the other side of the desk. "Pulled a gun on me back in the Longhorn . . . would have killed me if I hadn't beat him to the draw."

"A dangerous man," pronounced Judge Soper with a judicial frown. He had sobered up considerably. "Well, gentlemen, shall we — uh —"

"I'm ready," interrupted Donal. He looked at his copy of the tally sheet. "Four hundred and seventy head, DeSang."

The owner of the DS nodded, made a pretense of scanning the tally sheet Slash Driver tossed on the desk. "You picked good stuff, Cameron."

"I know cows," smiled Donal. "You told me to take my pick."

"Was at least fifty or sixty unweaned calves in the bunch," complained Slash.

"You said you'd throw in the young stuff," reminded Donal.

"I'm not kicking," DeSang said good-naturedly. He did some figuring with a pencil. "Totals eleven thousand, seven hundred and fifty. Cash," he added smilingly.

Donal glanced briefly at Rusty and Brasca who stood on either side of the door. "It's the same as cash." He pulled the brown envelope from his pocket and tossed it on the desk. "I'll take a look at the bill of sale while you count it." He picked up the document Soper pushed toward him.

"I've notarized the signature," Soper stated pompously. "You will find it all according to the law, suh."

264

DeSang picked up the brown envelope and slipped the flap open. He let out a startled grunt, hastily shook out the contents, then slowly lifted his head in a long look at Donal. His face was deathly pale. "What's this monkey business?" The smoothness had gone from his voice. The words came out in a tight, thin snarl. "What are you trying to pull off, Cameron?"

Donal glanced again at the two Circle C men, saw their hands hovering close to gun-butts. "Nothing wrong with those notes," he replied easily. "Should be as good as cash, DeSang. Your own name is on them."

DeSang made no reply. His hand reached inside his coat, but, lightning-fast as the movement was, Donal's gun was out and menacing him. Slash Driver started up from his chair, sat down abruptly and lifted his hands, his shocked gaze on Brasca's gun. Rusty was grinning over his own forty-five at the stupefied Judge Soper.

"Stand up," ordered Donal. "Face the wall, and keep those hands high."

DeSang got to his feet and turned to the wall, and, obeying Donal's gesture, Soper and Driver lined up with him. Rusty passed behind them, removed the Colt from Driver's holster and a small derringer fastened to a clip inside DeSang's coat. Soper carried no weapon.

"You can't get away with it!" DeSang's voice shook with rage.

Donal pocketed the bill of sale. "We're going for a little ride," he said quietly. His voice lifted. "All right, boys."

Dust drifted as the group of horsemen rode from the street and down the side of the store to the rear.

Donal spoke again, a threat in his voice. "Get moving." He gestured at the back door. "Not you, Soper," he added. "But I'm warning you to stay here in the office. Poke your head outside under an hour and you'll likely catch a bullet."

Soper promised almost tearfully that he would not so much as stir from his office chair.

"I'll be watchin' for you," warned Brasca with a fierce scowl. He winked at the others.

The frightened judge tottered to his chair, collapsed into it with a moan and reached a trembling hand for the bottle in the desk drawer.

The ominous smoothness to the affair told of careful planning. DeSang and Slash Driver made no further protest as they were hustled out of the back door. These soft-spoken men meant business.

The little party moved swiftly and silently toward the mouth of a deep gully less than a hundred yards from the office. Stark fear looked from DeSang's eyes as he saw in which direction they were going. He turned as though to make a bolt, felt the press of Rusty's gun against his ribs. He stumbled on.

Surprise widened his eyes when he saw the group of riders waiting in the gully. He knew most of these men. Jack Grayson and Harry True, Peters and Clements — and Blue Clover. His courage revived. These men were his friends.

"I call on you boys to help me," he said thickly. "This is murder."

They gave him no answer, only looked at him with cold, unfriendly eyes.

**266**

"Don't let Cameron get away with this," he begged them. "He's planning to kill me."

Only one voice answered him. "Shut up," Bearcat said gruffly. "Climb into that saddle, mister, and tie up your slack jaw. You, too, feller." He motioned with his gun at Slash Driver.

In a few moments they were riding up the gully. DeSang ventured a question. "Where are you taking us?"

"I'm making sure we get those cattle started for Circle C range," Donal replied.

"Turn us loose and I won't try to stop you," proposed DeSang. "You put a slick one over me, Cameron — but I'm a good sport."

"Don't worry," Donal said. "We've got it all fixed up just where to turn you loose, DeSang. About ten miles from here. You and Driver will have a nice walk back to town. You'll be too late to keep us from pushing those cattle through Lava Gap."

DeSang began an angry protest, but something, perhaps it was the hard determination on the faces of these men, silenced him.

Blue Clover, bringing up the rear with Rusty Cross, said worriedly, "Don't make sense, turning 'em loose."

"Leave it to Don," advised the Circle C foreman. "He wants to have them cows safe before he plays his ace card." Rusty spoke confidently. "I'd sure hate to be in DeSang's boots when this hand is played out."

# CHAPTER
# TWENTY-FOUR

# Dust in the Hills

Roderick Dhu flung himself from his saddle and ran into the store. Excitement played like lightning across his dark face. "DeSang moves fast," he said worriedly to Angus.

"He is no the man to sit idle," commented the trader.

"He is on his way to the Circle C ranch," went on the Apache. "Slash Driver and Stiles are with him, and many others."

"How do you know this?"

"I have been watching ever since DeSang and Driver got in last night from the place where Don set them afoot." The Indian's eyes glinted. "They were like madmen."

"Aye, and for more reasons than being footsore," commented Angus dryly. "You are sure, lad? You have seen them ride?"

"I watched from Indian Head with my glasses. They follow the trail that leads to Circle C. Men have been arriving since before dawn and now they are headed for the ranch."

"We must get word to Donal," Angus said. He rose spryly from his great chair. "Quick, lad . . . tell Gaspar to throw my saddle on the buckskin." He reached for the Winchester that lay in a leather boot fastened to the side of his desk.

As Angus and the Indian rode from the town, Rede Sems noiselessly entered Judge Soper's office by way of the back door. The judge, just in from his breakfast, was in the act of pouring himself a drink. The ex-town marshal stood watching him, and, as if drawn by the pull of those bitter eyes, Soper's head turned slowly in a look. The whisky bottle slipped from his fingers, splintered on the edge of the desk, its contents splashing the judge's trousers.

"That was right careless of you," Sems said, unsmiling. "Won't be time to get you another bottle."

The judge was having difficulty with his breath. He continued to gaze at his sinister visitor. This was no friendly call. The man was holding a gun on him.

"Get your hat," Sems said curtly.

Soper finally recovered his voice. "This is — is an outrage," he began. Sems waggled the gun at him. "Ain't got time to listen, and mind you, Soper, I'll kill you here and now if you don't come along awful quiet."

Soper reached for his hat with a trembling hand. Sems watched him, a glint of scorn in his eyes. "You and your wolf-pack figgered I'd cleared out of this town," he said. "I fooled you, huh?"

"You must be mad," stammered the judge.

"DeSang wouldn't say so if he saw us now." Sems smiled as if something amused him. "You know things that can hang DeSang. That's why I'm taking you along." His eyes glittered. "I'd rather shoot him down for the wolf he is, but I've a notion Don Cameron would like him to swing."

He herded the cowering judge to the back door, took a cautious look and then hurried him through the chaparral into the concealing gully. Soper hung back when he saw the two waiting horses.

Sems prodded him with his gun, and, with an anguished moan, Soper scrambled into the saddle and sat shivering while Sems tied his hands to the saddle horn.

"Where are you taking me?" he managed to ask between chattering teeth.

"Down the trail a ways," laconically answered the ex-town marshal. He stepped into his own saddle.

The trail leading to the broad flats of Tule Creek was well traveled that morning. Less than two miles separated Rede Sems and his apprehensive companion from old Angus and the Apache who were about the same distance behind DeSang and his riders.

The pale dust haze lifting above the rugged slopes beyond the flats worried young Pasqual Torres who was watching for his outfit's return with the new herd. Only fast-moving riders could make that swift billow of dust. Cattle on a drive make plenty of dust, but cattle moved slowly. Also that dust was in the wrong place. The cattle would be moving in from Lava Gap which lay almost directly east from the ranch house.

Pasqual wasted no more time in conjecture. He put his horse into a dead run. This was an affair for the attention of the more experienced Rubio.

Isabel was watching the dust haze in the distance. Unlike Pasqual she saw nothing significant in its several peculiarities. That long trailing plume of dust meant only one thing to her. The herd was approaching.

She found Marica in the kitchen. "They're coming!" she told the Mexican woman excitedly.

Marica gave her a wise smile. "Time ees ver' long when *El Señor* ees gone from rancho."

Color waved into the girl's cheeks. "Of course" — her tone was defensive — "one can't help but worry — these times, Marica. You know what I mean."

"*Si.*" The older woman nodded vigorously. "W'en I live on rancho always theengs 'appen so queek." Her eyes clouded, and she added slowly, "Sometime I theenk thees rancho 'ave mooch bad luck."

"Why — Marica!" Isabel was startled.

"Always theengs 'appen so queek," asserted the Mexican woman. "*Ay Dios mio!* I 'ave seen mooch bad theeng 'appen so queek on thees rancho — like w'en *los Indios* come." She crossed herself. "My leetle *madre* — she keeled that time weeth all of them."

Rubio came quickly into the kitchen. His face wore a grave look. "Great danger comes to us," he said to Marica in Spanish. "Many riders approach . . . men armed with rifles and pistols. I have watched them through the glasses."

"*Madre de Dios!*" exclaimed Marica. Her appalled look went to Isabel.

271

Something of her fright seized the girl. She snatched the binoculars from Rubio and ran swiftly into the patio and through the gate into the big yard. The dust was hovering much closer than when she had watched it with such glad expectations.

The powerful glasses brought the still distant riders astonishingly close. Her heart began to thump madly. She knew that black and white horse. She had often seen it in San Benito, with DeSang insolently resplendent in the silver-mounted saddle.

She lowered her glasses. DeSang's coming could mean only one thing. He intended mischief, or he would not have brought those score or more armed men with him. She was sick with dismay. It was even possible DeSang had learned about Lew Trent and planned a rescue by force.

She fled back to the patio, saw Old Sinful and Pasqual entering by the small side gate. The chuckwagon cook had been taking his turn guarding the prisoners in the *carcel*.

"The kid says there's a bunch of fellers headed this way."

"It's DeSang," Isabel told him. "I saw him plainly through the glasses."

Old Sinful was aghast. "Means hell's about to bust loose," he muttered. His worried look went to Marica and Rubio as the pair hurried from the kitchen. "We got to figger out somethin' awful fast, Rubio. No tellin' what them hombres will do."

The two men stared helplessly at Isabel. She could read their minds, knew their thoughts were all for her own safety. DeSang would soon have Trent out of the *carcel*. The thought sent a chill through her.

"We — can fight them." She spoke desperately.

"We couldn't hold 'em back for long," Old Sinful said gloomily.

Rubio spoke excitedly in Spanish to Marica Torres. Her eyes brightened. "*Si!*" She turned to Isabel. "Long time ago w'en Rubio small *muchacho, los Indios* come, but Rubio 'ide in cave and *los Indios* no find him."

"*Si*," broke in the old Mexican. "Queek — we 'ide in thees cave. Thees hombres no find us."

"I reckon we cain't do nothin' but hole up in your cave, Rubio," assented Old Sinful. "No chance for us to git horses an' hightail it from here. They'd spot us sure."

Isabel made no protest. To remain in the house would mean death for these men. They would not hesitate to fight. She knew their staunch hearts.

"Yes," she said quietly, "let's hurry." A sound faintly touched her ears as she spoke. At another time she would have thought that what she heard was the low rumble of distant thunder. But she knew she was listening to the drumming hoofbeats of those approaching riders. "Yes," she said again, "let's hurry!"

# CHAPTER
# TWENTY-FIVE

# Roundup at Circle C

The cattle had been harried along since early dawn and their resentful bawls filled the dust-laden air as they drifted through the yard gate.

Al DeSang was watching from a loophole in the patio wall. He muttered a startled exclamation. "Can't see much for dust," he said to his companions, "but I'm betting the count runs over a thousand."

Slash Driver peered at the milling herd. A man was leaning from his horse and closing the gate behind the last of the stragglers. In another moment the rider was lost to view in the swirling dust.

A puzzled look crept into the DS foreman's bloodshot eyes. The yard was choked with cattle, a vague, restless sea of white faces and rattling horns.

Lew Trent, watching from the small iron grill set in the high patio gate, turned an angry look on the other men. "Cameron's pulled off a double play on us," he said furiously. "He's picked up his own cows — the stuff we rustled from him."

"I cain't figger how he found 'em," grumbled Driver. "I pushed 'em over to Sheep Springs like you told me to." His tone was defensive. "You cain't blame me for him bein' smart."

Trent swore at him. "He's got back his own cows and stung you for nearly as many more," he said to DeSang.

DeSang's face showed growing uneasiness. "Something's wrong," he worried. He continued to watch the scene in the yard. "I wasn't expecting them to shove the cattle in like this. Spoils our play."

"Them cows is packed in like sardines in a can," swore Slash Driver. "Cain't nobody get in as long as the cows are in here. Sure does mess things up. We figgered the outfit would ride into the yard, give us a chance to blast 'em out of their saddles."

"They're maybe heading around the trees," suggested Trent. "They could get in the back way through the horse corral."

"We weren't expecting them to come in the back way," DeSang pointed out. "We thought they'd ride into the yard as Slash just said."

"We've got 'em trapped any way they get in," declared Slash. "Six of us posted in the house, and Stiles is hid in the barn along with Burch and Cheyenne." He made the count on his fingers. "Red and Jake are in the bunkhouse and the rest are staked out in the brush."

DeSang was not satisfied. "Something is wrong," he said again. "It's too quiet, and what has become of the Circle C outfit? Why don't they show themselves?"

Slash tried to reassure him. "Ain't no reason for 'em to get suspicious. We've got the horses hid in the barn."

Trent swore again. "I'd like to know where the girl is. There was a Mex woman here, too, and those damn punchers Cameron left to watch the *carcel*."

DeSang looked at him uneasily. "That's another thing I don't like. Where have they got to?"

"Hightailed it away when they seen us comin'," Slash surmised. "No sense worryin' about *them*." He shrugged indifferently.

DeSang was showing signs of panic as he watched and listened. Those cattle crowding the yard frightened him. Where were the riders who had brought them to the gate and then vanished in the swirling dust? And the restlessly milling cattle made such a bedlam it was impossible to hear a thing. His thoughts raced. He drew out a handkerchief and wiped his hot, dusty face.

"Get over to the barn," he said to Slash. "Warn Stiles to be on the watch in case Cameron's outfit heads in that way."

The DS foreman hurried up the walk to the small side gate. No chance to force his way to the barn through that cattle-jammed yard. Gun in hand he sped into the grove of trees and came opposite the bunkhouse. Somebody inside moved hastily, as though from the open door.

Slash halted, a grin on his face. "Red" — he spoke guardedly — "you and Jake come on over to the barn. There's a chance them fellers will head for the horse corral gate."

A voice inside the bunkhouse muttered an unintelligible reply. Slash heard the clink of a bottle against glass. He scowled. "Found some likker, huh?"

276

he said angrily, and strode to the door. "This ain't no time for boozin'." Something hard crashed against his head, and as he sank senseless in the doorway a pair of arms reached out and dragged him into the room.

Bearcat and Old Sinful exchanged exultant looks. No words were passed until the unconscious DS man was securely bound and gagged and rolled into a bunk. Two other bunks already held similar occupants.

"Makes three of the skunks," complacently murmured Bearcat.

"You sure cracked him a good one," chuckled Old Sinful.

"You cain't beat the barrel of a Colt forty-five for knockin' sense into a man," declared Bearcat.

"You mean knockin' sense *out* of him," Old Sinful said argumentatively.

"Figger it any way you want," tartly rejoined Bearcat. He wiped the gun-barrel against his trouser-leg. "This little ol' schoolmarm always gets the right answer."

Booted feet clattered up the path from the big house. Old Sinful watched cautiously through a window. "A pack of the wolves comin' on the jump," he whispered over his shoulder. "Shut the door . . . we cain't handle so many."

Bearcat quickly closed the door and slid the wooden bolt, but the newcomers apparently were not interested in the bunkhouse. They raced past, guns in hands.

"Headin' for the barn," Old Sinful decided.

"Mebbe we should have plugged 'em as they went past," worried Bearcat.

"The boss said for us to use stratojam," reminded Old Sinful sternly. "We'd spoil his play if we started shootin' too quick."

"*Stratogim*," corrected Bearcat. His hard look went to the three bound men in the bunks. "Means foxin' a pack of killin' wolves."

The men who had made such speed toward the barn came to a sudden halt as they pushed in through the side door by the horse corral. It was dark inside the barn, after the bright glare of the afternoon sun, but not too dark for them to see the menacing rifles in the hands of the four grim-faced strangers. Reluctantly six pairs of hands lifted.

A fifth man appeared from the shadows of a nearby stall. His face wore a smile in which there was a singular lack of mirth. "Lookin' for your little playmates?" he asked the horrified DS men softly. "We have 'em safe, all cosy and nice in the straw pile." His voice took on the rasp of a buzz-saw. "Get their guns, Brasca."

The Circle C cowboy minced forward from the same stall, an unholy glee in his snapping eyes. He bowed elegantly, broad-brimmed hat held against his chest. "So pleased, kind sirs, to remove your — uh — hardware."

"Cut the comedy," rasped Rusty Cross. "We've got to work fast."

Brasca chuckled, passed behind the line of prisoners and deftly removed their guns. "Velly nicee guns you bet damn life," he chanted. "Vellee nicee saddle on that red roan in the stall yonder . . . allee same saddle stole from me." He stepped back with his armful of guns and glared at the crestfallen faces. "Which one of you buzzards owns that red roan? I sure crave to take him apart for stealin' my saddle."

"Shut up," Rusty said impatiently. "All right, boys, tie these birds up and throw 'em in the straw pile along with the others."

"Six and three make nine," exulted Wes Coles. His arm was still in a sling, but the big Colt forty-five in his good hand had a hungry look to it.

"Twenty-two broncs in the stalls," Blue Clover said. "I counted 'em."

"Nine from twenty-two leaves thirteen," calculated Brasca. "Means one of 'em is unlucky and is goin' to swing." He smiled contentedly.

"If Bearcat sets in as judge they'll all of 'em hang," Wes said grimly.

One of the captives spoke hoarsely. "Wasn't Slash Driver here? DeSang said he just come over . . . told us to follow him."

"Mister Driver hasn't came as yet, kind sirs," Brasca informed him graciously. "We will look Mister Driver up and tell him of your — uh —" Brasca broke off, looked thoughtfully at Rusty. "I'm bettin' they nabbed the skunk over at the bunkhouse."

"We'll take a look-see," Rusty said. He stared intently at the man who had asked about Driver. "I've seen you before some place."

"Sure you have," broke in Wes, "he's that Stiles jasper who tried to grab the boss when we was in the store."

279

Stiles rolled scared eyes at them. "It was only a joke. We'd been drinkin' some." Sweat beaded his face.

"Listen!" Rusty's eyes had a frosty gleam. "You might have been jokin', but we ain't. Savvy?"

"How did you get in here?" grumbled Stiles. "We been watchin' for you the last couple hours."

"Couldn't see us for dust, I reckon." Rusty smiled. "We got tipped off DeSang was waiting for us to ride into the yard." His tone was grim. "You was all set to blast us out of our saddles when we rode into your trap."

"You're loco," mumbled Stiles. "I don't savvy what you're talkin' about."

"You're in a tight spot," asserted Rusty. "We have proof that'll hang some of you and send the rest of you to the pen for ten years. You didn't know a feller was listenin' to DeSang's talk. He's an Apache and he sure stalked you coyotes good. He met us bringin' in the herd five miles back and you can bet Don Cameron got awful busy. DeSang set a trap all right, but he's the one that's caught, and all the rest of you killers."

"I still cain't figger how you got in here without us seein' you," complained Stiles.

"You was watchin' the cows and figgered we was hid some place in the dust." Rusty grinned. "Was only a couple of fellers back there, pushin' the herd into the yard. The rest of us headed for Tule Creek and slipped in the back way. You wasn't watchin' for us that way. You can bet Don Cameron is smart."

DeSang's misgivings were growing apace as he waited with Lew Trent in the patio. He had sent the six men staked out in the house to join Slash Driver at the barn. No sound broke the unearthly stillness, save the bawling of the restless herd. The very presence of those cattle in the yard was proof that the Circle C riders were in the vicinity.

The mystery was beginning to fray DeSang's nerves raw. "Something is wrong," he said again to Trent. "I'm getting away from here. This place is a trap."

Trent gave him a venomous look. "Yellow, huh?"

"Don't be a fool," fumed the other man. "You want to get cornered against this gate? No chance for us to make a break into the yard the way it's choked with those cattle."

Trent, less sensitive to premonitions, smiled sourly. "You're awful jumpy, Al. We've got Cameron where we want him if you don't let this waiting stampede you."

"I'm not staying here any longer," declared DeSang. "I smell trouble and plenty of it." He started up the walk, felt the grasp of Trent's hand on his arm.

"You're not quittin'!" The Rocking D foreman spoke savagely. "We're going to play this hand to the finish. It's too late to run now, unless you want to hang."

The long-drawn-out scream of a bullet, followed by the blasting report of a rifle, shocked them both to silence. A man shouted and they heard the quick beat of running feet, a crashing in the bushes beyond the patio wall. Another shot, this time the heavy bark of a forty-five, and then stillness again, save for the monotonous bawling of the cattle.

Trent had his gun out and was crouching against the trunk of the big chinaberry tree. At his back was the open door of the kitchen. He gave it no heed. He had carefully searched the kitchen only a few minutes earlier, and now his attention was on the little side gate near the corridor of the house. Other doors opened from the house on the corridor, but Trent had searched those rooms, too. He disregarded them, kept his gaze alertly on the little gate.

DeSang came out of his momentary paralysis. There were shrubs in the patio garden, all of them too low to hide a man. His only weapon was the stubby little derringer he habitually carried under his coat. It had been his custom to hire his killing done for him. The weapon clutched in his hand, he dashed into the kitchen and came face to face with the man he sought to escape.

Again horror held DeSang helpless to move for the moment. Donal stepped swiftly into the room through the narrow opening in the massive adobe wall. None of the searchers had noticed the big cowhide flap concealing that opening into the room beyond. Long-gone generations of Salazars had used the place for storing fuel.

Another man appeared in the opening. The dumbfounded DeSang recognized the weather-beaten face of Angus Cameron, and now knew just how his cunning had been undone. Berserk rage of a sudden replaced his momentary inertia. His derringer flashed up, went spinning from his hand as Donal's headlong plunge drove against him.

In an instant the two men were locked in a desperate embrace. The old trader sprang toward them, his gun

282

lifted. Donal warned him off with a shake of his head. He wanted DeSang alive.

The man was big and strong, and desperation gave him the strength of a maddened bull. He broke free, seized one of the wooden benches and flung it at his enemy. Only Donal's quick sidewise leap saved him. He lashed out with both fists, rocked DeSang with stiff rights and lefts that sent him reeling through the door. Donal followed, grappled again with him in the corridor. He failed to see Lew Trent crouched near the chinaberry tree.

The sudden uproar in the kitchen bred confusion and near panic in Trent. He could hear the pounding of feet nearing the gate. He gazed about frantically, saw DeSang and Donal spill through the kitchen door and recognized the man who had unmasked his treachery and locked him in the *carcel*.

Trent forgot the men so rapidly closing in to the patio gate. There was still a chance, if he could kill this Cameron who proposed to drag him before a judge and jury. His gun flashed up, dropped from suddenly nerveless fingers. The heavy bullet that robbed him of his revenge spun him around, and, as he fell, Trent's last glimpse of life was the face of Rede Sems, still in a half crouch, smoke curling from the gun in his hand.

The sight of the sinister little gunman took all the fight out of DeSang. He spoke thickly from bruised lips. "You've got me, Cameron —" He dropped his arms, sank down on the steps, covered his battered face with trembling hands.

Men pushed through the side gate and gathered around. Rusty Cross spoke solemnly: "I reckon we've done with rustlin' in this Rio Seco country."

"One sure-enough roundup," crowed Bearcat. He looked speculatively at the trees beyond the garden wall. "Never seen so many cow thieves corralled all to once, but I'm sayin' loud there's plenty trees handy."

"Such talk is unseemly," sternly spoke the trader from the corridor. "'Tis the law and justice that will now ride this range, and Donal Cameron is the man who has brought us the same. 'Tis the law will sentence these many rascals to their just doom."

"That's right, Angus," Donal said quietly. He was looking curiously at Rede Sems. "How did you get mixed up in this business?"

Sems deliberately pushed the gun back into his holster. "Just a notion," he drawled. "I was headed this way with some evidence I figgered you'd need if DeSang is goin' to dangle at the end of a rope." His cold glance flicked at the man cowering on the steps. "Same evidence goes for Trent; you won't be needin' it for him — now." There was a hint of regret in the ex-town marshal's voice. "I shore would have liked to see him swing."

"You saved my life when you killed him," Donal said.

"I reckon that makes us quits." Something like a smile flickered across the gunman's thin face.

Donal looked at him. He knew the thoughts in the strange little man's mind. "Quits," he agreed. "We'll shake on that, Sems, and we're going to keep the slate clean."

Rede Sems took the proffered hand. "You're a white man, Cameron. Wish I could have met up with you some sooner. Things might have been different."

Donal felt embarrassed. "What's this evidence you say you have?"

"Left it tied up all safe and sound some place in the brush. Wears the name of Soper, Old Soak Soper, and he's sure ready to tell all he knows about DeSang." Sems smiled broadly. "Seen DeSang's outfit was here ahead of me and laid low till you come along. Did some prowlin' and seen you make that sneak into the house through the window and followed you."

"Mighty lucky for me," Donal said soberly. "All right, Sems, go bring in your evidence."

Rusty spoke as Sems vanished. "Countin' DeSang we have nineteen of 'em tied up," he said. "Trent is dead, and there's a couple more layin' in the brush. The Injun got one of 'em, and Rubio the other. They was gettin' too close to the cave, where the girl was hid."

The color drained from Donal's face. "She's all right, Rusty?" The words came from him huskily.

"She's all right," reassured Rusty. "Marica, too. Blue Clover is with 'em now, and so is the Injun and Rubio."

Donal's look went to DeSang, still slumped despondently on the steps. "Stick 'em in the *carcel*, Rusty," he said. "I'm leaving it to you to keep them safe. I've something else to do right now."

Rusty nodded. "That Denver hombre's still in the *carcel* . . . claims that Trent wouldn't let DeSang turn him loose . . . says that Trent aimed to kill him for tellin' on him about those hides."

"Keep him in a safe place," Donal said. "Denver is going to be awfully useful to us."

"You bet," agreed the foreman laconically.

Angus followed his young namesake from the patio. "Easy now, lad," mildly admonished the old trader, "or you'll be having no breath at all to speak to the lass."

Donal scarcely heard him. He was running at top speed through the trees toward Tule Creek. There was a prayer of thankfulness in his heart as he ran, a great thankfulness to Rubio for remembering the little haven where once in the long ago he had taken refuge from savage marauders.

Roderick Dhu stepped from behind a tangle of bushes, a rifle in the crook of his arm. Donal halted. "It's finished, Rod," he said. "I'm not forgetting that we'd have ridden slap into DeSang's ambush if you hadn't warned us."

"We Camerons stick together," rejoined the Apache simply.

Donal gave him a cheerful grin, sped on toward the green fringe of Tule Creek. A girl was standing there, skirts fluttering in the afternoon breeze, the sunlight in her hair; and, as she saw him running toward her, Isabel began running, too — but not away from him — and suddenly she was in his arms.

Old Angus Cameron looked at his foster-son, a twinkle in his shrewd eyes. "We're not wanted yonder, lad," he said. His keen gaze shifted to the dust cloud drifting down the slopes of Comanche Ridge. "That will be Jim Daker coming," he added. "He is due to hear news hard for his ears to believe, but believe he must and will, when he sees those hides and listens to the truth Soper and others will confess to save their own worthless necks." A laugh rumbled from deep within him. "Daker was always saying he'd clean these rustlers out of the Rio Seco. Circle C moved in and did it for him."

LPW RID Copy 1
Circle C Moves In [lg. print]
Rider, Brett.

JUL 2 9 2010